TO: The
on ea.
AKA

THANK YOU!

for... everything

More than
water

RENEE ERICSON

I honestly don't know what
to say. I'm so grateful for
your friendship, love, & honesty.

xxoo

Visit my website at:
http://reneeericson.wordpress.com/

Facebook:
http://www.facebook.com/ericsonrenee

Twitter: @EricsonRenee

DEDICATION

~To the Art~

Thank you for the escape.

One

The bass pumps steadily in the dark room as Chandra, my roommate for the past three years, and I make our way through the crowd of fans, looking for Cal on the stage. His band should be warming up soon.

Cal, my boyfriend for nine months, has no idea I'm coming tonight. I wanted to surprise him. I made an excuse to come back early to school even though classes won't start up for another two weeks. I'm not sure if my mother bought the story about a research project for a local art exhibit, especially since I had the super cushy gig at the Met, but it was time to leave. That place suffocated me—not just the workplace, all of Manhattan. The constant clack of six-inch heels, prim bun hairdos sculpted by gay men with names like Ms. Marcus, and pressed suits made of fine overpriced designer linen fabric oppressed every part of my being. New York City is a machine, and while there, I was an unwilling cog forced into a ritual of pedicures and vapid living.

It's time to unleash the caged beast I was forced to lock away over the summer.

With each step, my boots stick to the linoleum floor covered in a ten-year-plus coat of beer and alcohol. The mixed aroma of sweat, cologne, ale, and adrenaline slowly loosens the metaphorical chain around the life I was born to lead—the one I refuse to follow in New York. Freedom has been waiting for me here, a plane ride away, on campus. College is my sanctuary.

"EJ!" Chandra shouts over the bustling voices. She clutches my elbow, trying not to get lost in the flood of people. "There's room to the right."

Following her direction, I shuffle between the heat of bodies, careful not to spill anyone's drinks, and I claim a minuscule space against the wall at the tiny music venue.

Cal's band has played here before, but this is the first time they're headlining. He was so ecstatic when he told me about it last week.

"I really like your hair," Chandra says, patting my newly dyed platinum strands. "The color looks good on you."

"Thanks. Being mousy brown was torture," I say in disgust, playing with the ends of my elbow-length locks. "I couldn't wait to change it."

"You make it sound like someone was sticking you with needles to have a natural hair color."

"You've met my mother. She has a violent penchant for prim and proper. I wouldn't put it past her."

"This is true. She does have a knack for making you see her way, no matter what." Chandra relaxes against the wall, her face framed in ebony hair that ends near her waistline. "She even had me seriously considering a wool suit over the sari I had picked out last year for my final presentation in abstract sculpture. Could you imagine?"

"Absolutely. The woman is as clueless as a fish swimming in a bowl of milk. I'm pretty sure she exists on another dimension altogether."

"And where does she vacation? A Star Trek convention?" she asks, totally mocking, her dark brown eyes wide.

"Doubtful. She'd probably think that was some stargazing adventure in the woods—which she would never go on. There would be mosquitoes and no outlets for a hair dryer."

"Would she go if they offered mobile Botox services?"

"She might consider it if they served champagne. Good Lord, just last week, she threw a fit because her personal shopper didn't offer her some bubbly while they were trying on ensembles for an upcoming event. She even threatened to have the poor man fired. Her focus is so out of whack."

The amps click on, dimming some of the voices in the crowd, and we all turn our gazes toward the stage where Cal's band is gathering. Jackson, the lead guitarist, tunes his instrument as David takes a seat behind the drums. The bass guitarist, Landon, emerges from the side, taking his place on the stage, and adjusts the strings on his guitar, turning the keys at the top of the neck.

"Do you see Cal?" I ask.

Chandra stands on her tiptoes. "Nope, not yet."

I jump up a few times, getting glances over the spectators' heads. At the edge of the stage, Cal's bleach-blond hair with blue tips comes into view. He mentioned the color change from red to blue last week, something about a new inspiration he was exploring.

"C'mon," I say brashly, pulling Chandra by the arm and pushing our way toward the front of the room. "I see Cal. I want to let him know we're here."

I shoulder between the tightly packed people, dragging Chandra to the crowd just in front of the stage.

My entire body stills.

Cal's hands are all over a petite girl's ass, and in plain sight, he's devouring her—not like a zombie, but more like a teenage boy who found his daddy's porn.

They even have matching hair. *Cute.* Looks like she's his new inspiration. Maybe I should call her Smurfette? Small. Blue. But something tells me she isn't the only vagina in his little village.

"Holy shit," Chandra says at my side. "Is he…"

"Vacuuming that girl's lips?"

This situation is inching closer to hell with every passing second as he continues to grope the nymph.

"Let's go." Chandra grabs my arm, gently tugging me backward.

My feet hold their ground. "No."

I continue to watch my muse slosh his tongue in the vixen's mouth.

I thought I was his inspiration. That was what he told me.

We have plans. Together, we're going to tour the world—him spreading his music to the masses while I paint the wonderment of the experience. We're a team.

We're nothing. It was all a lie.

Freeing my arm from Chandra's grip, I march the remaining five feet to where my blond devil disguised as a mischievous angel tongues and fondles another. My roommate is fast on my heels, muffling cautious words near my ear. They are muted. I hear her voice, but my brain can only focus on one thing right now—the train wreck before me.

I tap Cal on the shoulder.

His dark brown eyes snap in my direction to meet my clear blue ones, ensuring that his lips remain on the blueberry bitch. Slowly, he releases his mouth from his plaything.

"Surprise, Cal!" I say in an overly excited fashion, using jazz hands for emphasis. "I'm back."

"EJ," Cal drawls. He blinks, dumbfounded, and minutely shakes his head, like he's trying to make his brain focus. He creates some space between himself and the girl who obviously has intimate knowledge of his body—or at least would like to. "I thought you weren't coming back until next week."

"Oh, Cal, darling, my sweetie pie"—I smirk—"I came back to see you and give you a surprise blow job, but it looks like you're set for the night. Hell, you might even get laid by your new friend."

He clears his throat and shoves his hands into his pockets. "EJ…"

I step forward with an outstretched arm toward the blonde-and-blue-haired tart, who was sucking Cal's face moments ago. "I'm EJ."

She hesitantly shakes my hand. "Avery."

"Nice to meet you. I hope you don't mind giving my boyfriend a blow job tonight for me. You can even fuck him if you like. It's up to you." I lift my wrist, pretending to check the time on my nonexistent watch. "I suddenly have other plans, and I wouldn't want him to go without ejaculating for a period of time. He obviously couldn't wait for my return, so you would be doing him and me a great service."

"I-I-I…I…" she stutters. "I didn't—"

"It's okay, Avery. I get it." I glare at Cal. "I'm sure he promised you the world. Maybe he even wrote a song or two for you. Anyone could fall for his utter bullshit, even me, so I don't hold it against you. But you enjoy. I'm not interested in his poetry anymore. For all I know, he was reciting fortune cookies." I step closer to his disgusting form. "You're nothing but a liar and a dickhead. Oh, wait. That's not right. You're cockless. I forgot." I flick a glance to Avery. "Or maybe you just needed some new inspiration. But a real man would have called it off before hooking up with someone else."

"Screw you, EJ. We were just having fun," he states like I'm clueless. "Besides, I'm the realest man you'll ever have."

"No, you're the only man with a vagina I've ever fucked. You're a pussy."

"You kiss your mother with that mouth?" he spits.

Instinctually, my hand slaps across his cheek, sending a white-hot stinging pain through my palm. Charged and ready to combust, I turn on my heel, shaking my hand, and I storm toward the exit with Chandra close behind me.

Opening the door, I sharply inhale the night air. The steel exit closes behind us, dampening the sound from the ripping guitar. The people standing in line all snap their attention in my direction.

My nostrils flare with rage.

I hastily march down the street, creating some distance between myself and the line of gawking patrons waiting to get inside.

"EJ!" Chandra pants, placing a hand on my shoulder.

I slow my pace.

Stepping in front of me, she forces me to stop. "Are you okay? That was…are you okay?"

"I don't know." I rub my wrist. "I can't believe he…in front of the band and all those people, he was all over her."

"Yeah, I saw."

"God. It's…I thought he loved me. I thought we made music together."

"Maybe you two lost your rhythm?"

"Maybe he's a cocksucker?"

"Yes, you're right about that." She runs her hands along my upper arms and consolingly says, "At least you told him how you felt."

"You think?" I ask, unsure. It's all so surreal. Everything from the minute we stepped inside the club until this moment is a blur.

"Yes," she confirms.

A heavy wave of heat flushes and collapses within my chest cavity. *Is this my heart breaking?*

When Cal used to play for me, his voice would capture an aching place in my soul. *What will happen to that pain now?*

His songs weren't just for me like I always thought. They were lies, facades. It wasn't real—not much in my life is, for that matter.

"I'm sure he knows that he's an asshole," Chandra continues. "That was quite a show you put on in there."

"Ta-da," I mumble, tears forming. "What an ending."

Two

With books in hand, I cross the lawn toward the College of Engineering library, my reassigned workplace.

It's my senior year, and classes are back in session. It's been a month since I caught Cal with someone else, and it's time to figure out what I'm going to do with my life.

When I first moved to campus, as a freshman, my parents, the well respected Nora and Thomas Cunning, were reluctant to even let me attend this university. Columbia or New York University were more their expectations, but I didn't belong at either of those schools. This Midwest university, far away from New York, with a prominent art program was more fitting for a girl like me, so I fought tooth and nail to get here.

My mind has been free to explore and discover. I found my home.

And then, after almost three years of studies, I found Cal.

What a pipe dream he turned out to be.

The beginning of our relationship was all the things a girl could want from an interested sexy boyfriend—flowers, music, and incredible sex. Of course, my mother hated him, which was an added bonus. In retrospect, he and I were falling apart for some time, even before I went back to New York for the summer. He often cancelled plans at the last minute, and we rarely spent time at his place in those latter months.

He was always busy, which I now realize was code for not wanting to hang out with me. I'm calling it a clear case of denial on my part. My absence only solidified the inevitable. While I was filing archives in a prestigious art museum, Cal was filing his dick in other compartments. Technically, they were women, but I like to take a more abstract approach to protect my emotions.

Thankfully, there's little chance of us seeing one another in the near future. Cal quit school last year to spend more time with the band, so I won't be seeing him in any of my art classes, which is where we met in the first place.

My phone buzzes in my back pocket, alerting me to a call. It's Chandra.

"Hey, sexy lady," I say, winded from being in a hurry to make my shift. "What's up?"

"Not much," Chandra replies. "Do you mind if I borrow your blue dress?"

"Which one?"

"With the low-cut back and the—"

"Plunging neckline?" I say, completing her sentence. "What's the occasion?"

"Jeremy asked me out," she singsongs. "He's taking me to that sushi restaurant downtown, the new one by the water."

"Architecture Jeremy with the dark hair and green eyes? And the kissable lips?"

"Yes, that's the one. You remembered."

"I couldn't forget. You talked about him all weekend."

"Did not!"

"You were even saying his name in your sleep."

She pauses. "I was?"

"Nah, but I bet you've been dreaming about him. I have been, and I've never even seen the guy. You must paint a really good picture. He's a god in my mind."

"Okay, that's enough. Are you going to let me borrow your dress or not?"

"Of course you can borrow it. Be careful though. That dress basically guarantees you some action."

"That's kind of what I was hoping for."

"Then, you will be all set."

"Thanks, EJ."

"No problem."

We end the call as I reach the entrance to the library about five minutes before my night shift.

I've been working with the school's library system for the past two years, having gotten the job to earn my own money. It was a solution to a problem—or a way to hide my hobby, as my father calls it.

My parents' emphasis on academics is a bit overbearing, and to say they aren't happy about my studies is an understatement. They only acquiesced to my major in art history once I assured them that the research could be of value to my family's prominent advertising company in the future, which according to my mother is barely more admirable than slaving away with the vagrant trash in the art world. However, she let it be known that she wouldn't be as lenient when it came to me selecting a focus for my master's degree. My entire family has an MBA from an Ivy League school. Yale is the preference, and the same is expected of me.

However, art is my life and my official minor while at the university. I bleed my struggles onto the canvas, into my sculptures, and through my drawings. I create compulsively. It's my therapy and my way to make all the complexities right within my mind.

My family does not embrace my form of creativity.

They shun it.

Opening the door to the old library building, I proceed down the hall and hook a left at the bust of Edward Charles Howard—the first noted chemical engineer, as shown on the placard—heading straight to the front desk. I drop my bag in what I glean to be the staff section and then venture to the check-out station to get started.

The library position is simple enough, cataloging items and assisting students to find the information they need for various research projects. Last year, I was assigned to the main library, and I started this quarter there as well, but I have been transferred to the engineering library today. Apparently, they are short-staffed. The change of pace in the smaller building should be nice in comparison to the workload from the never-ending stacks at the main library.

Approaching the desk, I wait patiently for the gentleman attending the counter to finish answering the question from a fellow student. Once the redhead, who appears to be a freshman, leaves toward the area directed, I close the gap to introduce myself.

"Hi," I say as he focuses on the screen. "I'm EJ. I was just transferred here from the main—"

"The main what?" he asks, clacking away at the keyboard.

"The main library. I'm scheduled to work tonight, and it's my first time here. Am I supposed to check in with you?"

"Likely." He hits a few keys and moves the mouse. "Hang on. Let me check something."

I lean my hip against the wooden counter while he finishes his investigation.

"Found you," he announces. "Yep. You're in the system. I must have missed the notice while helping a student." He clicks the mouse. "Evelyn Jane Cunning. Goes by EJ. Art history major. Fine arts minor. Senior. Off-campus living. Three-point-nine GPA. Honor student."

"That's me."

11

"Great." He swivels around in the chair, peering up at me.

Total geek chic is the first thing that comes to mind as I evaluate his plain khakis and comic book character T-shirt, the hipster-vintage kind. Honey-brown hair tops his handsomely stubbled face framed in a pair of Buddy Holly–type glasses. Behind the lenses, his dark blue eyes give me a once-over, up and down.

"Welcome to Howard Library," he continues. "I'm Foster. Things here should be pretty straightforward since you have worked over at the main library. It's the same system but in a smaller space. If you have any questions, feel free to ask."

"Your name is Foster?" I question, unbelieving. "As in, the beer?"

"Yes."

"You don't sound Australian."

"I must have left my accent back at my apartment." He turns back toward the monitor and clicks the mouse. "Along with my crocodile, koala, and kangaroo."

"Well, that makes all the sense in the world."

"Yes, deriving facts from absurd logic—that must be your artistic side." He gives me a sidelong glance. "It's a family name."

"Can I call you Fozzie?"

"Can I call you Evelyn?"

"Not if you want me to answer."

"It's safe to say, the same goes for calling me Fozzie. I'm not a Muppet."

I laugh at that response, having not thought of The Muppets in years. Crossing my arms over my middle, I observe him as he returns to his work like I'm not right next to him.

"So, what needs to be done?" I ask.

"I was just sorting through a few hold requests for other branches that I began about an hour ago. If you'd like, you can start sorting through the book returns. The drop-off access is right behind you."

Twisting at the waist, I spot the return deposit. I open it up, pull out the books, stack them onto an adjacent cart, and then wheel it over to the monitor next to Foster. Logging into the system with my ID, I begin the process of manually checking in and organizing the materials to be returned to their proper places.

After checking through about half of the returns in silence, I ask, "Is it always like this?"

"Like what?"

"This…dead."

Foster scans the room. "Yeah. It's Friday night, which is usually the quietest. I suggest bringing your homework for your next shift. You'll likely have a lot of spare time."

"If it's not busy, why do they need two people working?"

"Safety reasons."

"So, I was sent over to babysit you?"

"That's an interesting way of putting it, but yes. It's school policy."

I go back to my task—clicking away, entering, and organizing. When the rest of the pile is sorted, I wheel the cart around the desk, preparing to put the books back into their proper places.

"So, what's your story?" I ask.

"What do you mean?"

"You had access to my full bio at your fingertips. So, what about you? Give a little. Make it even."

Adjusting his position in the chair, Foster leans an elbow on the desk. "Foster Blake. Senior. Chemical engineering major, business minor. Four-point-oh average. Honor roll for every year in attendance. Chemistry scholarship. Howard Medal Award Winner, two years in a row. American Institute of Chemical Engineers member and student treasurer. Member of the American Chemical Society, Engineers Without Borders, and the Investment

Club. I also play recreational soccer and golf and volunteer tutor once a month at an after-school program for middle-schoolers."

"That's all?"

"Yeah, I had to drop a recreational ping-pong league to make sure I would have time to work on my thesis. Sometimes, we have to make sacrifices."

"I hope you know I was just kidding. You've got more action going on than a whore at a bachelor party. With a schedule like that, do you even have time for restroom breaks, or did you just opt for a catheter?"

He pushes the bridge of his glasses up with his forefinger. "What days do you work?"

"Monday, Wednesday, and Friday nights. Why?"

"Same as me."

Foster focuses back on the monitor to continue his work. As he's jotting down notes in a notebook, I quickly glance at the unfamiliar scrawl. The symbols are completely foreign, leading me to believe he's no longer going through the request list. For all I know he could be translating an obscure nerdy creature language from some fantasy novel.

"I'm going to take these books back to the shelves and familiarize myself with the library layout."

"Sounds good. I'll be here all night."

Three

It's about half an hour before closing time, and Foster wasn't kidding about the pace of students on a Friday night. I've completed most of the assignments that I planned to address over the weekend, including a research for a paper on Picasso's Black Period, which is grossly underrated. All that remains is my human study, and I don't happen to travel with charcoal.

A female student approaches the information desk while I'm flipping through a fashion magazine, and Foster is immersed in a book, probably on geek world domination.

"Can I help you?" I ask, leaning my elbows on the wooden surface.

"Actually…" She flicks a glance toward Foster. "Um…Foster?"

He closes his book and scratches the side of his head. "Hi, Maggie. What's up?"

"I was wondering if you could help me find some information on thermodynamics?" Maggie asks, her fingers twiddling with the ends of her ebony hair.

"Have you already done a web search?"

"A little, but there's just a lot to go through. I don't know where to start."

It's a good thing she's talking to him because I don't know where to start either. I'd likely lead her toward the thermal underwear section at the mall.

"Thermodynamics is a pretty wide topic," Foster states, strumming his fingers. "I know the information can be a little overwhelming. Are you looking for anything specific?"

"Not really. Just the basics for an economics paper I'm working on, and I need to learn a little more about the science behind the business."

"Sounds simple enough. There are a lot of books with the basic science business model information available, but we don't generally keep many of them here. Let me take a look for you though."

Foster scoots forward to the monitor, bringing the screen to life, as Maggie bends over the desk, tilting her head toward his, focusing on the illuminated screen. She edges closer…and closer…and closer, pushing her breasts together with her upper arms, letting him know the girls are ready and waiting.

Classic peacock move.

Maggie is overtly interested in everything Foster Blake—so much so, I wonder if she would even comprehend science or business at this time. She's like a puppy waiting for attention. He, on the other hand, is completely unfazed by her presence, which is weird since I sense her pheromones from over here.

"It looks like we only have one in right now," Foster states, grabbing a small pink square of paper and a pencil from the bin between our two stations. He scribbles down the information and hands the slip to Maggie's reluctant hand. "Here you go."

She licks her bottom lip. "Do you think you could show me where it is? I'm not really familiar with this library."

"Sure." Remaining in his seat, he points toward the bottom of the staircase. "Just take the steps to the top and make a left. The section you're looking for is three rows down and on the right."

Maggie tightens her mouth, looks at the slip, and then peeks over her shoulder at the set of steps. "At the top of the steps?"

"Yep. It's all in numerical order. One, two, three…you get it."

"I'll show you," I offer, rising and rescuing the poor girl from the obvious idiotic moment that Foster is going through.

"Um, thanks," she says.

I round the corner of the desk and take the slip from her to see what we're looking for. "No problem. Right this way."

I lead Maggie up the staircase and down the aisle to the third row, just as Foster instructed. Together, we scan the numbers until finding the book she's looking for. Pulling it out, I hand it to her waiting hand.

"If you have any other questions, feel free to ask," I tell her.

"Thanks."

Leaving her among the shelves of books where she pretends to view other volumes in the stacks, I descend back to the first floor and take a seat once again next to Foster where he's lazily flipping through a science periodical from the shelves.

He's an enigma.

He's geeky in some ways, yet there's something else. Maggie saw something. He definitely has some really strong and striking features underneath the obvious nerd thing. With his underlying subtleties—strong chin, good hair, bright eyes, defined lips, and firm hands that turn each page with dexterous fingers—I can see how a girl could be attracted to that. Along with his sinewy forearms leading up to firm biceps that—

"Do you have X-ray vision?" he asks, startling me from my observations of him.

"Maybe." I shuffle through my bag, pulling out the first book my hand finds. *Great.* French Baroque Artists. *Blech. So gaudy.*

"See anything you like?"

"Not really." I open to a random page. "You're not exactly my type, so don't even think—"

"Don't worry. I wasn't." He laughs. "You're not really my type either."

"Is anyone your type? Or are you oblivious to all women?"

"Huh?"

I shut the book and lean forward. "Are you gay? Because, if you are, we need to talk about your sense of style. You do not fit the stereotype at all—unless you're going for that whole superhero-at-night, geek-by-day thing."

"Um…" He places the magazine next to the keyboard and turns in the seat to face me. "I'm not gay."

"So, you're just oblivious to all women?"

"No. Why would you say that?"

I gesture toward the steps. "You didn't even notice that girl drooling all over you. She was totally into you. She was practically handing her boobs to your mouth."

"Oh, I noticed." He adjusts his black-framed glasses. "I'm just not interested."

"Why not? She's cute."

He leans back in his chair, folding his arms over his chest.

"You thought she was cute, right?" I ask, pressing.

"Sure. I'm just not interested."

"Yeah, you said that. But why? Is she some stalker psychopath from your past? C'mon, Fozzie…"

He raises his brows, like a warning about the nickname. "Yes, Evelyn?"

"Girl-talk with me. She's a crazy loony who slept with your best friend or something, right?"

"No." He shakes his head. "You're way off. Maggie's nice. She and I had a lab together last year, but I don't need the hassle right now."

"Hassle?"

"Yeah." He leans forward, resting his elbows on his knees. "Dating. It's a time suck, and I'm too busy for all of it."

"Too busy to go out with a girl? Man, Foster, you might want to think about dropping another extracurricular besides ping-pong, so you could have a social life. There's more to life than studying."

"Hey, I have a social life, and I go out, but—"

"But?" I drawl.

"I'm too…occupied for dating right now."

"What is this? Some trendy asexual thing? You do masturbate, right?"

"Do you know no boundaries in a conversation?"

"Not really."

"Fine." He sighs and then scratches the back of his head. "Since we're going to be working together for who-knows-how-long, let's just get this out of the way. I don't date because you girls are complicated."

"How could taking a girl to dinner be complicated? It's ordering food and then consuming it. Or do engineers do it differently?"

He squints. "We eat the same, and it's not just dinner. There's texting and phone calls and meeting up with each other for meals and defending yourself if you talk to other girls and all that bullshit about love and feelings you girls throw our way. Not to mention, every girl, in the back of her mind, is always thinking about marriage."

"Is that what you think?"

"That's my experience, and I don't have time for that kind of commitment or the emotional roller coaster right now."

"Ah," I singsong, "I get it. She dumped you."

"Who?"

"Your ex-girlfriend. Don't worry. I understand. I just had a bad breakup, too. Stupid prickwad was screwing someone else. He couldn't handle all of my awesomeness anymore."

"Or maybe it was your colorful personality?" he says sarcastically.

"Again, my awesomeness."

Four

DEAR E,

I HOPE THAT THE MIDWEST AND
SCHOOL ARE TREATING YOU WELL.
YOUR OLD MAN MISSES YOU DEARLY,
AND I'M LOOKING FORWARD TO SEEING
YOU AT THANKSGIVING IN A FEW
WEEKS. DON'T FORGET TO BOOK YOUR
FLIGHT. LET US KNOW IF YOU NEED
ANY HELP WITH THE APPLICATIONS. WE
ARE JUST A PHONE CALL AWAY. YOUR
SISTER, BARBARA, AND HER HUSBAND
SEND THEIR LOVE. SO DO YOUR
MOTHER AND I. TELL CHANDRA WE
SAID HELLO.

LOVE ALWAYS,

YOUR FATHER

Sipping on a cup of coffee at the breakfast bar, I sift through the package that arrived from my family's New

York home yesterday. It's filled with a stack of applications to four Ivy League universities even though I could have easily filled them out online. I'm sure the hard copies were my parents' way of forcing my hand even more. Much of the basic information has already been filled in, including my name, address, previous schooling, and other data that qualify me as a human being. All that's left for me to do is write the appropriate essays and request my transcripts to be sent to each place of higher learning.

I would consider not filling them out at all since I don't see earning an MBA in my future, but the personal note from my father has me feeling a guilt-ridden sense of duty, especially since he was the one who had backed my case to attend the school I'm at now for my undergraduate degree. It doesn't help that Barbara, my older and only sister, set such a perfect daughter example—graduating at the top of her class, being accepted to Columbia, and receiving an MBA from Yale. She went to work for my father right after graduation and recently married a fellow employee, a rising star, over the summer.

She's a show-off and an overachiever, which makes trailblazing my own path even more difficult. If only she had screwed up one thing in her life, my life would be simpler.

Pulling out the first application, I read the requirements for the graduate program and make notes on a small notepad. Deadlines are approaching fast, and I don't want to miss them because I'd never hear the end of it. My mother would nag the hell out of me for every remaining second of my life. Being responsible—or at least at a level that is acceptable by my parents—is my only saving grace right now. All my life, my mother has expressed the importance of outer presences, so I do my best to appear to be the fine young lady my parents desire. I play their game right back at them. The distance helps, too.

"Morning," Chandra says, her dark ponytail swinging behind her, as she enters the chilly kitchen. She zips up her hoodie and goes straight for the French press, pouring herself a cup of coffee.

"Hey, there." I smile briefly. "Morning."

"Whatcha doing?"

"Looking at applications." I pile them back together and shove the papers into the large envelope.

"For?"

"Grad school. My father sent them."

"Ah," she says, understanding. She takes a long sip of savory caffeine before moaning heavily.

"That good?"

"So good. Like liquid pleasure."

I tighten my lips. "I think I'll leave that one alone. You enjoy your *liquid pleasure*."

"I sure will." She leans a hip against the counter. "So, what's on tap for you today—besides the evil applications?"

"It's Wednesday." I wrap my recently touched up platinum locks into a makeshift bun. "Photography at ten, and then I plan on spending much of the afternoon in the studio until I meet with my advisor at four to chat about my senior project."

"How's your project coming along so far?"

"It's pretty easy really. It's just a lot of writing and citing my work. Right now, I'm ahead of schedule for turning it in." I rise from my seat and place my empty cereal bowl in the sink. "How about you? Any big plans?"

"Today is an all-day studio day, and tonight"—she smiles—"Jeremy is taking me out to see a play and then to dinner."

"Oh, sounds fancy."

"It should be," Jeremy says as he enters our small kitchen, surprising me. "Everyone has been raving about the restaurant and the show."

Chandra and Jeremy have been dating for a few weeks. She's been extremely optimistic about the world in general since spending more time with him. If I'm being honest, it's kind of obnoxious. I'm completely happy for her, and I want her to be happy as well. *But what is it about women and new relationships?* We all turn into delirious little girls who blow bubbles and skip from place to place.

"Morning, EJ," Jeremy continues as he sidles up to Chandra and slips a hand onto her lower back. He places his lips near my roommate's ear. "I've got to get going. I'll call you later."

"Looking forward to it," she remarks.

I might have just thrown up in my mouth a little from all the sweetness in the air.

Jeremy kisses her on the cheek, and then he leaves out the door. I load my dish into the dishwasher and then lazily sip the rest of my coffee while Chandra prepares her own breakfast.

"So, he's sleeping over now?" I ask, placing my mug on the counter.

"Yeah." She closes the refrigerator. "I'm sorry. I should have asked if it was okay first."

"Why?" I chuckle. "Do you need a chaperone in the bedroom?"

"No." She guffaws. "Because this is your place, too."

"We've lived together for three years. I've had guys stay the night before, and so have you. You don't need my permission. Why would you even think that you needed to ask?"

She crosses her arms. "I don't know. Ever since your breakup with Cal, I wasn't sure."

"Sure about what?"

"I just didn't..." She sighs, dropping her arms. "I didn't want you to think I was flaunting Jeremy in your face."

"What?" I ask, finding her statement absurd. "That makes no sense at all."

"EJ, you and Cal were together for a really long time, and you were a serious couple. You two were always with each other. I've known you for what seems like forever, and you haven't said one word about him since we saw him at the club all—"

"All over the blueberry bitch?"

"Yes. You never said much about the breakup, and…you haven't gone out with anyone since. I was trying to be respectful."

I laugh. "Do you think I'm the overly sensitive type?"

"No…but I've been kind of waiting for the impact of the breakup to hit you, and it hasn't. You don't seem to be processing anything. A breakdown is inevitable at some point."

I scrunch my brow. "Did you change your major to psychology this year and not tell me?"

"EJ…I'm trying to be your friend."

"Listen, I'm okay." I rub my hands across my face. "I've had some time to think about Cal and me, and I'm good. No need to worry."

"Are you sure? You can talk to me if you need to."

"Positive. He's a stupid dickwad, and I was an idiot." I shrug. "Sure, he has good hair, and that ass in leather pants won't quit, but I'm fine."

"Yes, there was something intriguing about those leather pants. A little too tight and…revealing?"

"Right?" I laugh. "Is this where I make a small penis comment?"

"Feel free," she encourages. "It would probably feel good to get it out."

"Nah. There's *nothing* to talk about in that department, if you know what I mean."

"I do indeed." She nods exaggeratedly. "I get your drift one hundred percent."

We both laugh. Chandra giggles so hard that she gives herself the hiccups. After a few more chortles, we finally calm our giddiness, and I gather my things from the counter.

"I'd better get going," I say, heading toward the hallway. "My first class starts soon, and I've yet to shower."

"Okay. You're good though, about Cal?"

"Yes."

"And me and Jeremy?"

"Yes, but don't ask me to join in on some threesome. I don't think I'm quite ready for that yet."

"Of course you aren't. That would be totally insensitive of me."

"It really would be." I lean a shoulder against the hallway partition. "I do have a line, and you don't want to cross it."

"Would it be crossing the line if I told you that Jeremy has a really cute roommate who's also an architecture major?"

"Depends. Have you seen him in leather pants?"

"Not yet. I could scope that out for you if you'd like."

"Maybe." I peer down at the envelope in my hand. "But I might not be ready to date anyone. This is going to sound weird, but it's actually been kind of nice, being single and concentrating on school."

"Ah, so that's how you've been dealing with the breakup?"

"Possibly. But senior year is busy anyhow with final projects and now working on these stupid graduate school applications. Breaking up with Cal might have actually been a blessing in disguise. If I don't figure out a plan for next year soon, I might be heading off to get my MBA."

"Your parents are still pushing for that?"

"Yes, it's family tradition," I say, resolved. "I would have to make a strong case for something else, and right now, it's not looking good."

"Well, there's still time, right?"

"A little."

She shoves her hands into her pockets. "Let me know if there's anything I can do."

"Thanks. Have fun tonight," I add, referring to her date later this evening. "Should I expect another sleepover? I can make popcorn and rent a movie."

"Actually, Jeremy and I are planning on spending the night at his place," she says suggestively.

"Ooh la la," I sing, raising my brows with each syllable. "Somebody's getting some. Just be sure to practice safe sex."

"Thanks, mother," she jokes back.

"You're very welcome, dear."

Five

Dropping my bag on the floor near my feet, I take a seat at my usual desk in the classroom where we meet for photography class. This is an art elective that I'm using toward my art history degree. I've been fortunate to have many of my desired classes overlap with the required ones for my major.

"Hey, sexy thing," Wolfgang, my fine art major friend says, sitting at the desk next to me. He then offers a foam cup to my empty hand. "I brought you a coffee—skim milk, no sweetener."

"I love you, Wolfie," I enunciate with far too much emotion. "You're way too good to me. Remind me to send you my firstborn in payment."

"No need, short stuff. This one's on me."

"You're the best."

"That's what all the girls who have had the indulgence of my lips say."

"Yes, *all* of them do say that." I wink at him. "Do I need to remind you that there's only ever been one?"

"And she was the best one ever."

Since freshman year, Wolfgang and I have been good friends even though we have different majors. We used to see each other more often in the classroom environment, but as the years have passed and our majors are now more focused, we see less of one another. However, we do try to schedule a pertinent elective together each quarter, and this term, it's photography. When it comes to art, I highly value his opinion, and sometimes, I refer to him as my studio husband. He's good eye-candy, too—even if he does play for the other team.

Early in our friendship, he claimed to be bi-curious, and confided in me about the social pressures he felt. So, we made out a few times as an experiment. I was his only subject. He might like to look at girls, and he enjoys their company, but the man salivates for other men.

Since our make-out sessions, he's been dating men exclusively, and I'm positive it has nothing to do with our lip-mambo moments. I'm not that bad of a kisser, no matter how much he might tease me.

"How's your photography series coming?" Wolfgang questions, pulling out his binder of prints. "Are you getting the shots you need?"

"I'm not so sure anymore," I respond tentatively, unhappy with where my subject sits. "It feels like it's missing something. Will you take a look at it for me?"

"Anything for you, darling."

"Thanks."

Our professor, Dr. Jensen, tromps into the room with his haphazard light-brown hair sweeping across his brows like some grungy band member. He's not even carrying a briefcase, like most typical educators at the college level. He just has some brown paper bag with a grease stain.

Stopping at the front of the room, he writes Friday's date in red ink on the whiteboard, circling it about a gazillion times.

"Due dates, people," Dr. Jensen announces. He replaces the cap on the dry-erase marker and then turns to address the class further. "We will be critiquing and judging each one of your series this Friday. All prints should be cut to five by eight and matted on an eight-by-ten white board. You are required to turn in a minimum of six prints and no more than ten. Don't forget. This will count for thirty percent of your final grade in this class." He tosses the marker onto the empty desk where it quickly rolls across the hard surface before landing on the linoleum floor. "I'll be coming around to see if you have any questions. Once I've checked in with you or if you don't have anything you'd like to discuss, you are free to go and use the rest of the class to work on your projects."

More than half of the class rises from their seats, collects their belongings, and exits out the door. When a professor lets a class loose early, it's often a good excuse to head home and go back to bed. We're responsible for our deadlines, of course, but the liberty to work when we want is something I love about this program. It allows free-flowing thoughts, creativity, and inspiration to come naturally, not forced.

"Are you staying?" Wolfgang questions me, gathering his things.

"Yeah, I want to get an opinion." I sip my coffee. Still piping hot, it slightly burns my tongue. "I'm not feeling one hundred percent about my work."

"There's a good reason for that." He leans closer, and at a lower volume, he says, "It's because you're an artist. Doubt is part of the process."

"Then, I'm a super artist right now."

"That bad, huh?"

"Yeah. It's not sitting right with me." I flip through the images I've taken over the last week. "The direction is there—I feel it—but everything I've attempted misses the mark."

"It happens to all of us," he consoles. "I'll wait with you."

"You don't have to do that."

"Nah, it's all good. He can look at my stuff, too, and then we can talk shop and make sure you're on track. You can look at my horrid work, too."

"I love everything you do. It's like you can't create anything wrong."

"Or you can stroke the hell out of my ego."

About ten minutes later, Dr. Jensen steps over to where Wolfgang and I are sitting together, conversing about the latest teen book turned to overly hormonal movie. We both want to see it.

Dr. Jensen briefly looks at the prints Wolfgang accumulated for his photo series based around coffee. There's a lot to go through since my friend has gone down two different paths with his images. He has made a study of production with photographs of beans, equipment, and the final liquid product, and another study of the social aspects, which include baristas and people consuming the caffeinated beverage. The overall critique in regard to the composition of each image is worthy, as expected because Wolfgang has a keen natural instinct for the arts, but he needs to tighten up his focus a little for a targeted impact.

Dr. Jensen then turns to me. "EJ, let's see what you have."

I sift through my collection of black-and-white images, sorting out my favorites and what I consider my better work.

"What is the exact focus of your study?" he asks, browsing my selection of favorite images.

"Water," I state firmly. "But it feels like something is missing."

"These are all different. Wouldn't you agree?"

He separates three images from the others, closely looking at each one. I study the pictures—a puddle, a running faucet, and a fountain image taken at a downtown water sculpture on the square.

"Yes, but they're all linked by water, which is my subject."

"But they all convey more than that, and they have a different"—Dr. Jensen circles his hands in front of his torso as if he's turning the wheels of his vocabulary—"message."

"Yeah." I bite my bottom lip. "I guess in some ways. Maybe I need another environment to connect them better?"

"No, you have plenty to work with here." He fingers through the prints set aside, pulling out two images from the downtown fountain shoot. "You have more in this environment. I don't think you need another way of showing water, but rather, you need to explore it further in one place. Dig deeper."

"Deeper," I mutter.

He hands me an image of water suspended in air, a droplet caught midstream, sparkling in the sunlight. The fluid almost glows independently in contrast to the background. There's something ethereal about it, and I didn't originally pull it as a favorite.

"This one," he continues, "is very interesting, more so than all the others. The way the liquid is caught in the light is like—"

"A religious experience?"

"Some might see it that way. It's all up to interpretation, but that's the art in it."

Holding the black-and-white image he chose, I begin to get lost in the story of the water and the symbolism in my own mind. This simple droplet of water could very well convey the fragile beauty of life. It's a living spirit that causes my heart to flutter with delight, connecting myself to the moment. It's not just water. It's everything, if I allow it to be.

"I see what you mean," I say, awestruck that it was there all along.

"Do you think you have a good direction now?"

"Yes. Thanks."

"Very good. Email me if you have any questions."

Dr. Jensen steps away, heading toward another student waiting for his insightful advice. I gather up my prints, stuff them back into my bag, and exit the classroom with Wolfgang by my side.

"So, what do you think you're going to do about your project?" he asks, playing with the ends of my hair.

I zero in on his hand near my shoulder as his fingers continue to run through the white-blonde locks. "What are you doing?"

"You really do have the best hair," he says with a charming flirtatious innocence. "I can't help myself."

I give him the what-in-the-hell-are-you-talking-about eye.

He removes his hand. "You know about my hair fetish."

"I do?" I enunciate. "Is that why you keep your head shaved?"

He rubs the dark stubble on top of his skull. "Not on me. I like it on others. You're your own masterpiece. Every person is."

"Now, you're just trying to cover how stupid you sound with compliments."

"It's the same thing with boobs. I could look at those all day, too. They're really pretty. I love the way some bounce, and others just sit up, high and tight."

"I'll be sure to wear turtlenecks from now on."

"No, don't! Yours are great. It's just an infatuation. I only like to sample, not commit."

"You're ridiculous." I laugh. "Spoken like a true artist—always struggling and can't commit to anything."

"That's not true," he objects, a sly grin spreading across his face. "I'm thinking about committing sin with Jasper this evening."

I'm intrigued. "The hottie with a body from the graphic design department?"

"The one and only. What a sexy ass he has, too. We're supposed to have drinks tonight."

"Just drinks?" I ask suggestively.

"We shall see. Maybe I'll let him drink me."

"Okay, too much information. I don't want to hear how you use each other as lick sticks."

"You know you fantasize about it."

"Not so much." I scrunch my nose. "I'm not into the curiosity sandwich. I'm a mature young lady."

He barks a laugh, wrapping an arm around my neck. "I love you, little lady. You're so full of shit."

We continue down the hallway toward the cafe area. Wolfgang orders a pumpkin muffin from the counter, and we take a seat at one of the small round metal tables.

"Let's talk shop. How do you plan to handle your water series?" he asks, wiping the napkin across his mouth.

"I almost feel like starting over, to tell you the truth," I admit, feeling overwhelmed. "Dr. Jensen was right. My stuff is all over the place."

"You're not looking at it right. You have some brilliant pieces in there." He taps my binder. "The fountain stuff in particular has some profound messages and composition."

"Do you think so?"

"Yeah. Maybe you just need more of those?"

"If I were to go that route, it'd be best to get some images in different lighting. Everything I have is during the day."

"That's not a bad idea. You totally should."

"It's not going to happen." I sigh. "The assignment is due on Friday, and I need to print and matte everything tomorrow in order to make the deadline. There's not enough time."

"What's the issue? Take the shots tonight."

"Can't. I have to work and by the time I get off, it'll be nearly midnight."

"So?"

"So, the fountain is downtown. You know, the one on the square? That's the problem." I raise my brows.

"Still not following."

"Late night, girl with her head shoved behind a camera and not aware of her environment," I say, like the issue is obvious. "There's been a lot of crime in that area lately. I'd be asking for some serious trouble without a safety buddy, and Chandra has a date tonight. It's a big reason all my shots are daytime ones. Plus, everyone is always so busy with studios and assignments. It's a little late to ask someone else."

"I'll go with you," he offers.

"You just said you have a date with Jasper. I can't let you give that up."

"I love you, little one, but I'm not offering to give up anything." Wolfgang leans his elbows on the table. "I'll have a drink with him, and then he and I both can chaperone your silly ass. So, you'll have two guys watching your back."

I glance at my photo binder, wanting so badly to fill it with greatness. "Do you think he would mind?"

"Nah," he says confidently. "Besides, you need help, and you would do it for me."

"I'll owe you big time."

Six

After returning the recently checked-in books to the stacks on the second floor of the engineering library, I descend the steps and join Foster behind the desk where he's studying for his upcoming industrial chemistry processes exam. I needed a break from all his knowledge-spouting. My head might have gone into shutdown mode when he started to explain the specifics of enhancing metals with chemicals—otherwise known as smelting. I never should have asked what he was working on as a courtesy because he definitely got a geeky hard-on from talking about the science of the procedure. To me, the word *smelting* sounds more like a drug-induced sniffing party than a sophisticated scientific process, but to each their own.

"Are things still going smelt-tastic?" I ask, taking a seat in the cushy gray chair and sliding over my book on surrealism.

"Smelt-errific," Foster quips back, scratching the side of his head and shuffling his warm-brown hair over his ear. "So great that I've moved on to pyroprocessing. I'm on fire."

"I'll get the fire extinguisher." I fan myself. "The heat of your brain is spilling over into my space."

He peers at me oddly over his shoulder and then concentrates on his textbook.

Over the past month of working together, Foster and I have fallen into a comfortable pattern at the library. We complete our jobs independently, have occasional conversations, and do our school assignments in between. As far as coworkers go, he's fairly easy to work with. He gives sporadic comments about my attire or hairstyle, and I, in return, ask falsely interested questions about complex molecular structures. He usually laughs because my inquiries are completely fiction and totally miss the mark.

"After you finish your flame-induced studying, do you want to help me reorganize the periodical section?" I ask, pulling my hair up into a ponytail. "The group of freshmen that was here finally left, and magazines are all over the place."

"Should I put on my superhero cape?" He's mocking me. "Is it a complete catastrophe?"

"Worse. The hydros might be mating with the motherboards soon. If we don't fix it, engineers around the world might go ballistic."

"Now, that would be a travesty." He shuts his book and places it underneath the desk. "Let's get on it before there's any dangerous crossbreeding."

Leaving the front-desk area together, we begin the process of gathering the magazines strewed about the library—on the chairs, windowsills, tables, and even on the floor. Within fifteen minutes, the entire section of periodicals is neat, clean, and alphabetized.

Returning to our seats, I pull out my notes to study for an exam on American artists in the 1920s. It's not my favorite time period at all. I prefer the Renaissance period.

Before settling my brain into study mode, I take out my phone to check for any texts or emails. There's a voice mail from Wolfgang. He's likely just confirming that I'll pick him and Jasper up once I get off from work, so we can go down to the square and get the much-needed shots for my photography assignment.

I listen to the message.

"EJ, it's Wolfgang. Listen, something came up. Call me as soon as you can."

That's where the voice mail ends. The tone of his voice was a little…tentative…urgent. Without any pause, I dial his number, and the phone rings twice before he answers.

"Hey, EJ," Wolfgang says, somber. "I'm…"

"What's going on?" I ask, slightly nervous.

"I'm a full-blown idiot." He exhales heavily. "I'm in the emergency room."

"Oh, crap. Holy shit! Are you okay? What happened?"

"I'm fine. My ego is a little bruised though. I cut my hand."

"Is it bad?"

"Sort of. There was a lot of blood."

"Shit. What happened?"

He groans. "Jasper and I went back to my place to have another drink, and I decided it would be a good time to slice a pineapple to bring out the flavor of the alcohol. Apparently, drinking and slicing don't go hand in hand because I sliced mine instead of the pineapple."

"Holy fuck!"

"Tell me about it. I'm a total moron, and now, I'm waiting to get stitches. Some date, huh?"

I shake my head. "It's not your finest. That's for sure."

"It's pretty pathetic."

"At least you had a hottie by your side the whole time."

"True. He is quite a looker. Anyhow, I'm so sorry, but I can't do the shoot with you tonight. I haven't even been triaged yet, and this place is packed. I swear, if one more kid pukes, I'm going to ask for a healthy dip into a vat of sanitizer. I could be here all night."

I sigh. "It's okay, Wolfie. Don't worry about it. Get your hand fixed, and I'll talk to you soon."

"Sorry. Maybe we can do it after I get out of here? Not sure when that might be, but I hate letting you down."

"No. Don't worry about it. You take care, and don't apologize. Accidents happen."

"Thanks."

Ending the call, I stare at the phone. What happened to Wolfgang is horrible, and life is totally going to suck for him in the coming week. As an artist, working with an injured hand is a huge disadvantage, and I hope he heals quickly.

Then, my reality settles in. Friday is less than forty-eight hours away. A huge project is due, and I have no backup plan to speak of. I was counting on Wolfgang.

Taking the risk of going downtown by myself is a possibility, but it would not be smart or safe. Wolfgang was kind of a one-shot deal. Chandra is busy, and it's too late to really call anyone else. I'm sure most of my other friends are buried in their studio work at this time.

I could take on a new subject, which would basically be starting over and doing two weeks of work in twenty-four hours. I could always resign to turning in my existing shots. It is not my best work, and it doesn't meet my full potential, but it would at least be something.

All these options suck huge dick.

I toss my phone onto the desk where it spins round and round. Pushing the chair away from the counter, I rest my elbows on my knees and my face in my hands.

"Is everything all right?" Foster asks hesitantly.

"Yeah," I mumble into my palms. "No. Shit. Yes. No one is dead, so that's a plus."

"Okay..." He edges himself closer to me. "Did someone get hurt?"

I tilt my head to find us closer than I expected, discovering that the shade of his blue eyes are more cobalt than cerulean at this range.

I inch backward a bit. "My friend sliced his hand while trying to show off his pineapple ninja skills on a date."

"That's certainly a unique tactic for impressing someone. Is he going to be all right?"

"Yeah. He just has a mild case of drunken klutz and needs to get stitches. Should be good as new."

"Well, that's a relief." He purses his lips. "Are you two really close?"

"Yeah. We have some classes together."

"Are you going to be okay? Do you need to leave early? I can cover the rest of the shift."

"Huh?" I ask, confused by the random offer.

"You seem pretty upset. If it's too much to deal with, you can go, and I'll close up for the night by myself."

"What? No, I'm okay. He'll be fine, and he has someone with him." I shimmy my seat closer to the desk, placing my palms on the hardwood surface. "He was supposed to help me with a project tonight after work, and now, he can't. I understand why, but..." I frustratingly kick the inside of the desk, causing a bellowing boom to echo through the entire room. "Shit," I hiss. "Fuck."

"That bad, huh?"

I groan, placing my face back into my palms, and mumble, "You have no idea. It's thirty percent of our grade, and I have shit to present. I'll never be able to recover. My GPA is going to tank, and I might as well say good-bye to grad school. I'll never hear the end of it."

"Was he going to be a nude model for you?" Foster asks, totally oblivious.

"No." I half-laugh. "Is that what you think all artists do? Look at nudes all day?"

He shrugs. "That's how they're portrayed in movies. I figured they were into it for the real-life porn."

I crack up. "You must think we're all a bunch of horny bastards. If that were true, don't you think that every guy in a fraternity would be an art major?"

"Maybe they secretly want to be."

"You might have a point. If you must know, Wolfie—"

"Wolfie?" He raises his brows.

"My friend—his name is Wolfgang—was going to go downtown to the fountain on the square with me tonight, so I could take some night shots for my project. The day ones are ready to go, but I need different lighting."

"In the nude?"

"No." I giggle. "He was just going as a chaperone, so I could take some pictures of the fountain and not have to worry about watching my back. When you're behind the camera, all you see is what's through the lens. It's a safety thing. I'm thinking about risking it and going alone."

"Don't do that." He gives me the are-you-a-total-moron look. "That's stupid. I'll go with you, if you really need to go."

"Stop it. You don't have to do that. It's late enough as it is, and you have a test in the morning."

"So? It's not like I have a curfew." He places his book into his bag. "And you shouldn't be down there alone at night. I'll stand with you and watch your back while you take your pictures."

"You would really do that?"

"Sure." Foster pushes the bridge of his dark glasses higher. "Why not? Weren't you sent here to—how did you put it? Babysit me? I can return the favor."

"I don't know what to say."

"Most people usually just go with thank you."

"Then, thank you." I smile.

"You're welcome."

Seven

The crisp night breeze sweeps over my bare hands carrying my photography equipment as Foster and I tread across the stone square plaza toward the illuminated large fountain at its center. Hues of yellow, purple, pink, and gold light up the individual streams of water dancing around the sculpture, creating a lucid rainbow of curves in the air.

"I'll set up over there," I say, pointing to a well-lit space about twenty feet from the rim of the fountain.

The temperature lowers as we edge closer toward the moving water.

"I should be able to get a few shots here, and then I'll likely have to change position."

"Sounds good," Foster says near my side, tucking his hands into his taupe canvas jacket. "What should I do?"

"Just be a good guard dog."

"Do I need to bark?"

"Only if you want to."

I set up the tripod, lengthening the legs to the appropriate height, extract the camera from my bag, and clip it onto the head of the stand, firmly securing it.

Peeking through the lens, I frame the shot and adjust the angle of the camera to achieve a desirable composition.

Fingers crossed this goes well.

Sometimes, the process of getting the right shot is more trial and error along with a little bit of luck.

I shoot, capturing eight images in a row, and then readjust the angle of the lens upward. I take five more shots as the sound of water plunging into the small pool at the bottom of the fountain fills the quiet evening.

"What's this all about?" Foster questions.

I change the aperture. "Are you asking a philosophical question about life?" I grin, teasing him. "The age-old question, what does it all mean?"

"No." He chuckles. "I think Gandhi and a bunch of ancient Greek guys covered most of the what-does-it-all-mean stuff. It's highly unlikely your views on that could possibly trump those."

"How do you know?" I peek at him. "I could make a very strong argument. Don't you think it's kind of premature of you to disregard my views so quickly?"

"Depends. Do you think the meaning of life can be found through a camera lens?"

I shrug. "It's possible. Don't knock it until you try it."

"Sounds like peer pressure to me. I'm not falling for that."

I smile and look through the camera once again. "I'm totally lost, and I have no idea what you are even talking about. Your big brain went on some kind of tangent."

Foster steps closer to my side, and his arm nudges my hip. "The meaning of life."

"Deep, Fozzie. Cosmically existential."

"Sure, Evelyn," he says, drawling out my name.

After taking a few more shots, I change the camera lens to one more suited for close-ups, pick up the camera and stand, and walk closer to the fountain.

"By the way, I wasn't trying to have a philosophical conversation about life with you," Foster says.

I lock the tripod legs into place. "I'm aware. I was just teasing you."

"You do that a lot," he deadpans.

I'm fully aware of my constant sarcastic tone, but never has anyone called me out on it so blatantly.

Foster is doing me a huge favor by coming to this part of town in the middle of the night, and I should be a little more appreciative of his generosity and try not to be so flippant. As my mother would say, I was raised with manners, so there's no reason not to use them. Even though I hate to admit it, there are occasions when she's right, and this is one of them.

"I'm sorry," I tell him. "I didn't mean to blow you off."

"You didn't." He smiles in a way that is authentic and somewhat...adorable. "But I am starting to wonder if you can hold a serious conversation."

"I can, but it isn't my usual means of communication."

"Why?"

"A lifetime of rebellion."

"Huh?"

"Never mind." I bury my head behind the camera. "We can have a serious conversation if you want. What did you have in mind?"

Foster stands silent at my side as I snap a few photographs. When the frame is exhausted, I gather my equipment and meander to the opposite end of the platform with my faithful guard at my side—still quiet.

I drop my camera bag at the new location.

"Before," Foster says, "I was asking about your project and all these images that you're taking."

"What about them?" I ask, quickly setting up.

"What's your project about?"

"It's a study of water."

"Water," he muses. "I guess that's pretty obvious. Are you doing all the classical elements? Earth, wind, and fire, too? Not the band, of course."

"No." I laugh, ducking behind the camera. "Why would you think that?"

"It's logical. They all go together, chemically speaking, balancing each other out, and humans are dependent on all of them to co exist with one another."

"For humans and the earth maybe, but this isn't a science project. It's art. Plus, I'm not exploring that kind of story with this series."

"There's a story, too? These are pictures, right?"

"That's usually what you take with a camera."

"You're teasing me again, Evelyn."

"But it's so easy, Fozzie," I singsong. "Besides, you're thinking too hard. You're going to hurt that big brain of yours."

"I doubt that," he counters. "And it's not that big."

"Right." I laugh. "Keep telling yourself that, Mr. I Hold Every Academic Chemistry Award Known to Man."

"Somebody needs to. Why not me?"

He pauses, and I take another shot.

"Explain to me what you mean, so I don't give myself a brain aneurysm."

"Okay." I rise from my bent position.

The soft glow from the fountain illuminates his windblown warm-brown hair. The excessive moisture in the air has caused the ends to curl across his brow, framing his midnight-blue eyes.

"Each image is supposed to tell a story, and I'm using water to convey mine."

"Water?" he questions skeptically.

"Yes. Clear liquid often found in oceans, streams, lakes, and rivers. Sometimes falls from the sky in the form of rain."

"Can also be a gas or solid." He taps his forehead. "My gigantic brain has just informed me that it's two parts hydrogen and one part oxygen. I did pass basic chemistry. It's kind of simple."

"Chemically simple, of course," I playfully mock. Then, I return to shooting my photography assignment. "Each shot should be more than just a picture. If done correctly, within each frame, a tiny tale will unfold. The composition should make people question their purpose in life and the meaning of life and existence in general. Art is a way to convey what words cannot.

"It's not simple, like you said. It's not just two parts hydrogen and one part oxygen. It's more than water. It's a story—a living and breathing substance beyond the reflective surface." I snap an image and then return my focus to Foster, who is pondering over the fountain before us. "Sure, you joked about it before, but in some ways, I really am exploring the meaning of life through a lens."

Foster grins. "Damn, Evelyn, that's kind of deep."

"Thanks, Fozzie."

I pick up the tripod with the camera attached and maneuver around the base of the fountain to the other side, wanting to capture every angle. Lining up my shot, I play with the shutter speed, taking longer-exposed shots to create a sense of motion.

"So, why water?" Foster asks at my side, continuing our conversation.

"What do you mean?"

"There has to be a reason you chose it, right? According to you, it's more than just molecules, and you think it tells a story—or at least, you want it to tell one."

"I don't know." I feel a pang in my gut. I snap another shot and then peek over my shoulder at him. "I guess I've always had a thing for water. Ever since I was little, um…I've kind of been obsessed."

"Fond childhood memories?"

"Hardly," I huff. "Kind of the opposite."

"Oh?"

"Growing up, my family and I used to spend a lot of time on the water, and I hated it. Every trip was torture."

"I thought you said you loved the water."

"I do. My mother, on the other hand, is…never mind."

"Ah," he says, like he's had a eureka moment, "mommy issues."

"Total understatement." I laugh to myself, realizing how open I'm being about the subject. "It would have likely taken years of therapy to come up with that diagnosis, and you figured it out in less than three minutes."

"I must be a genius."

"I told you that you had a big brain," I remark over my shoulder.

"You sure did." He massages his temples. "And it's getting bigger by the minute."

"That's your ego inflating."

"Doubtful." He lowers his gaze toward the ground, kicking at the cobblestones. "Would you like me to send you a bill for my psychological services?"

"Please do. I'll forward it along to my accountant."

He adjusts his glasses over the bridge of his nose. "So, what? When you went on family vacations, did you have visions of tying a rock to your mother's ankle and dropping her to the bottom of the ocean?"

"That's kind of morbid. And no, I didn't. I always hoped to escape into the water myself." The same pang hits my stomach once again. It's a new-to-me nervousness. "Do you promise not to laugh?"

"No," he utters curiously, "but I'll try not to."

"Great. I can't believe I'm telling you this. It sounds so silly, but part of me always hoped that I could turn into a mermaid and plunge into the depths of the sea forever."

Foster tilts his head. "That doesn't sound silly."

"Really?"

"No. And your family can't be all that bad."

"Well, that's debatable."

"It's doubtful that they're so bad that you'd rather spend your entire life as part fish, drowning sailors with screeching siren songs."

"The gig was attractive when I was ten."

I take two more shots and then stop to review my digital images. Satisfied with the variety and angles, I announce, "I think that's everything I need."

Detaching the camera from the tripod, I place it into my bag and rise back up to begin breaking down the rest of my equipment.

But someone beat me to it.

Foster collapses the tripod legs and then locks everything into place without me having to even tell him how. Carrying the metal stand, he begins to walk toward where my vehicle is parked in a nearby garage.

"So, what's your parents' story?" Foster questions as we're crossing the street. "Divorced or something?"

"Worse. They're happily married. They always do the right thing and are loved by everyone they meet."

"Sounds like a total nightmare."

"A very scary one."

Eight

It's the Friday after Thanksgiving, and I'm fleeing New York City two days earlier than regularly scheduled. The visit was not a warm one.

I'd arrived at my parents' penthouse on Wednesday afternoon and ended up going out with a high school friend, who was also back in town, to catch up since my parents had a social function to attend that would last through the evening. The following day, I'd joined them, Barbara, and her newlywed husband, Geoffrey, for Thanksgiving dinner at the same hotel we had dined at since I was six.

The meal itself had been overly indulgent and grand, as was the conversation. By the time dinner had ended, it had been obvious that my presence wasn't needed in New York—or even desired, for that matter. My father had promptly left for Italy on business, and my mother had made arrangements with Barbara to visit Geoffrey's family in the Hamptons. Being an afterthought for the holiday, I'd decided to return to campus where stilettos and pencil skirts weren't a requirement.

I'd devised a white lie about studying for finals and spending the weekend working on my thesis. None of my family had batted an eye about my soon-to-be absence, so I'd booked the earliest flight available.

I will be landing back where I truly belong in less than three hours.

"Flight attendants," the pilot announces over the aircraft cabin, "prepare for takeoff, please."

Settling back into my seat, my tension dissipates when the plane pulls away from the gate. It's not long before we're on the runway and ascending into the air. I gaze out the window, watching the world below become smaller with every passing second. When the New York skyline is well out of view, I close the shade along with my eyes, exhausted and free, drifting to sleep.

~~~~~~

"Evelyn," my mother says, her high heels clicking across the hardwood floor of my bedroom, "I'm heading out for the day." She stops by the window, drawing the taupe curtain to view the street twenty stories below.

"Where are you going?" I ask in my eleven-year-old voice, turning within my seat at the vanity.

"Meetings, darling. The charity auction I'm heading this year needs a lot of my attention right now. After that, I have an appointment with Gregor at the salon and then drinks with Charlotte and Daniella. I can't very well let them down."

"Oh," I say, smoothing out the wrinkles in the skirt my mother purchased for me on one of her daily shopping excursions last week. The white eyelet trim is similar to the scallop on my bedding.

"Marisa will see that you do all your lessons," she says, referring to our live-in au pair.

Marisa has been with me for the last two years, joining us after the previous employee went back to Europe.

"Be sure to brush up on your French. I hope she's been conversing with you in it daily."

"She has."

"Good. I'll talk to her about it as well. We're all going with your father to Paris to meet up with our dear friends in two weeks. You need to be prepared."

"I remember," I reply obligingly.

"Yes. Well, you'll want to be sure you can speak the language fluently to make good conversation with their son, Gerard. The Beauchamps are very important people to us."

"Fera, Maman," I answer, loosely replying, *"Will do, Mom,"* in French.

"Bon." She nods, still gazing out the window into the sea of buildings. The fine fabrics hanging from the windows frame her elegant long physique tastefully. *"Keep practicing. Don't forget, you have violin in an hour."*

"What about my pottery class?"

"What pottery class?"

"Don't you remember? I asked last week if I could take one. I gave you a flyer about it."

"Evelyn, dear." Her angelic eyes set within her angular face demand my attention. *"I'm not so sure. You have more important things you need to be concentrating on right now. French, violin, and swimming on top of all your regular studies are really important if you want to get into an Ivy League school, which is a must. You don't want to jeopardize your future."*

"I know this," I say, lowering my head.

She approaches where I'm sitting, placing both hands on my shoulders. *"Sit up straight. You're a young lady, not a Neanderthal."*

I nod, not saying anything more.

"Now," she continues, *"I will see you tomorrow."*

"But I thought you said you were just going to be gone for the day?"

"Sorry, dear," she consoles, fingering a tendril of my light-brown hair. *"I actually won't be home until late. There's a dinner with the Thompsons, and Sandra is heading a Christmas fundraiser. I have to be there."*

"I understand."

"Besides, Marisa and you have plenty to go over. I don't want you to get behind."

"Okay," I say reluctantly.

She kisses the top of my head. "Don't forget to go over your French. Gerard is really nice."

Her body, a product of a strict low-calorie organic diet and exercise with a side of liposuction, retreats out of the room.

My mother is a stranger to me in so many ways. The only interactions we have are in regard to what I should be doing, according to her wishes.

Her wishes.

Does she even know my wishes?

Does she even care?

Does she even know me at all?

Who am I?

For the first time ever in my existence, I realize that my life isn't really mine. It's the one my mother has been planning and molding since the day I was born. I'm being groomed for Gerard or whatever man who comes from a good family with money and fine breeding.

I'm the human equivalent of a Fifth Avenue mare seeking a European stud.

I dreamily stare at the landscape print of blue-and-orange swirls over a dark village. What I wouldn't give to live in that starry night in the painting.

~~~~~~

"Excuse me."

My eyes flutter, shades of gray vinyl flashing through my vision, and the stale air hits my nose as I awaken.

"Excuse me, miss," a voice calls to my left. "The captain has announced our descent," a flight attendant in her sixties, wearing a terrible shade of red lipstick, continues. "Please return your seat to the upright position. We'll be on the ground shortly."

Still returning from my dream state, I nod while straightening my seat. The flight attendant lingers down the aisle, uttering similar instructions to other passengers.

As the aircraft descends closer to the ground, I retrieve a small notebook, a memento of my childhood, from the seat pocket in front of me. Each trip home always brings about new revelations, and this was no different. I discovered that my bedroom had been downsized to make room for my mother's expanding closet.

Because two weren't enough. Apparently, she needed another one for her handbags.

Much of my room had been packed into boxes in preparation for a remodel.

At first, I was livid when the house attendant explained the upcoming construction since this was the first I knew of it, but then I quickly accepted the change because, in all honesty, most of the memories I had were not fond ones. I took the opportunity to reminisce about my youth, as I made sure nothing of importance was being thrown out or stored away, and I found my first art journal.

The bound pages were a secret between Marisa, my last au pair, and me. She'd introduced me to so many new ideas about life, the world, and people in general. Before taking me under her wing, she had been a struggling musician in Europe, and she'd come to the States to fulfill her grand and lofty hopes and dreams of having a professional career in the music industry. However, when Marisa had found herself unable to pay the rent, she had taken on me—my mother's burden—as her own. While we had only been together for a short number of years, I'd learned more in her presence than with any other au pair my parents had afforded me.

Within the first few pages is a postcard print of Van Gogh's *The Starry Night*. Marisa had taken me to the Museum of Modern Art on one of our required cultural excursions, and I had fallen in love with the colors and lines of the masterpiece. I recall gazing at the canvas for what had felt like an eternity, as if it had sucked me into a dimension where only I existed within the eloquent echoes of Van Gogh's mind.

Over lunch in the museum's cafe, my au pair and I had talked about a variety of art, what it meant to us as individuals and what each artist was trying to convey when they'd crafted their masterpiece. Before we'd left the museum, she'd bought me the postcard and the journal in my hands with her own money. Although Marisa had said it was because she wanted to give me a gift from herself, in retrospect, there's no doubt in my mind that it was because she had known my mother would have disapproved.

Why else would she have asked me to keep it a secret?

When we'd returned to the immaculate penthouse, smelling of bleach from a recent cleaning by the maid, Marisa had asked me to summarize my feelings and observations about Van Gogh's *The Starry Night.*

Studying the painting had become my obsession for years as I tried to properly describe the way this art piece in particular made me feel. My words had started off simple, but as I had grown, so had my thoughts.

As I flip through each note, I can't help but smile.

When I come to the final entry—written when I was nearly seventeen, according to the date—my eyes water. Some feelings never change.

THE STARRY NIGHT BY VINCENT VAN GOGH

HUES OF BLUE AND YELLOW SWIRL LIKE COSMIC WAVES OVER THE SMALL EVENING VILLAGE. THE ILLUMINATIONS ARE SO BRIGHT IN THE PAINTED SKY THAT THEY PIERCE A VIBRANT HEARTBEAT INTO THE STILLNESS OF

THE RIGID BUILDINGS BELOW.
UNBENDING BOXES HAVE BEEN
CONSTRUCTED TO CONTAIN AND CHAIN
THE MORNING CREATURES, SO THE
NIGHT CAN PLAY FREELY, ALLOWING
THE DARKNESS TO ABSORB ITS OWN
LIGHT.

HUMANITY RESTS AND FLOURISHES IN
THE RECTANGULAR CLUSTERS. BUT
WHAT IF THE BEINGS ARE HOLLOW?
THEIR EMPTY HEARTS HAVE BEEN
MOLDED AND REGIMENTED TO FOLLOW
RULES FORMATTED BY THE DAYTIME
INHABITANTS.

SLAVES TO THE VOID.

I AM NOT ONE OF THOSE HOLLOW
HEARTS. MY PUMPING BLOOD IS A
CAGED AND FAMISHED BEAST PRIMED
TO EAT AWAY AT THE BINDINGS OF THIS
EXISTENCE.

I WANT TO LIVE IN THE NIGHT—TO
DANCE AND TO BE FREE, TO RIDE THE
WAVES OF THE WIND. I WANT TO BE
WILD AND WITHOUT BOUNDARIES.

MY BODY WAS GIVEN A LIFE IN THE
STILLNESS, BUT MY SOUL YEARNS TO
RETURN TO *THE STARRY NIGHT*.

Nine

"So, who are we meeting again?" I question Chandra.

We turn the corner at the end of the block where streetlamps light up the sidewalk, paving the way for college students to enter the many off-campus bars.

"Jeremy," she replies, stuffing her hands into her coat pockets as the crisp fall night air cuts through us.

"And?" I ask, pulling the newly dyed red strands from my balm-covered lips.

"Just a few of his friends." She peeks at me, a mischievous grin playing at the edge of her cheeks. "Including his super cute roommate, Anthony."

"Great," I drawl with the insinuation of impending doom.

"What? It's not all right for Jeremy to tell me which of his friends are going to be there?"

I laugh. "Don't pretend like I don't know what you're up to."

"I have no idea what you're talking about," she says, her voice rising to an octave of false innocence.

"Sure you don't. You've only mentioned Anthony's name to me almost daily for the last month. Stealth you are not."

"Yoda you are not." She bumps her shoulder against mine. "I just thought it'd be nice if we could all go out together sometime. Honest."

"I get it, but I'm really not in the dating mood tonight. I was hoping to just get hammered."

"Well, you can still do that," Chandra says, stating the obvious. "And maybe meet someone at the same time?"

"We'll see."

Coming back to campus early was definitely for the best. The moment I walked into my apartment from my shortened New York trip, I immediately felt at home. The streets of Manhattan might be a lifelong dream for many, but for me, it's a prison surrounded by invisible bars of expectations, false lives, and my inability to live up to any of my family's desires.

Wanting to leave my unpleasant New York holiday behind me, I did what any girl would do. I dyed my hair. Being that it's autumn, I opted for a seasonal shade of red to match the changing oak leaves, in hopes of shrugging off the cold still lingering from my last interaction with my mother.

"Here we are," says Chandra, swinging open the door to a local pub that caters to college students and known for craft beers on tap.

It's a rite of passage to vomit on the restroom floors at least once while attending the nearby university. On my twenty-first birthday, I made my pledge to this establishment's porcelain god while Chandra held my hair.

We enter together, the heat removing some of the chill from the dropping temperature.

"I see Jeremy," Chandra says, tilting her head toward the front corner. "This way."

I follow her lead, joining her boyfriend and a few of his friends surrounding two tables pushed together. Unbuttoning our coats, Chandra and I take a seat along the booth as the four men rearrange their seating positions to make room for us.

"You made it," Jeremy states, sliding his arm around my friend's shoulder.

"Did you have doubts?" she teases him.

"None whatsoever." He leans forward, peeking at me. "Hey, EJ. New hair?"

"Yep. Decided to go seasonal."

"I like it."

"Thanks." I smile at him.

Jeremy is easy to get along with.

"How was New York?" he questions me further.

"The same as always in a reliably obnoxious way."

He laughs. "So, I take it, you didn't see the parade?"

"Nope." I fold my jacket, tucking it next to my hip. "Monster-sized turkey balloons were not on my agenda. Just good old-fashioned family drama with a side of cranberry sauce."

"Sounds like you could use a drink."

"I could likely use two."

"I can get it," a blond guy with broad shoulders says, rising from the table. "What do you want?"

"Something with alcohol, please."

He chuckles. "That sounds manageable. What about you, Chandra?"

"Whatever," she says, shrugging her shoulders. "Just a beer."

"Be right back."

The blond leaves the table, and Chandra proceeds to introduce me to Jeremy's friends. They're all in the same architecture program and apparently live in the same building.

"And this," Chandra states as a dark amber lager is placed in front of me by the alcohol-fetching blond, "is Anthony, Jeremy's roommate."

"Nice to meet you," I say, pulling the beer closer. "And thanks. Next one's on me."

"Sounds good," Anthony replies, pulling out the seat across from me. "Or maybe you could let me buy you drinks all night? It would be my honor to serve you, angel."

Is this guy for real? Lame ass. There's no way that actually works on girls.

"Is this the part where you ask me, 'Did it hurt? You know, when you fell from heaven?'"

"Well, did it?" he asks with a wide grin and a slimy wink that makes my skin crawl.

Great. I'm stuck with this guy.

Chandra subtly nudges me with her elbow and smiles in my direction, encouraging the oh-so hopeful and likely never-going-to-happen mating between her boyfriend's roommate and myself.

This should be a fun evening.

Over the next hour and two beers, I listen to Anthony's not-so-subtle come-ons between touting on and on about his greatness and egotistical gloating about how he will be taking over his father's architectural firm once he's done with school. And, in case I missed it the first five times he mentioned it, he boasts once again that it's the largest firm in the tri-county area.

La-di-fucking-da.

"They're having a fundraising ball in a few weeks," he tells me, referring to his family's firm…again. "Everyone will be there—the mayor, a few Major League Baseball players, and the governor. It's the biggest event in the area this season. Of course, I'll be there to mingle and network. I'll likely have to spend most of my time occupying the mayor's son since we went to school together, but it should be fun." He winks at me…again and plasters a stupid machismo smile across his face. "You should come, too."

"Excuse me?" I ask, confused.

"To the event. You can be my date."

"Um…"

This guy is oblivious. It's been over thirty minutes since I last uttered a word. *Has he not noticed?*

"You think about it, doll," he says way too confidently, rising from his chair. "I'm going to use the loo. That's what they call the restroom in Europe. I'll be right back."

He motherfucking winks again—*I swear, he must have a tic*—and then he crosses the room toward the bar.

Hopefully, when he takes a piss, his head will deflate a little.

While Jeremy is great for Chandra—nice, decent, and normal—it's painfully obvious that his roommate is a totally douche and nothing I want near my vagina.

"So, what do you think?" Chandra asks when Anthony is out of sight, and Jeremy is talking actively with his friends. "He's cute, right?"

"Yeah…" I down the rest of my pint. "And totally into himself. Maybe he should date a mirror."

"Oh, c'mon. He's not that bad. I thought you two were getting along. I heard you laughing."

I give her an are-you-serious look. "I was laughing at him, not with him or beside him. There's a total difference, and unfortunately, I don't think he could tell."

"Maybe he's nervous. You can be a little intimidating sometimes."

"Even if that were true, I haven't had a chance to get a word in edgewise. He's been talking about himself the entire time. I swear to all that is holy, if I hear about his father's firm one more time, I might stab myself with a fork." I assess the table. "Just my luck. No forks. Looks like I might have to beg you to poke me in the eye with your finger."

"I'm sorry," she says, truly remorseful. "I thought you two would hit it off. Honest. He's never been like that before when I've spoken to him. He's usually really great. Maybe he's just had a bad day. You know how that is."

"True." I tap my glass with my fingernails. "I've had a pretty crappy one myself. Maybe I should call it a night before it gets worse and just go home."

"At least stay for one more drink," she insists, "and then I'll go home with you."

"I thought you were staying at Jeremy's place tonight?"

"A girl has every right to change her mind," she singsongs. "It's our prerogative."

"You're such a dork." I shake my head, laughing at her attempt to cheer me up. "One more drink."

"Good."

"I'm going to use the restroom and get a refill," I say, emptying myself from the booth, holding the drained glass in my hand. "Do you want anything?"

"Sure," she says, lifting her half-full pint. "Same as the last time would be great."

"You got it."

"And, EJ?" Chandra calls as I turn toward the rear of the bar. "I'll be sure to…" She winks and gestures toward the vacant seat where Anthony was seated, indicating that she will help to take care of the narcissistic dickwad.

Thanks, I mouth.

Then, I head to the restroom, pausing only for a moment more when I spy Anthony heading back to our table. Sure, I'm avoiding him like a child afraid of clowns at a circus, but this guy is one freak show I've had enough of for a night.

After freshening up, I circle toward the bar and order a drink for Chandra and myself.

"Here you are," the bartender says, sliding the beverages in my direction.

I pay the gal, leaving a generous tip because working around the holidays likely blows ass chunks, and I grab the two cold drinks. Turning around to walk back to where Chandra and Jeremy's friends are seated, my attention is caught by a table of men hollering boisterously to my right. Three guys laughing and chanting while the fourth slams a shot glass and then places it in the middle of the table with a collection of other empties.

I recognize one of the laughers and chanters as my coworker.

Foster slaps the hard wooden surface in front of him and then shoots up from his seat before heading straight in my direction.

"Hey," I say. "Fancy seeing you here."

"EJ?" He squints his blue orbs behind his black frames. "Did you change your hair?"

"Yeah. Red. It was time for something new. No one wants to look like a snow cone for too long."

"So, you splashed a little color onto yours. I got ya."

He's in a good mood tonight. I'm glad that someone is.

Foster sidles between the bar and me. "I thought you were in New York for the holiday weekend."

"I was, but I decided to come back early. Change of plans."

He raises his hand, signaling for the barkeep. "Couldn't grow fins fast enough?"

"What? Are you drunk? How much have you had to drink?"

"In ounces or alcohol content?"

"Don't talk nerdy to me."

"Har, har. Hardy, har, har."

A small spurt of laughter escapes my lips. I'm laughing with him, beside him.

"I assume you spent the holiday with your parents?" Foster continues.

"Yeah, just like every year."

He leans a little closer, and the scent of whiskey wafts off his breath. "And you couldn't grow fins?"

I narrow my eyes.

"To change into a mermaid," he says slyly.

"You remembered," I say, impressed that he recalled the somewhat serious conversation we'd shared a few weeks back.

Tapping his forehead, he replies, "Big brain."

"Extremely."

The bartender arrives, and Foster places an order for sixteen shots of flavored vodka, which is pure insanity. Without any question, she sets the glasses on a tray and then begins to fill them with the strong clear liquid.

"Party hard," I say as the last glass is being filled. "Nothing like a vat of rocket fuel to warm you up on a cool evening."

Foster pulls out his wallet, gives the woman a few bills, tells her to keep the change, and then lifts the tray from the bar.

"Are you starting a fraternity house?" I ask.

"Nope. Drinking game. Care to join?"

"I would kick your ass at quarters, and I wouldn't want to embarrass you in front of your friends."

Slowly walking back toward his table, carrying his tray of rocket fuel for the soul, he says, "Not quarters."

With my interest piqued, I follow at his side while holding my beer in one hand and Chandra's in the other. I should be getting back, so I don't worry my roommate, but a few more minutes can't hurt. Besides, the longer I avoid Anthony's company, the better.

"Then, what are you playing?" I ask when we are with his companions.

His friends all stop talking, lifting their gazes to Foster and me.

"It's elemental," Foster states, divvying up the shot glasses among the men at the table. He places two in front of each of them and sets the rest at the center of the table.

"Sherlock Holmes?"

"Nope." He places the empty tray on the unused table next to them and then takes a seat. "The periodic table of elements. Care to join?"

"Aren't you going to introduce your friend?" one of the dark-haired men says to Foster.

"Guys, this is EJ." He swipes a chair from the nearby table, placing it in the tight space between himself and a dark blond guy. "EJ, this is the guys." He pats the wood surface. "Take a seat."

Curious, I oblige and set my drinks on the table in front of me.

"I'm Graham," the blond states, offering a hand.

I shake it, noticing a firm grip but not enough to cut off circulation.

"Peter," the stocky dark-skinned guy says.

"James," the third man, a bit on the slight side, offers with a slight nod.

"So, are you in, Evelyn?" Foster asks, teasing.

"Fozzie," I chide in warning. "Is your brain broken?"

"Nope, it's on overdrive." He scoots closer to the table.

"How do you two know each other?" Graham questions.

"We both work at the library." I take a drink of beer.

"You don't look like the typical engineering major," James states, openly judging me.

"She's not," Foster interjects. "She's an art major, slumming it with me."

"Art history," I correct him even though I wish his statement were true. "I'm minoring in art."

"And communications," Foster adds.

"No, I'm not. Where did you get that idea?"

"From your conversational techniques. Why else would you ask a guy about his masturbation habits the first time you meet him?"

Every set of eyes at the table lands on me.

"She did not," Graham hoots.

"She most definitely did." Foster leans his elbows on the wooden surface. "Her communication skills are like no one's I've ever known. So, are we going to play or what?"

"That's highly advised," says James. "Anything, so I can stop visualizing you whacking off."

"Don't pretend like you don't do it all the time anyhow," Foster taunts.

"All right, you two," Peter says. "We're playing now. Where were we?"

"We were just about to start on actinides," Graham states. "And James is up."

Oh, shit, what kind of nerdfest did I just sit down to?

"Are you in, EJ?" Graham asks me.

"I don't think so. I have no freaking clue what an actinide even is." I tuck my hair behind my ears. "Unless it's some sort of anti-blemish cream for horny and overly hormonal teenagers, I think it's best I sit this one out."

Again, all eyes land on me.

"Now, you have to play," Foster states, grinning like a fool and patting my hand. "If nothing else, I need to hear your answers. That explanation of actinide was perfection."

"Right," I say sarcastically. "Fine. I'll play your silly drinking game. First, explain to me the reason we're talking about acne medicine and then tell me the rules."

Foster purses his mouth. "The actinides series of metals on the periodic table of elements—"

"Oh, right. So silly of me not to know that."

"Yes, indeed it is."

"Keep talking."

"Each round revolves around a different series, but we only discuss one element at a time. The way it works is the guy…" He pauses for a moment and then corrects the statement, "or girl who answered incorrectly last chooses the next element for discussion. Once the element is given, we go around stating facts about that element from the periodic table. Now, you don't have to be right or wrong. It's more about how confident you are in your answer. Kind of like poker and bluffing. If someone thinks your statement is false, he or she can challenge the validity of the answer. Then, we look up the answer online, and the loser has to drink."

"And you want me to play this Poindexter game? Me? The art history major?"

"Yes." He laughs. "I have a pretty good feeling that you'll do better than you think."

"Fine." I huff, exaggerating my annoyance. In reality, this game sounds hilarious, and I really want to see it in action. "I was looking to get drunk tonight anyhow. Bring it."

"You heard her, James," Foster says, focusing on his friend. "Give us an element. Do your worst."

James closes his lids, deep in thought for a few seconds. He then blurts out, "Thorium."

Like rapid fire, the men begin spouting off facts regarding the given element.

"Atomic number ninety," Peter states.

"Unstable isotopes," says Graham.

"Once used in gas mantels," James adds.

When the men all look to Foster, he says, "Discovered in 1828."

Then, they all turn their gaze to me.

"You're up, EJ," Foster encourages. "What do you say?"

I snort. "I should probably just forfeit and take a drink."

"That's no fun. C'mon. Give it your best shot."

This is ridiculous. "Fine. What the fuck am I talking about again?"

"Thorium," Graham reiterates.

"Thorium." I grab my glass, ready to drink. "You know, the most godly of them all, being named after Thor, god of thunder. Bring on the giant hammer man with rippling muscles."

James laughs. "I'm calling bullshit on this one."

I lift my glass to my lips.

"Wait," Peter says. "The rules state that we have to verify if she's wrong first."

"Do we really need to?" I ask, lowering my drink. "Everyone here knows that it's wrong."

"Actually," Foster says, chuckling at my side, staring at his phone. "She's right. James, take the shot."

"You've got to be kidding me," he protests.

"Not at all." Foster flips his phone around for everyone to witness that I am indeed correct.

James picks up the shot and downs the vodka in one gulp. "Looks like I get to pick again." He balances the empty glass upside down on another one at the center of the table. "Einsteinium." He turns to me. "Named after Albert Einstein."

"Well, I'm up shit creek now with zero paddles, life vests, or lifeguards to speak of," I mutter.

Graham says, "Discovered in the debris of the first hydrogen bomb explosion."

"Atomic number ninety-nine," Foster offers.

"Symbol is E-S," Peter adds.

It's my turn, so I say, "The geekiest and smartest element of them all, complete with a pocket protector."

Foster slides my beer closer to me. "That's a really good guess, but you should prepare to drink."

"You think?" I ask, dripping with sarcasm.

Graham lifts his head from his phone. "Surprisingly, the einsteinium element does not have a pocket protector. Time to drink, EJ."

"Nobody saw that coming," I snark. I lift my glass, drinking close to half the pint. "I guess this means I get to choose next?"

"That's right," Peter confirms.

"Well then, you are all completely out of luck because I'm still convinced that an actinide is a pimple potion."

Everyone laughs at me, beside me—and soon, I realize, with me.

"I can pick one for you," Foster offers. "Since your chemistry knowledge is a little remedial."

"You're being a little generous by even saying it's remedial. So, yeah, go for it. Your pick."

"Very well. Let's go with californium."

"I'm guessing that being named after California won't be sufficient?" I mumble.

"Is that your input?" asks James.

"No. I'm still formulating my Nobel Prize winning answer." I dramatically rub my temples, like massaging my brain will relax it into geeky submission. "Why don't you brainiacs free your cerebellums of analytic thoughts first?"

Graham guffaws. "Sure, EJ. I'll go first. Slowly tarnishes in air at room temperature."

"Can disrupt the formation of red blood cells," James offers.

"Heaviest naturally occurring element on earth," Peter follows.

"Atomic number ninety-eight," Foster finishes.

They all turn their expectant faces toward me.

"And the smart table award goes to all of you," I say playfully, spreading my arms wide like a game show hostess. "Ding, ding, ding. We have a winner." I grab my beer, prepared to drink.

"Aren't you even going to take a guess?" Foster inquires.

"Oh, sure." I set my drink back down. "Why the hell not? Californium. The tannest and most valley girl element at the party just below the Sunset Strip." I raise my glass. "Cheers, gentlemen." Then, I take another swig of my beer.

"I don't think we need to verify that one," Peter says, shaking his head. "Everyone knows that elements don't have melanin, and therefore, can't tan."

"Of course they don't," I tease. "Everyone knows that."

"Shut up, Peter." Foster laughs, flicking a cardboard coaster at him. "No need to kick her while she's down."

"It's okay." I giggle with them. "It's pretty obvious that I know jack dick when it comes to the acne cream elements. Talk about taking advantage of a gal and her tiny brain."

Drinking games have always been a forte of mine, and admittedly, so far, this is one that I'm failing at miserably. Sitting back, I search through my head for a way to get a leg up on these guys. They all have more knowledge than fourteen-year-old boys have hormones, but there has to be something. I hate losing.

Then, I recall one little trick I might have up my sleeve.

"Let's change the subject," I announce, leaning my elbows on the table and capturing everyone's attention. "Could I interest you all in a bet?"

"This should be good," says Peter, intrigued. "What is it?"

"I bet I know a little something about physics that you all don't."

"Oh, yeah?" Foster says, sitting up in his chair. "Is that right?"

"It sure is." I glance at my beer, still more than a quarter of the way full, Chandra's untouched beer, and Foster's two shots, ready for consumption. "Are you game?" I ask my coworker.

"What do you have in mind?"

"There's a law I learned in physics a long time ago that I'd like to demonstrate, if that's okay with you."

"I'm all ears."

I point to my beer. "I bet that I can drink the rest of my beer here and the full one next to it"—I point to Chandra's intended beverage—"faster than you can drink your two shots."

He squints, looks to the sky, assesses the beverages on the table, and then peers at me once again. "This is a little too simple. You aren't serious, are you?"

"I sure am. There are a few rules though—to be fair, of course."

"Like what?"

"Well, since the volume of my drinks are more than yours, it would only be fair that you allow me to finish my first beer before you start on your shots. And you can't touch your first shot glass until my glass is back on the table. That's it."

He puckers his mouth. "Okay...that sounds fair."

"Also, we can't touch each other's glasses—at all. That's an automatic forfeit. I'm not allowed to touch your glass, and you can't touch mine."

"Anything else?"

"You can only hold one glass at a time. So, neither of us can pick up our second drink until the first one is finished and back on the table."

"You make this too easy." He unbuttons the cuffs on his sleeves and begins to roll them up his forearms. "I'm game. What's the wager?"

"If I win—"

"EJ!" Chandra's voice echoes, approaching the table. "There you are. I thought you might have left."

"Nah, I just ran into a coworker." I point to my left. "This is Foster. We work together at the engineering library. And these are his friends—Graham, Peter, and James. Guys, this is Chandra, my roommate."

In symphony, out of tune and not even close to harmonic, they all share a "hi," and "hello."

"So, what's going on?" Chandra asks, standing near my shoulder.

"These boys just kicked my ass in a drinking game, and Foster and I were just about to place a wager on the law of physics."

"What do you know about physics?" She laughs.

"Plenty." I smile, feeling confident about the bet. I turn back to Foster. "Back to our wager, I think we should bet one—"

"If you lose," James slurs, the alcohol consumption beginning to take hold, "you and your friend have to make out...and we get to watch."

"James," Foster warns. "That's stupid. She'll never agree to that."

"Never hurts to ask."

"You're cut off."

"I accept that bet," I say without any thought. Even if I do lose this bet, which is highly doubtful, swapping a little spit with Chandra doesn't give me the heebie-jeebies. I peek up at Chandra, and she shrugs, agreeing with the terms as well. "And if Foster loses…" I glare at James. "You have to make out with him, and we all get to watch."

"No fucking way!" Foster contests. "James has chronic garlic breath. Sorry, man, but you do."

"Scared?" I taunt.

"No. I just hate garlic."

"La-ame."

"I say, take the bet," Graham encourages. "I don't see how you could lose, and I could use a little girl-on-girl visual."

"Whose side are you on?" Foster scowls at Graham.

"Yours…and my dick's."

"Typical men," Chandra comments, amused.

They're all so drunk.

"Do we have a bet?" I ask with my hand outstretched.

Foster reluctantly clasps my hand. "Fine. You're on, and I want tongue, lots of tongue."

"Ditto." I slide his two shots out in front for everyone to see along with my beer, which is almost empty, and the completely full glass that was intended for Chandra. "Do you remember the rules?"

"Of course."

"No drinking any of your shot until I've finished my first beer and the glass is resting on the table."

"Right." Foster removes his dark-rimmed frames, setting them on the table. "And no touching each other's glasses, and we can only have one drink in our hands at a time. I got it."

"Awesome." I pick up my drink. "Are you ready?"

"Yes."

"Remember, you have to wait until I'm finished with this before you can start."

"I got it."

I tauntingly raise my brows and then touch the glass to my lips, slowly consuming the hoppy ale. Savoring the anticipation building among the men as they intently watch me, I relish in my soon-to-be victory.

"You know," Foster begins as I continue to consume the first part of our bet, "according to kinematic viscosity, the flow rate of liquid greatly depends on the temperature of said liquid—the warmer the liquid, the faster the flow. Essentially, even if we were drinking the same volume of liquid, which we aren't, your beer would take longer to consume since it's been kept at a near freezing temperature while my shots have been stored at room temperature. So, even with the odds of volume being in my favor, from a scientific standpoint, you would lose, no matter what."

Closing my blue eyes, I drop my head backward and finish off the last drops of beer.

I wink at Foster. *He's in for a world of hurt.*

The moment my empty glass makes contact with the wooden surface, Foster reaches for one of his shot glasses, remembering the rules. As he's lifting the vodka to his mouth, I casually flip over my pint glass and cover his remaining full shot still resting at the center of the table.

At my side, Foster slams the empty glass on the hard surface and then instinctually reaches for his other shot, now covered by my empty pint.

"Remember," I remind him. "The rules state that we aren't allowed to touch the other person's glass."

His hand hesitates over the tempting shot surrounded by my glass.

Picking up my second beer, I add, "This is an example of Newton's first law of motion. An object is either in constant motion or remains at rest until acted upon by an external force. According to the rules, it looks like your shot will have to remain at rest while my hand will gladly act upon my beer, allowing me to consume it at a much higher rate than you anticipated."

Foster runs his fingers through his caramel-brown hair, leaving it completely disheveled. "Holy…damn."

I lower my glass and turn to James. "Don't forget. We want to see lots of tongue."

Ten

Tongue. Lots of tongue.

Excessive tongue.

Slippery.

Deeply plunging.

My tongue.

Foster's tongue.

Our tongues.

His mouth is on mine, impassioned and solid, as my eager hands clench his remarkably solid ass.

Holy hell, what in the shit is going on? What am I doing? What is he doing?

"Fozzie," I mumble against his mouth, gasping for air.

"Yes, Evelyn?" he pants, pressing me harder against the wall.

The pressure of his blaring erection against my hip bone has my groin area seeking his. I'm like a teenager in the backseat of her parents' car, looking for a stolen moment.

"What are we..."

"Do you want to stop?"

My head is screaming nothing in the negative or positive, but my body is yelling the same as I say, "No, not at all. You?"

"Not really."

How did we get here?

Full of alcohol, Foster clumsily lifts me by my thighs, using the wall at my back to catch his balance. I wrap my legs around his waist, securing my body to his, and we continue to lock lips like savaged beasts on one of those animal-mating documentaries. With stumbled steps, he maneuvers us away from the kitchen in his apartment and down the hall toward what I assume is his bedroom.

I should be questioning what we're doing.

I should be stopping this right now.

I should be ripping his clothes off because I'm so blazingly horny, and my vibrator is out of batteries.

He just feels so good.

The heat of his body.

His mouth on mine.

His hands on me.

His breath commingling with my own.

Fuck, it feels good.

Turning a corner, my knee collides with the doorframe.

"Ow. Fuck," I cry out in protest.

"Sorry." His sinful mouth drops to my neck, distracting me from the recent injury. "Do you want me to get some ice?"

"Only if you're going to get kinky with me."

"Are you into that sort of thing?"

"Not ice. That shit's cold."

Foster drops us to the bed, half-falling on top of me with a mistimed and misjudged thump.

"No ice," he confirms, righting himself a bit. "Got it."

He removes his black frames, and I grab them from his hand before he has a chance to stash them away. I settle them over my face. The prescription on the lenses is so minor that my already drunken vision is barely distorted.

"Do I look smarter?" I ask, playfully pointing my index finger to my cheek.

"Definitely."

Ducking his head, Foster connects his lips to the skin on my neck and then the space under my chin while slipping his hand under my blouse and over my bra-covered breast. I fumble with the hem of his shirt tucked into his pants. Then, I pull his clothing upward, and like a total amateur, I manage to get it stuck around his neck. He lets out a half-gagging, half-choking sound before rescuing me from my sloppy seductive efforts by removing the layer of fabric himself.

My hands are like magnets being drawn to his firm chest, and they connect with his comforting skin.

Skin. Skin. Skin.

Warm skin.

Toned.

Fucking sexy-as-hell and all-over-me skin.

I-want-to-feel-more-of-it skin.

My mouth runs along his collarbone.

He tastes good, too—a combination of man and mint.

Foster lifts my top over my head before dropping it to the bed, and then he reaches behind my back. I sit up to assist him in the effort of de-clothing me. He tugs at the hooks on my bra a few times.

"Fucking girl clothes," he says, flustered, yanking at the force field of intimate apparel. "These damn hooks."

"You can formulate a hydrogen bomb, but you can't undo a bra?"

"The university doesn't offer classes on this shit."

"I'll complain to the dean."

The garment finally unhinges, and my breasts are freed. With apparent frustration, Foster removes the bra from my body in one fell swoop and then cups one breast with his palm while mouthing the other. He tweaks a nipple with his fingers and nibbles gently on the other with his teeth as we slowly lower back to the mattress.

I arch my back, encouraging him to keep fondling me the way he is, because *fuck me* the feel of his body touching mine is giving me incredibly salacious ideas. And I genuinely don't care if what we're doing is wrong because I'm adopting a new rule until morning. *If it feels good, it is good.*

My hands skim and press along his lean arms and firm back as he continues to suck and lick my chest. Reaching his waistband, I follow the line of denim to the front of his pants and attempt to undo the button.

"Need help?" he asks, kissing his way up to my ear.

"Yes. Your pants are like a chastity belt. Are you trying to keep me out?"

Foster laughs against my cheek and snakes an arm between us, popping open the button. I unzip his pants and grip his length under his boxer shorts. He growls into my ear, and *holy fuck*, does that ever make me want to pump his dick.

So, I do.

What is he doing to me? Foster Blake, the library and chemistry geek?

He's making me hot and bothered. That's what he's doing. My wet panties are accumulating the evidence.

"Shit!" he whisper-shouts. "Evelyn, is this what you want?"

I pause, my hand stilling around his cock, as he lifts his head from the crook of my neck and searches my features. He removes the glasses from my face and sets them aside.

He waits for me to respond.

"I don't know what I want," I say without a thought.

"Me neither."

Our breaths slow in unison as a slight seriousness takes over the mood.

"I don't want to stop," I add as I begin to push down his boxers and pants together.

"Neither do I."

"You're very agreeable." I laugh.

He releases an adorable grin. "Only on special occasions."

"And this qualifies?"

"It's notable."

Foster pushes back from the bed, undoes my pants, and slides them down and off my legs. He then slips off my panties.

"I guess that part didn't get a new dye job," he teases, referring to my non-tinted but well-groomed trail.

"You think you're funny, don't you?"

"Not really. I'm more surprised it doesn't match your hair."

"There's not much there to dye."

"Touché."

Quickly, he drops his pants and boxers to the ground and then steps out of them and toward the bureau. There, he opens the top drawer, searching hastily through the contents. When he returns to me, he tosses a condom on the bed and then begins to crawl over my waiting form.

"That's quite an impressive beaker you have," I say in the most non-seductive way possible.

"You were checking out my instrument?" he questions, dragging his mouth north of my hip to my breast.

"Just doing my research."

Hovering, he kisses me on the mouth a few times, almost like he's still making sure I'm not backing out. I realize that I need to make the first move. I reach to the side of the mattress, find the condom, and tear it open. Making my intentions known, I nudge his shoulder, so he's lying on his back. Sitting up, I roll the latex contraceptive over his instrument and then straddle him.

"So, what do you think?" I question.

Confusion crosses his face. "About what?"

I tease his length with my sex, gyrating over his lower body. "My tits? They're pretty great, right?"

"Your tits are fucking amazing."

"Just checking."

Taking control, Foster rolls us over, so he's on top, demanding missionary position. I'm not complaining one bit.

Without wasting any more time, he eases into my entrance, filling and touching an unrecognized void. He slides his hands under my shoulders. I circle my arms over his and then wrap my legs around his waist.

Rocking into me and moaning into my hair, Foster pounds away my recent frustrations from the last few days.

Apparently, a good dicking helps with that.

As we continue to move our bodies in cadence with one another, a strange sensation comes over me.

Foster is different.

I feel different.

The sex is different than any I've ever experienced before.

It doesn't feel right. It doesn't feel wrong.

It just...*feels.*

Eleven

Under the yellow lights, Foster leans in toward James, licking his lips a few times in preparation for their inevitable kiss. The men waggle their brows at one another as the table chants, encouraging them to lock lips. We all can't wait to watch them swap spit.

Taking the plunge, their mouths collide, and we all hoot and holler in astonishment and laughter. They stay joined for some time as we continue to cheer them on, like it's some sort of circus act.

"Where's the tongue?" I demand. "Tongue! Tongue! Tongue!"

The men and Chandra join me in chanting, "Tongue! Tongue! Tongue!" with full knowledge that it's part of the bet.

Foster lost, and now, it's time for him to live up to his end of the bargain. After all, we shook on it.

They disconnect their lips, and then James licks Foster's face—twice, once on each side, salivating all over his cheeks.

"Ew," cries everyone watching, all in different tones ranging from disgust to delight.

"There," James announces, wiping his mouth with the back of his hand. "Lots of tongue. Happy?"

"Not really," I say, laughing. "But it will do. Technically, the bet has been fulfilled."

I turn my attention to Foster as he dries his face with the sleeve of his shirt. He lifts his eyes to mine, shakes his head, and then teasingly draws the shape of his lips with his tongue.

More tongue.

The room darkens and shifts until I'm seated at the bar with Foster at my side and a line of shots before us.

Another drinking game.

"Go," I say. "Your turn."

"Never have I ever kissed two girls on the same night," he says.

Shit. He's got me. *I take the shot.*

"You have?" he asks, astonished.

"I was a freshman once," I reply nonchalantly. "My turn. Never have I ever shaved all of my pubic hair."

He laughs. "I think you're lying."

"So? Who cares? Have you?"

"Yes." He pauses and then takes the shot.

"Foster, you're a kinky, kinky shit."

He places the glass on the bar's surface. "Or I swam competitively in high school. My turn. Never have I ever walked in on my parents going to town."

A discerning sound escapes my lips in disgust. "Thankfully, neither have I. So gross."

"No kidding."

"Hey, girl," Chandra says, appearing at my side. "Are you ready to go?"

In contrast to earlier in the evening, I'm actually having a lot of fun, and the night still feels young. I'm certainly not ready to go.

"No. You go ahead," I tell her.

"Are you sure?"

"Yeah, you were planning on going to Jeremy's anyhow."

"I don't want you walking home alone," she states since we always have a safety-first rule. "It's pretty late."

"I'll walk you home," Foster offers to me. "I don't mind."

"Or I can call a cab." I shrug and then address my roommate, "Go on. I'll talk to you tomorrow."

Darkness.

81

The scene shifts as I open the ladies' room door into the dimly lit wooden hallway. Foster is exiting the men's room at the same time, cleaning his glasses with the end of his shirt. A sliver of skin peeks out between his garments. I follow his hand as he returns the black frames to his face. His hair is slightly disheveled, his eyes are dilated, and his cheeks are tinged a slight shade of pink from the excessive amounts of alcohol we have been consuming over the past few hours.

"You know," *I slur, leaning against the doorframe,* "you're kind of hot, Foster."

"You're drunk."

"A little. So what? So are you."

"True."

"But you're still cute. How come you don't have a girlfriend?"

"Because it'd cut into my masturbation schedule."

I chuckle and step closer to him. "Well, I definitely understand that."

My lips crush against his.

My gut flips.

I step back, creating some space, in hopes that the intimate moment won't linger.

"Sorry." *I shake my head.* "I've had too much to drink."

Foster approaches me.

"Me, too," *he responds as his warm breath laced with alcohol brushes my cheek.*

His lips are suddenly on mine, and his body presses my back on the wall near the secluded restrooms. My hands sculpt around the shape of his shoulders and arms.

Gravity pulls on my stomach, our bodies tumble into the dark, and we are no longer standing.

I'm lying naked with the mattress squeaking at my back. The scent of mint, alcohol, and sweat waft through the air as heavy pants surround the room. Grunts are flying from my lips and from the man over me, burying himself inside me.

"Fuck, Evelyn! Your body is incredible."

~~~~~~

My eyelids rapidly flutter open, seeing hazy shades of creams and whites. The heaviness in my chest and within my head leaves me with little desire to move.

I squeeze my lids tight, slowly count to ten in unison with the intake of air to my lungs, and then open my eyes again.

I hate hangovers.

The covers are so warm and cozy…and then, a few seconds later, I'm sweating. I need to get out of this heated bed.

Rolling to my side, I reach around to grab the blanket's edge, only to touch a hefty hand.

Realization strikes me.

I'm at Foster's apartment.

In his bed.

And completely naked.

There are two ways to handle this situation—sneak out or awkwardly spend the morning together. I decide to opt for the former.

Slowly, I slink out from underneath the weight of Foster's arm, and with absolutely no grace or coordination, I thump onto the floor.

Ridiculous hangover. No body control.

My head pounds madly like a heavy metronome when I turn it from side to side, searching for my garments. One might think to prepare for a mistaken sexual encounter by laying out their clothes the night before, so they could make an easy getaway. Apparently, I'm an amateur in this department of crazy one-nighters.

For better or for worse, this is my first experience with a situation like this. Most of my nights with men are usually the result of a natural progression during a date. This is new territory for me, and now, I resemble the foolish girl on one of those romantic comedy movies. If I'm lucky, I'll stub my toe on the way out to complete the one-night-stand cliché.

Spotting my panties and pants, I slowly crawl across the floor and begin to dress, trying to keep as quiet as possible. As I'm zipping up my jeans, Foster stirs under the covers, rotating his head on the pillow. I pause, waiting to see if he's waking up. I examine his features, which appear so much softer while he slumbers.

Watching him lying there without saying a word, I try to wrap my mind around how or why we slept together last night. Sure, he's got that sexy-when-naked thing going, but he's definitely not like anyone I've ever been with before.

However, for some odd reason, I was all about jumping his bones last night.

Can a girl just blame it on alcohol and call it a day?

But that's not reality or fair. I was making conscious decisions.

Trying not to overanalyze it, I finish zipping and fastening my pants and then creep back toward the bed, hoping to find my bra and shirt. Scanning all around, I spy my top at the corner of the mattress, and my bra is wrapped around Foster's leg.

What are the odds?

"Hey?" Foster grumbles, rubbing his palm across his jaw and righting himself in the bed.

I sit back on my heels and cover my chest, feeling utterly exposed in the daylight. "Hey. Um…I need to get going. I, um…I have to get to the studio."

"Yeah. Sure." He rubs his forehead. "Okay."

Based on his lack of vocabulary, he's not in tip-top shape this morning either.

I pull my bra away from his legs, gather my shirt, and walk toward the other side of the room. Turning my back to him in order to have some privacy, I hastily put on my bra and pull my shirt over my head, stretching the hem downward to cover my hips. I turn back around to say good-bye.

Foster has extracted himself from bed, already put on his boxers, and is now slipping into his pants. I hate to admit it, but a topless Foster is pretty easy on the eyes, but I avert mine so not to ogle. This is awkward enough.

"Well…" I say, my voice thick with lingering alcohol. "I'm gonna get going."

Foster adjusts the shirt over his torso and then reaches for his glasses on a nearby side table. "Let me drive you home."

"No, that's okay. I can walk."

"Just let me take you." He picks up a set of keys from the bureau.

"Nah, I'm good. I always walk in the mornings anyhow," I lie through my teeth.

"Are you sure?"

"Yeah." I exit out of his room, not allowing the conversation to continue.

Foster silently escorts me down the length of the apartment, passing another bedroom on the left. I find my shoes, purse, and jacket along the way.

I barely remember anything about this place. I don't know if I was completely hammered or just really focused on getting laid.

Opening the door, I step out into the building's hallway. "I'll see you on Monday."

"Yeah." He leans in and kisses me on the cheek, sending a tingle through every nerve in my body. This must be part of the one-night-stand formality. "See you Monday."

I nod my head and then descend the stairs. When I reach the first floor of the building, I open the door and follow the path from the courtyard to the sidewalk. I hook a left to find a street sign. At the corner, I take comfort in recognizing the name of the street, knowing that I have to tread only about five or six blocks before I'm home.

With my arms wrapped around my waist, I bank a right and head up the hill toward my neighborhood, pondering the entire time whether my actions last night were a mistake, a rite of passage, or something else altogether.

Foster and I are friends, colleagues, and different in so many ways. I wonder if last night has changed all of that and what we will be once Monday comes.

Twelve

Ever since my photography class let out over an hour ago, I haven't left Wolfgang's side. He's currently in the middle of prepping for a final in an upper-level art class, doing research at the design library, while I pretend to view and study compositions for our photography class final. The assignment is to do a series that directly negates our last project. Since mine was water, I'm pursuing images of fire.

In less than thirty minutes, my shift will begin at the engineering library. This will be the first time I see Foster since we did the ole in and out, bump and grind, hitting of the nasties.

Since we had sex.

After leaving Foster's apartment early Saturday morning, I stayed in my room all day, only coming out to see Chandra as she left on another date with Jeremy. I claimed to be a bit under the weather, which wasn't a huge stretch since I was nursing a hangover.

Come Sunday, I was feeling much better, and after completing some homework, I ventured to the studio, laying crimson and blue hues on a large canvas for no reason other than a desire to create and paint. It was my own personal therapy to make sense of my actions.

When three hours had passed and I had painted until my arm was sore, the final conclusion on my sexfest was that it was fun and that my budding friendship with Foster would likely be over after that night because, at the end of the day, I didn't care for him like a girlfriend should. To me, he was still just Fozzie, platonic Fozzie. No matter how great the boink-o-rama evening was, I just didn't have those love feelings toward him.

Peeking at my phone, I note the time and begin to gather my things, preparing to leave for my shift.

"Off so soon?" Wolfgang asks.

I shove my book into my bag. "Yeah, I need to get to work. My shift starts in about fifteen minutes."

"I'll walk with you," he says, rising from his seat and closing a book. "I need to get out of this place. My head is beginning to hurt."

We put on our coats, and exit the library into the dark evening. The sun always sets earlier this time of year, nearing December.

About halfway to the engineering library, Wolfgang asks, "Are you feeling all right?"

"Yeah," I respond, adjusting my bag higher up my shoulder. "I'm fine. Why do you ask?"

"You've been off today. Barely said a word. It's so unlike you. Was the trip back home not that great?"

"No, it was predictable, just like I said. I came back early because my family had other plans, and I didn't feel like sticking around."

"Is that normal? You don't talk about your family much. I just figured you had normal child-parent issues with them."

"You could say that."

"Did something happen?"

The engineering library comes into view, and my heartbeat quickens, anxiety setting in.

"Yeah, something like that." Sighing, I stop in place, staring at the entrance. "But not with my parents. I slept with my coworker."

His head does a quick snap in my direction. "Say what?"

"Over the weekend, I had sex with the guy I work with," I admit, tilting my head in the direction of my workplace. "I had too much to drink, and we have to work together and—"

"You got some. Congratulations."

"Wolfie…"

"What? Do you like him?"

"He's nice." I lift my shoulder. "Not really my type. He's kind of geeky but nice."

"But do you like him?" he asks again.

I hem and haw and then say, "No, not like that."

"So then, it was just one night of fun." He shrugs, like it's no big deal, giving unintentional sex less thought than ordering a latte. "We all do it."

"I never have," I admit. "This was kind of a first for me."

"You popped your one-nighter cherry?" He laughs. "I thought you had done it all."

I smack his arm when he won't stop chuckling. "It's not funny. We work together."

"That's going to be awkward. Do you think he likes you? Most dudes get over it pretty quickly as long as their dick got action."

My eyes roll so hard that I might have come close to giving myself a lobotomy. "Well, that's reassuring."

"It's the truth. Nothing to be embarrassed about."

"I'm not embarrassed."

"Then, why are you freaking out?" Wolfgang covers his mouth with his hand. "Oh God, is he, like, that ugly, fat guy you keep a secret but is really great in the sack? I had one of those once."

"Shut up!" I laugh. "No. And you did not."

"Sure did. Sophomore year. Best head of my life, but good Lord, I couldn't take him on a date even for takeout. He was not pretty."

"You're terrible." I shake my head. "I had no idea you were so shallow."

"Eh, it was a phase. I would never do that again. I actually felt guilty about the whole thing once we finally called it quits."

"Good. You should have."

"So, is that the thing? He's ugly, isn't he?" He begins to walk hastily toward the door. "I gotta see this guy."

"Wolfie!" I shout in protest, chasing after him. "Stop. No."

He opens the entrance. "Oh, now, I really have to take a look."

My friend races through the hall, turning at the bust of the famous engineer, and comes to an abrupt halt at the library's glass doors. I catch up to him, pausing at his side, finding Foster standing at the check-out desk, sorting through a pile of books.

"Is that him?" questions Wolfgang.

"Yeah," I say reluctantly. "His name's Foster."

"Foster? Well, isn't he all proper?" He examines Foster for a few moments. "Hello, Mr. Foxy Man with Spectacles. I wouldn't mind a one-nighter with him. Fill that geek-chic bucket-list fantasy."

"Oh. My. Gawd." I giggle. "Can we focus on my dilemma?"

"I don't see the issue. You two had sex. Get over it, and he will, too. Don't make it a bigger deal than it really is. Move on. Or not. He's hot." His lips tighten. "That shirt he's wearing is doing all kinds of good things to showcase his chest and arms. I might have to give him a whirl myself. He's got a good body under all that cotton, doesn't he?" He cocks his head. "I wish that damn desk wasn't in the way, so I could get a good look at his ass."

I grunt, frustrated that my friend is of no help. I thought for sure he would have had some reasonable guidance. Instead, he's adding the guy from my tryst into his spank bank.

"Stop trying to stare at his ass," I chide.

"Well, if you're not interested…maybe I can convince him to come and play with me."

"Stop it. He's not your type, and he's totally not my type. The guy lives and breathes the periodic table of elements." I sigh. "How am I supposed to go about this?"

Foster lifts his head, peering toward us, as Wolfgang and I are gawking at him from the other side of the glass door. Foster adjusts the bridge of his glasses, and his expression goes blank.

At my side, Wolfgang slides an arm over my shoulder, and before I have a chance to react, he's kissing me—full-on lip-to-lip, caressing-my-face kissing me.

It takes a few seconds before my brain registers what's happening to my body. The fact that my gay friend has decided to give girls, namely me, another try at this moment in time without my consent is not exactly what I was expecting.

I push him off of me, wiping my mouth with the tips of my fingers. "What in the hell was that all about?"

"I was helping you with your problem." He tilts his head toward the library desk.

Foster disappears into the back room.

"Great."

"Well, now, you don't have to worry about him asking you out—you know, since you were sucking face with me."

"Not the best solution."

"Hey, I was just trying to help."

I elbow him in the ribs. "That's not helping. Kissing is what got me into this mess in the first place."

"I think it was a little more than kissing."

"No kidding."

Leaving Wolfgang's side, I make my way through the glass doors and into the library. It's early in the evening, our busiest time of the shift, and with finals just around the corner, I expect it to remain this way until the end of the quarter.

At the front desk, I drop my bag into a cubby and check myself into the computer system. Before I take a seat and get situated, a student asks for assistance in finding a missing volume on the shelves. I guide her to where it should be, locate the book on the opposite shelf, and then return to the information area where Foster is actively engaged in aiding another student. I sort through a short stack of books, and then I'm pulled from my work again to assist another person.

This goes on for the next hour, busily assisting students with their searches and assignments. Foster and I exchange a few words here and there, but they're completely work-related. There's a bit of formalness to our interactions, but otherwise, any awkwardness is shadowed by the hustle and bustle.

When the room finally begins to settle down, Foster and I are seated next to one another for the first time since I arrived, and the nerves commence. It appears that everyone within view is occupied, so I open up the drop-off area and process some of the returns to keep my hands busy.

I'm waiting for the inevitable *real* talk, the one that I keep telling myself won't be a big deal, but for some reason, it has me full of trepidation.

Silence screams between the two of us.

"So, how was your weekend?" I ask, breaking the ice, setting a pile of books on the desk.

His hand stills over the mouse, but he doesn't reply.

"Mine was great," I continue, straightening a stack of manuals full of information that I will never understand. "Thanks for asking. The holiday was typical—you know, all the usual family crap, but nothing out of the ordinary. Upside though, I did get laid. How about you?"

Foster pushes away from the desk, spins the chair, and crosses his arms over his waist. I pull out the last of the books from deposit and place them on the desk, waiting for him to say something. The look on his face is so serious and stoic that I wonder if I went too far, making light of our situation.

"Why didn't you tell me?" he asks, his voice low and serious.

I sit up in my seat. "Tell you what?"

"That you were already seeing someone? I'm not into the cheating game. I wish I had known."

My face sours. "I'm not seeing anyone."

"I saw you kissing the guy in the hall."

We got so busy, and I was so concerned about the inevitable tension between Foster and me that Wolfgang's little stunt at the door completely escaped my mind.

"He's not my boyfriend." I laugh.

"Well, whatever he is, that wasn't cool."

"Are you jealous?"

"No. Shit." His fingers comb through his hair. "Forget it. It doesn't matter anyhow. Glad I know now."

"Why doesn't it matter?"

He shrugs. "It just doesn't." He rotates the chair, facing the computer screen once again.

I explain, "The guy in the hall is just a friend of mine. He was kissing me because he's an idiot. And so am I."

He gives me a what-the-fuck-are-you-talking-about look.

"That's Wolfgang. You remember him? He was supposed to help me out for my photography project, but he sliced his hand. We've been friends for almost four years. He's not my boyfriend, and we aren't seeing each other. He doesn't even play for the hetero team. He's gay."

Foster lifts his brows.

"I told him about us—you know, the other night—and he thought he was being helpful."

"You are making absolutely no sense."

I sigh heavily. "Listen, this is really weird for me." I point a finger back and forth between the two of us a few times. "So, I'm just going to come out and say it. Thanks for the good boning, but I'm not interested in anything else. That likely makes me sound like a bitch, but it's the truth. I wasn't cheating, and I'm not dating anyone."

He laughs. "You're nervous."

"Hell yeah, I am. Aren't you?"

"No. Well, I was until I saw you kissing that guy, and then I just got pissed. I'm not into playing someone's revenge fuck, but I'm good now."

"A revenge fuck? No, it definitely wasn't anything like that." I tongue the inside of my cheek. "Just a bit of fun between the sheets."

He tightens his lips, amused. "That's good to hear. Glad I could entertain you in a way that you like."

"Well, it wasn't that much fun," I backpedal, trying not to inflate his ego.

"No, no, you can't take it back. It was the best night of your life, and you know it."

My hands fly up in play surrender. "I admit it. The truth has set me free."

"Well, as long as you acknowledge it." He lowers his voice and adds, "And even if you didn't, the fact that you practically made me deaf by screaming the hell out of my name is proof enough for me."

My jaw hits the floor as Foster stifles a grin.

"You did not just say that."

"There's proof in the action. Cause and effect."

I shake my head and return my attention to the task at hand. Stacking the books together, I check in the top manual as Foster scoots toward his monitor, resuming work.

It would appear that Wolfgang was right. If I don't make a big deal out of it, then neither will Foster. However, he was obviously unhappy when he thought that I was being unfaithful to someone else, which I understand, but then he was able to quickly resign that my dating someone didn't matter. *Curious.*

"Hey, Foster?"

"Yes, EJ?"

I edge closer to him. "Can I ask you something?"

"Sure."

"Before, you said something about, it doesn't matter if I'm dating someone. What did you mean?"

He closes his lids. "This is why I was nervous to see you."

"I don't follow."

"I like you, Evelyn. I do. But I can't...we can't..."

"Date?"

"It's nothing against you. It's me. I just...can't. I'm sorry."

I laugh. "Stop, Fozzie. You're going to hurt yourself. I had a lot of fun, and I like you, too. I'm not looking to date you either, so don't worry."

He adjusts his dark frames. "Still friends then?"

"Yes, friends."

Thirteen

The server clears our plates and then sweeps the crumbs from the crisp linen tablecloth. My father dabs the corners of his mouth with the black napkin and then places it on his knee. Out of habit, I smooth my palms over the napkin lying across my lap.

My father called yesterday, informing me that he was going to be passing through town for a business meeting on his way to Los Angeles, and hoped that we might be able to get together for a late lunch. With his constant work schedule, time with him is so difficult to come by, but I do enjoy his company for the most part. So, I made arrangements with my professor to miss class in order to meet my father. Even though I will see him during winter break in about two weeks, I couldn't pass up this opportunity for some one-on-one time.

This morning, knowing my father's tastes for international fare, I emailed his secretary the address of a Scottish restaurant downtown for us to meet. He was late since his meeting ran over schedule, so our time together will be quicker than expected. Lunch is now coming to a close, and he will be leaving to board a plane shortly for the West Coast.

He signals for the server, and she arrives promptly. My father has a commanding air to his demeanor, and everyone respects it when in his presence. He's been this way for as long as I can remember. Even my excessively assertive and opinionated mother respects his word. He has a balanced mix of authority, gentleness, and just enough charisma.

"A twelve-year-old scotch, please," he tells the petite woman. Then, he asks me, "Would you like one, E?"

"No, thanks." I smile kindly. "I'm scheduled to work tonight."

"Of course." He addresses the woman at his side, his blue eyes crinkling at the corners, "Just one for me, and you can bring the check with it."

She nods and leaves the two of us alone in the sparse restaurant where the bussers are readying the tables for the evening service.

Shaking his head, he states, "I will never understand why you took a job with the school library system."

"I thought a good work ethic was important to you?"

"It is," he agrees, leaning over the table. "But I could have easily set you up with a local advertising firm. At least then, maybe you could have gotten some hands-on experience with the business."

Frustrated by the constant fight on this topic, I blurt, "Who says I want to join the business?"

"E, I thought we discussed this already. The only reason I even supported your…desire to pursue art was because we agreed that it would be beneficial to the company. Art history is a good path because it could help with future research as well as it looks good on your transcripts when applying to grad school. Thankfully, this school is commendable enough that Ivy League won't be out of the question."

I peek out the window as pedestrians meander down the sidewalk under the late afternoon sun. In his charcoal-gray suit, the patriarch of my family sits a little taller in his seat and spreads his fingers along the linen-covered surface.

"I remember the conversation," I answer quietly.

The server brings my father his drink along with the bill. He quickly slips his credit card into the billfold, and she scurries off to run it through the machine.

He takes a slow sip of his scotch and then rests it on the table, his fingers still wrapped around the fine crystal. "E, listen. You should have choices, but I still want what's best for you and your future."

"Working for the family business certainly doesn't feel like a choice."

His shoulders slump. "I know how much you love your art, and I think you have talent—a lot of it actually. I still have some of your work hanging on the walls in my office and not because you're my daughter. It's really good."

I peer at him, hopeful.

"However," he continues, "the life of an artist is no guarantee. I want to support your wishes, but I won't back a decision that could leave you penniless and dependent for the rest of your life."

"I don't need much," I argue.

"No doubt," he scoffs, "thanks to the trust your grandparents set up for you. But a kid who lives off their family's fortune for the rest of her existence is trouble in the making. Look at the Jacksons' boys, living out west, spending money like it's going out of style. No job. No prospects. No desire. They're lazy and unmotivated—not to mention, their occasional run-ins with the law. I don't want that for you. You're better than that."

"I would never end up like that," I protest.

"No, you won't," he states firmly, "and I'll make sure of it. I'm not taking your hobby—"

I judge him sternly, insulted by the term *hobby*.

"Your talent," he substitutes, "away from you. I just want to make sure you have a future—one with purpose as well as independence."

"I understand," I resign.

My father continues to indulge his scotch as I patiently wait for our time to be up.

"How's Barbara?" I inquire about my sister, changing the subject.

He sighs. "Married."

"Yeah." I giggle over his reluctance in saying it. "I remember. I was there for the wedding, too."

"I wish she would have waited."

Quirking my head to the side, I ask, "I thought you liked Geoffrey?"

"He's a good guy, but I don't think they needed to get married so quickly. They dated only a few months before getting engaged. They barely knew one another. But what's done is done."

"She's happy though, right?" I ask, wondering if there's something that I don't know.

"She seems to be." He downs the rest of his drink, gently placing the empty glass on the table. "She's so different than you."

"No kidding. Winning Miss Congeniality in a Miss Teen America Pageant was never my thing," I say, referring to one of my sister's many accolades. "Nor was having a championship poodle a necessity for me."

"She's more like your mother. You ended up being more like me."

I laugh. "Is that a good thing or a bad thing?"

"Depends on who you ask." Subconsciously, he fingers the top of his dark brown hair with specs of silver running throughout, a habit I witness only in the comfort of family. "Trust me, always speaking your mind has its drawbacks as well as its perks."

"Yeah, I'm still learning that lesson."

"You will figure it out with time. Life has a way of forcing you to see your place, one way or another."

The server returns the check, thanks us for coming, and wishes us a good afternoon. My father and I rise from our seats, and together, we make our way toward the exit while shrugging into our jackets. Emerging from the comfortable restaurant, I slip on my gloves and walk half a block down the street to where the town car is waiting. We duck inside the cabin, rich with black leather upholstery and tinted windows, and then my father instructs the driver to take me to my apartment, reciting the address by memory.

"How are your applications coming, by the way?" my father asks when we're about halfway to our destination. "Any problems or questions? I'm happy to help."

"Thanks, but I sent them all off a few weeks ago. Now, I'm just waiting."

"Let me know as soon as you hear anything. I'm happy to make a call, if need be. You're a legacy at Yale, so that should be a shoo-in."

"I don't want you to make a call," I say with slight disgust.

"Don't sound so turned off. It's the way it's done sometimes, whether you like it or not."

I sigh. "But if it doesn't happen on my own merit, then I shouldn't go in the first place."

"I hope you didn't botch your applications," he says in warning. "I can fix a lot of things, but outright mocking will not be ignored."

"Of course not. I would never do that. You and Mother always taught me to do my best, no matter what. So, I did."

"Good. Because you will get your MBA. It will open more doors for you than you could possibly imagine."

"Maybe I want to find a different kind of door with a different key," I mumble.

"I heard you," he says, humored. "You might want to work on your whisper technique." He leans in my direction, over the vehicle's bench seat. "Your mother is really good at her whisper technique. Sometimes, I miss an entire conversation."

I chuckle. "That might be a result of your own self-preservation, Dad."

"Possibly." He shrugs. "But it might be the secret to all marriages. However, when she really wants to talk to me, she sure as hell makes sure she has my attention." A grin tugs at the corner of his mouth. "You're like her, too. When you really want something, you make sure you have everyone's attention. I love that about both of you. You might not realize it, but you get your passion from her."

I slump back in my seat. "Too bad we have dissimilar interests."

"It might seem that way, but you are both motivated by love, and there's no arguing the reasoning behind that."

Fourteen

There's currently a lull of students at the engineering library, so I'm using the opportunity to scan through the images I recently took for my final photography project. I've been working on my fire study for over a week, and I'm confident with the collection of frames and compositions. The purpose of this project was to show a situation or object that was on the opposite spectrum of our last study.

Fire and water are counterparts in almost every sense. One is gaseous and hot while the other is fluid and tends to do well at room temperature. In different realms on the color spectrum, one is generally thought of as red while the other is blue. Knowing this as well as the fact that they don't mix, extinguishing one another upon contact, I'm attempting to show how they are similar. My study focuses on the fluidity of the flame in comparison to that of water.

Foster is currently in the stacks, helping a student, while I man the desk. It's been a little over a week since our one-nighter, and right now, it's like it was a surreal moment, more fiction than fact. Our first few shifts together were somewhat awkward, but we've been moving forward toward a better comfort level. There are occasions when I do glance in his direction, recalling his naked body, but I shake it off as hormones and curiosity.

There is definitely a strangeness to working with someone who you've seen in the nude with his full nakedness on you, in you, yet never had anything romantic with—and have no feelings of regret or assumptions for a relationship. One-night stands are more low maintenance than I thought, especially since he and I are on the same page about what occurred.

Our interactions aren't exactly the same. There is a little more filter, like we're both being careful not to cross any line, but working with him has been easy enough up to this point. Of course, whenever I enter the building, I ask him to turn around, so I can get a good look at his ass, but it's only as an icebreaker for each shift. He happily obliges, shaking his head. I hope he's not documenting my requests for a sexual harassment case.

With my laptop on my knees, I continue to scroll through the images, noting my favorites for print. The assignment is due next week, and I plan to get most of the printing and matting done this weekend.

"That's hot," Foster comments over my shoulder, leaning across the counter. "New project?"

"Yeah," I answer, focused. "It's for my photography final. I'm finally getting a good grasp on this one."

"So, you went with fire this time? No wind or earth?" He rounds the desk, taking his seat next to me, scooting closer to his monitor.

"No." I shut my laptop and shove it back into its bag. "It just kind of worked out that way since I did water on my last shoot."

"Ah, you needed to do that opposites thing?"

"How did you know?" I ask, straightening in my chair.

"It's kind of obvious. Water and fire don't mix on any level." He pauses in contemplation. "Well, that's not true now that I think about it. Chemically speaking, they can work aside one another. It's a battle but possible."

"You've gone all scientist on me again. It's not complex. One is hot, and the other is wet. The end."

"Sorry, bad habit." Foster removes the dark frames from his face, placing them next to the keyboard. "I was just thinking that, even though fire and water generally work against one another—one always winning the war, so to speak—there are some environments where they can coexist. It's all about having the right chemistry."

"Well, I'll take your word for it." I roll my seat forward to reach my monitor. "You do know chemistry a lot better than I do."

"Yes, we established that pretty well about a week ago."

"Yeah, yeah, yeah. But my knowledge of Newton's first law totally kicked your ass."

"No, that was EJ Cunning's law mixed with my desire to see you kiss your friend."

"Call it what you like."

"I almost feel like I should call it cheating."

"Fozzie."

"Evelyn."

"I outwitted you. That's all that was, nothing more." I playfully grin in his direction, tucking a fading rouge lock behind my ear. "Besides, if I recall, you still had a happy ending to the evening."

"And…" He exhales. "You went there."

"So, it wasn't happy?"

"No comment."

"That's what I thought." Smug, I return my attention back to the computer screen. "Cunning wins again."

He clicks the mouse a few times, and I take the cue that our little conversation is over. With not much to do, I pull out a book on Van Gogh for my thesis, wanting to do a little more research on his childhood, hoping to find a way to properly connect it to his work.

"It wasn't bad," Foster remarks out of nowhere.

"What did you say?"

He chuckles. "I said it wasn't bad. The ending. The one you were referring to last week."

I flip a page. "Well, when they end the way yours did, most people consider them to be very good, fantastic." I peek at his concentrated profile. "Orgasmic even."

"True." He stays focused on the monitor, holding his mouth tight so not to show any delight in our conversation. "If I recall correctly, yours was pleasant also."

"No complaints here."

"That's good to hear." A huge grin begins to form across his mouth.

"Don't look so self-assured," I remark.

"Never," he teases.

We work together in silence as I'm reading the biography, and he's conducting online research. Finals are right around the corner for the entire university. Two students approach the desk, but Foster is able to quickly point them in the right direction, and they are gone soon after.

When they're out of earshot, my coworker turns to me and questions, "So, when is your project due?"

"My thesis?" I ask, assuming he's inquiring about the book in my hand. "I plan on turning it in early in the spring quarter."

"No, not that. Your photography study on fire?"

"Next week. Most of the shots are already set, and I'll be matting them this weekend."

"I see." He edges his chair further under the desk.

"Why do you ask?" I ponder, closing my reading material.

"You got me thinking about fire and water. We've done some interesting experiments in the lab, actually igniting fire in water. It was quite a sight."

"I bet."

The wheels in my head begin to turn, curious as to how a shot like that might look through a lens. I've seen welding underwater on TV, and it's rather powerful. Those big fishing boats always have to fix something. I wonder if what Foster was referring to is anything like that.

Now, I need to know because to actually capture fire and water—heat and that which calms it cooperating for an instant, working side by side, showing their battle as well as their likeness—in the same frame would be miraculous.

"Was it a hard experiment?" I ask innocently.

"Not technically. There's not a lot of heating or cooling. It's just mixing together the right substances. It's extremely dangerous though, and it lets off a highly toxic gas."

"Oh," I utter, mildly disappointed. "So, it's not something you should try at home?"

"No," he stresses, "not at all. Is there a reason you were asking?"

"Yeah but never mind. The idea of gagging myself to death with toxic fumes in order to take a picture doesn't sound all that appealing."

He lifts his frames back to his face and then turns toward me. "If you're really interested, I can find out if one of my professors can conduct the experiment for you. It needs to be done in a controlled setting for safety."

"No, that's okay. It was just a thought. I already have some great shots, but the concept is really different. Maybe some other time."

"Let me know if you change your mind. I'd be happy to ask someone in the department."

"Thanks." I reopen my book.

No less than a minute later, Foster says to me, "You know, if you're really interested, I might be able to show you a different experiment where fire exists underwater."

"How? I thought you said it was dangerous."

"Not like this. There's some smoke involved but nothing that will make you sick, as long as the room is ventilated. I think it will get you the shot you want."

"So, what is it? Can I do it myself?"

He tightens his mouth. "It's probably best that I conduct the experiment for you."

"Oh, so it's all *sciencey* and stuff."

Foster laughs. "Sort of." He grabs a nearby pencil and a piece of notepaper from the desk and scribbles on it. "Here," he says, handing me the slip. "That's my number. If you want, give me a call, and we can set something up, so I can show it to you this weekend."

I skeptically peer at him. "This weekend?"

"Yeah. I'm busy until then, but Sunday would likely work."

With the small square paper between my fingers, I drop my hand into my lap. "Why are you offering to help me?"

"Why not?"

"Won't it be weird? You know, after…"

"Could be. I don't know."

I gaze at the numbers.

"I just figured," he continues, "since we're friends and all, I could act like one by helping you out. Isn't that what friends do?"

"Yeah, it is." I fold the paper in half, stuffing it into my bag. "Will you be naked this time, friend?"

He guffaws. "Don't you wish?"

"One can only hope."

Fifteen

At the top of the steps, I knock lightly on the russet-colored hardwood door of Foster's apartment on this Sunday afternoon, as we scheduled. The door swings inward, revealing Foster dressed in a gray hooded sweatshirt and a pair of denim pants, covered by a generic red-and-white-striped cookout apron. Strands of damp hair haphazardly lie across his brow, accentuating his sapphire eyes lacking the omnipresent dark frames.

"Hey," he says, adjusting his hair back into place. "You're right on time."

"There's a saying that punctuality is a virtue." I lift my right shoulder, adjusting the strap of my camera bag.

He narrows his gaze. "No, there isn't."

"Sure there is—according to the preachings that I've read."

"Preachings? I'm starting to wonder where you learn some of the things you spout."

"It's all in the *Prostitute's Guide to Vegas*," I say, like it's the most obvious statement in the world. "Time is of the essence when you get paid by the hour, and clients are calling out God's name while worshiping your body at a budget price. There are even coupons for regulars."

Foster's mouth twitches, the corner betraying the hint of a smile. "I might need to get a copy of that book."

"Feel free to borrow mine."

"So generous of you." He steps aside. "You're so full of shit. C'mon in."

I enter the apartment, scanning his residence for the first time without alcohol or hormones interfering. The small white living space is sparse but neat, showcasing an overstuffed sofa and a side chair, and at the room's center is a television of average size, in comparison to what I've seen in other college man apartments. The walls are bare, save for a very large antique-finished framed print of the periodic table of elements.

Should have seen that coming.

The furnishings are typical for a male apartment—simple and muted. Nothing stands out. This place is a blank canvas begging for some color. The open floor plan flows into a kitchen at the right with a small prep island in its center.

With my tripod and camera bag in hand, I follow Foster into the kitchen area. On the dark granite countertop of the center island rests three large clear glass beakers of different sizes and configurations, filled about three-quarters full with water.

"So, I take it, this is where the magic is going to happen?" I ask, stopping in front of the trio of glasses.

"Yeah. I'm not fully set up yet, but you should get the best lighting in here."

Dropping my bag to the ground, I slug out of my coat, lay it over one of the barstools, and begin to set up my equipment while Foster opens up the kitchen window and then pulls out a large glass bowl from a lower cabinet.

"How's this going to work?" I question, attaching my camera to the top of the three-legged base. "Do I need to do anything?"

"No," he responds, shutting off the faucet once the bowl is sufficiently filled. "I'll conduct the…experiment, and you can just take the pictures."

"Will it be really fast, or will I be able to get a few shots?"

"You should be able to get plenty. The burn lasts a significant amount of time—about thirty seconds—but I've set up four environments in case you don't get everything you need the first time."

"Four sounds like plenty." I raise the height of the neck on the tripod.

"I hope so." He laughs. "I only have enough materials for four." Placing the clear bowl next to the beakers, he continues, "I'll be right back. I need to get the secret ingredient."

"It's not illegal, is it?"

"No, but these things are really hard to come by this time of year."

I peek after Foster as he makes his way around the partition and enters his bedroom at the end of the hall. Two other doors down the narrow space remain slightly ajar. One at the end of the apartment is clearly the bathroom, and from my previous visit, I recall the other as being a second bedroom.

I duck back into the kitchen area when Foster emerges from his room with a small cardboard box in one hand and Scotch Tape in the other. Behind the camera, I adjust the lens, focusing on the container farthest on the left, assuming we will begin with that one.

"Where's your roommate?" I ask, straightening from my bent position.

Foster opens the brown shoebox. "I don't have one."

"Then, why do you have a two-bedroom? Extra storage place? Mad scientist lab?"

"No." He chuckles, pulling out a small brightly colored rectangular box from within the larger one. "I had one, but he graduated last year."

"And you didn't get a new one?"

"Nope."

"Why not?"

"'Cause I didn't want a new one."

"The rent must be very reasonable if you can afford not to have a roommate."

He furrows his brow. "Yeah, it's not too bad."

Opening the end of the thin cardboard container, Foster withdraws a thin metal stick that is half-covered in a thick, dark powdery-looking substance.

Glancing at the box, I ask, "Is that a sparkler?"

Lifting the item in question, he says, "Yes."

"A sparkler? A kids firework?"

"You got it." Reaching behind him, Foster opens a small side drawer, finding a long-nosed lighter, and he places it next to the tape on the countertop. "Are you ready for some magic?"

"So, where's the science in this? What did you do? Lace it with some kind of coating?"

"Nope, it's just a regular old sparkler." He pulls the tape, sticking it to the firework's tip, and begins to wrap two of the sticks together. "They contain oxidizers, which allow them to burn, and the tape will assist in keeping it lit underwater."

Skeptical, I narrow my glare as his hands finish wrapping up the sticks. "Is this something you learned at school?"

"No." He chuckles, placing a pair of safety goggles over his face. "At a fraternity party, freshman year." He flips on a nearby fan.

"What's that for?"

"Ventilation. The smoke isn't pleasant. Are you ready?"

"Sure. Why not?" I bend at the waist, peering at the large glass bowl through my camera, checking the aperture speed once again. "Let's see this magic you speak of."

A crackle ignites in the air for a few seconds before the metallic spray of the lit sparkler appears through my camera's lens. Then, without warning, Foster plunges the firework into a bowl, dimming the silver-white sparks. Fiery hues of amber, tangerine, and crimson-honey explode through the clear liquid in a burst of magnified color, all contained by the glass barrier. It's a display of liquefied flame and flowing color.

My finger presses the shutter button, quick and furious, diligently trying to capture the moment unseen by the human eye. The water begins to cloud into a thick, muggy gray haze, and the color deepens to a dense shade of charcoal in a matter of seconds. Then, the light is gone. All that is left is a blackened stick submerged in the coal-like water.

"Holy hell," I whisper, stunned by the demonstration. Coming out from behind the camera, I tell Foster, "That was so much cooler than I thought it would be."

"I thought you might like it," he replies, prideful. He retrieves three more of the fireworks and begins to prep them like he did the first. "Do you want to see it again?"

"Absolutely."

Twice more, Foster plunges fire into water, showing me in a somewhat artistic, scientific, and playful way how, under the right conditions, two forces at constant odds can miraculously morph into a harmonic symphony, despite their battle. Each time, I'm amazed even though it's a juvenile trick learned at a houseful of college boys.

This is an act of chemistry, and its beauty enraptures me.

"Last one," Foster announces as we both edge down the length of the counter toward the tall and skinny beaker. "Just beware. This one might get a little more...vibrant."

"Oh, yeah? Why's that?"

"The flame will always seek more air in order to thrive. The design of this thin cylinder will elongate that process."

He finishes wrapping the sparklers. "It's best just to show you."

"This should be interesting."

A small blue flame appears at the tip of the lighter when Foster clicks the button, and I'm struck with an idea.

"Wait," I demand. "Can we shut off the lights for this one?"

"Sure." He sets down the lighter and flicks the switch, plunging the room into relative darkness, and then he ignites the piercing blue flame again. "Ready?"

Peering through the camera, I prepare for the impending wonderment. "I'm not sure, but let's do it."

The crinkling sound of the fireworks being lit spurs into the silence. Into the frame, bright white shards spread from the tips of the sparklers, subdued for just an instant, as they are plummeted into the glass tube. Then, a violent stream of apricot and umber fill the cylinder from top to bottom, filling the encased fluid.

As the sparklers continue to burn, the flame rises higher upon itself, and the fingers of heat lick their way to the top, bursting beyond the water's surface. The fire is breaking free, trying to grow and thrive in a place it's meant to reside, searching to gain its full potential outside of the stifling wetness, gasping for air beyond the suffocation.

The fire grows so robust and fierce, and the angry heat causes the water to boil, creating a fury of passion.

It's intense, powerful in a way unlike the other experiments.

Suddenly, a jagged horizontal line severs through the upper third of the glass, breaking it into two.

For a moment, the flame expands into the air, a wafting surge of hope freeing itself from the glass prison, and then it disappears.

My camera captures every moment until the sparkler dims in the murky water, just like the ones before it.

"Wow," I gasp, left in the darkness.

Foster flips the switch, illuminating the room once again. "See what I meant?"

"Yeah," I sputter, overwhelmed. "Holy shit!"

He laughs.

I shake my head, still not totally comprehending what just occurred.

"Looks like this one is done," he states, gathering the two broken pieces of glass from the split beaker.

Stepping around my equipment, I pull out a paper towel from the roll on the counter. "Let me help," I say, wiping up the watery debris from the granite surface.

Together, we quickly clear the area and clean up the mess. For the most part, it was contained within each of the glasses, save for one.

"Do you think you got anything worth using?" Foster removes his apron and sets it on the counter next to the goggles.

"I'm sure I did." I release the camera from the tripod. "Let's take a look."

Rounding the counter, Foster peers over my shoulder as I scroll through the images I took over the last fifteen minutes. There are nearly two hundred digital frames, and even though I was the one taking the pictures, the collection marvels me.

Stills of bubbles, colors, and movement captured by the sophistication of the high-speed lens fill the viewing screen. The juxtaposition of light and water are beyond gorgeous, and the symmetry to poetry is a symphony in the making.

I'm breathless.

It's more than water.

It's more than fire.

It's life surviving and flourishing where it shouldn't, where it couldn't.

It's almost...a miracle.

"That's what it looks like through a camera?" he asks, his warm breath tickling my ear.

"Pretty amazing, huh?"

"It's almost…"

Turning my head, I grin when our gazes meet. "Like art? Like…a story?"

Tilting closer, Foster's heated mouth unexpectedly touches mine, sending a chilling spark along the surface of my skin, and I savor the taste of his air upon my tongue.

Releasing my lips from his, I peer up at his dumbfounded appearance mirroring my own.

"I thought we were friends," I say, lowering my camera to the granite surface.

Foster's chest rises and falls with an undertone of frustration. I'm unsure if it's with me, himself…or something else. There are too many scenarios in this situation.

"We are," he responds, still stunned. "I'm sorry. I shouldn't have done that."

"It's okay, Foster." I gather my camera and then lean toward the ground, putting it away in its case. "You're a really good kisser, by the way."

"You're just saying that to tease me and make light of the situation. I'm not sure what I was thinking. It's not like…"

"I know. And I wasn't teasing you." I rise, resting a butt cheek on the nearby stool. "You really are a good kisser." I cross my arms and smirk. "You're pretty good in the sack, too."

"Okay, now, it's getting weird." He ponders over his shoulder and out the kitchen window. "Why not just take it a step further and say you wouldn't mind having sex with me again? You know, because it was so great the first time."

Pursing my lips, I try to contain my giddy thoughts. There's a part of me that does find what Foster said as somewhat ludicrous, but the truth in his suggestion is undeniable.

I actually wouldn't mind sleeping with him again.

He has a great body that feels spectacular against mine, and he's definitely a hottie in his own way. Bumping and grinding with him was quite memorable, even while under the influence of libations, and all inhibitions, even though I tend to have very few, were pushed aside. Not to mention, sex with him was easy in the sense that I didn't want anything more, and neither did he.

"I don't think I would mind," I spurt out.

"Shut up," he quickly retorts, clearly finding my reply absurd.

"Fine. I'll shut up then. No more talking from me."

He shakes his head. "You're just trying to get a rise out of me."

"No, I'm being honest. The other night was impressive, and sometimes, riding the roller coaster more than once isn't a bad thing. I could ride yours again."

He barks, laughter exploding from his lips. "Are you serious?"

I lift my brows. "Yeah, I think I am."

Foster licks his bottom lip, and I stare at his thick lashes hooding his eyes as he contemplates his feet. A silent question hangs in the air, filtering the atmosphere like moonlight when the sun sets, creeping into the forefront.

"If I'm being honest," he states, stepping closer until his chest teasingly touches my own, "I wouldn't mind riding you again either."

"Oh, yeah?"

"Definitely."

My tongue flirts with the opening of my mouth. "Do you want to…"

"Still be friends?"

"Yes."

"But something else, too?" he suggests.

"I'm open to it."

His breathing becomes heavier and visible with the rise and fall of his chest. "Friends who kiss?"

116

"Or more—"

Foster's mouth crashes upon mine, hard and fanatical, as an agreement in theory is made into reality. Our tongues collide, desperate to feel and taste what the other has to offer, exploring a familiar and exciting memory.

His hands pull and squeeze my hips while mine thread through his soft and somewhat damp hair, releasing the scent of his shampoo. My shirt rises at the sides as Foster's thumbs explore upward under the garment.

"Still friends?" he questions, dipping his head and grazing his lips along the delicate skin of my neck.

"The best kind." My fingertips search for his naked flesh at the hem of his sweatshirt.

"No expectations?"

"None from me," I pant. "Except for the occasional high five or fist bump."

Foster lifts the shirt over my head, tosses it to the floor, and then raises me onto the granite countertop. I reach for the bottom of his sweatshirt, pull it off his body, and let gravity take it, falling next to mine.

"I don't know if I told you before," I say, palming his firm chest, "but you're really fucking hot without your clothes on."

"No"—he undoes my bra—"you didn't mention it."

"Well, now, you know."

He slides my lingerie down my arms. "Your breasts are like something out of a magazine. They're anatomy perfection." He cups one with his hand. "And just the right weight."

"I take them to the booby gym weekly."

"I bet." Lowering his head, he tauntingly licks my nipple. "Do you work these out, too?"

"They're kind of part of the package."

Foster continues to tongue and massage my breasts as I explore his tight arms and shoulders with my hands. Trailing his fingers down my front, he slides a hand underneath my pants and into my panties, searching for my opening. I spread my legs, allowing him to deftly touch me in a sensual and surprisingly skillful manner.

Lifting his head in line with my own, he presses our lips together, and I moan into his mouth as he continues to evocatively touch me.

"You get so wet," he murmurs. "So, so wet. I want to kiss you."

"You already are." I smile, humored.

"Down here." He pushes a finger inside me and then slides it outward before slowly entering my cavity once again. "With my mouth."

"Are you always this…step-by-step?"

"No, but I need to make sure that it's okay."

"It's definitely okay." I lick his ear. "Does this mean that you will expect me to give you head in return?"

"Only if you want to."

Then, the words, "I think I want you to fuck me," cross my lips without a thought.

"You have an interesting way of expressing yourself."

"So I've been told."

Nudging him backward to create some space between us, I hop off the counter, landing next to him. He stands motionless in front of me as I unbutton and then unzip his pants. With both hands, I grab the waistband of his jeans and boxers and shimmy them down his legs. He steps out of them, standing completely naked before me.

"Still impressive," I comment, referring to his erection.

"Thanks. Glad it works for you."

"Me, too."

I slip my hands into the sides of my pants and drop them along with my panties to the ground. Placing my hands at my waist, I tilt my head with an expectant look upon my face.

"Still nice." He purses his lips. "I'm surprised you don't have any tattoos. I thought that was part of the artist uniform."

"Who says I should be that much of a cliché? I'm naturally a masterpiece."

"You never did get around to that dye job, did you?" he asks, focused on the space between my legs.

Playfully, I swat at his bicep. He catches my arm, bends at the knees, and throws me over his shoulder.

"This is extremely caveman of you, Fozzie."

"Sex is a very basic human function, Evelyn."

Draped over his body, I pat his ass as he walks us back to his bedroom. The shades are drawn shut, but the faint purple light from an early dusk peeks along the edges of the window.

Foster drops me onto the bed before dragging my backside to the edge of the mattress. Pulling my legs around him, he lowers himself to his knees. His mouth hungrily connects with my pussy—wet and flirtatious, licking and sucking. His dexterous tongue presses and circles around my clit, like a man on a mission.

"Still friends?" he asks between a lick and a suck.

"Yeah." I bite my lip, trying to steady the electric sensations tapping their way through my system, as he plunges his tongue inside me. "I'll make you one of those friendship bracelets, like we used to do at camp."

"Perfect." He draws his tongue through my folds. "I look forward to it."

Foster continues to tease and taunt my sex with his mouth, bringing me an unexpected physical enjoyment, as we meander this gray area of friendship with no rules, other than the ones we're making up each step of the way.

"Fuck me, you're really fucking good at this," I comment, running my fingers along his scalp. "You're like some kind of clit whisperer. Do you practice this shit?"

"Yes. I exercise my mouth at the gym, the same way you do your breasts."

I laugh and sit up, resting on my elbows. Our eyes connect, playful and giddy.

Foster kisses my inner thigh and then raises his brows with a silent question to which I easily agree, nodding my head. Rising from the floor, he steps toward his bureau and withdraws a condom.

Coming to my knees, I meet him at the foot of the bed and take the contraceptive into my hand.

"So, you'll take it from here?" he asks.

My fingers lightly skim down his hard-on. "Is that a request?"

"Or merely a suggestion."

Ducking down, I teasingly draw my tongue along the underside of his length, circling my lips around the bare tip, needing a taste.

Once.

And then twice more.

He moans.

My body responds.

Ripping the wrapper, I take out the condom and roll it over Foster's erection.

Nudging me backward by the shoulder, he directs me down onto the bed. His hands follow the shape of my outer legs, from my hips to my ankles, grabbing and resting them on his shoulders.

He slowly guides himself into me, his eyes never wavering from where our bodies connect, mine consuming his, observing the entire process. Most guys do like to watch, but in my experience, they aren't usually this blatant about it. I don't mind. It's just Fozzie, and there's no reason to be shy or pretend that it's inappropriate.

With my legs positioned steadily at his shoulders, Foster licks his thumb and then begins to rub my clit while steadily pushing in and out of me, causing my skin to flush from the inside.

My breathing rate increases.

Whimpers of pleasure fly across my lips.

He slams into me harder and then glances in my direction with a look so primal and exceedingly sexy that I lose all sensibility.

Screaming out cries of pure physical bliss, I let go of any resistance and give him the power to make me orgasm. My legs turn to jelly, my flesh tingles, and a heat runs through my veins as he continues to enter me with an intense vigor.

Foster tightens his grip around my ankles and squeezes firmly when he drives into me a final time, grunting with gratification.

When both of our panting returns to a more measured rate, he collapses onto the bed next to me, where we lie side by side, staring at the stark ceiling above.

Out of nowhere, he positions his palm about a foot away from my face.

"What?" I ask, winded.

"High five?"

Slapping my hand with his, I say, "That definitely deserves one."

Sixteen

"Knock, knock," Chandra announces just outside my cracked bedroom door.

"Hey," I call out from the entrance of my closet. "Are you getting ready to leave?"

"Yeah. I'm heading to the airport now."

Dropping my shoes into the suitcase on the bed, I join her near the threshold where she's standing with a roller bag resting at her side.

I throw my arms around her neck and say, "Have a safe trip."

She pats me on the back. "You, too."

"I will." Backing up, I finger through the strands of hair near the front of my face. "And tell your family I said hello."

"Will do. Tell the same to yours. I'm running late, and I need to get going." Chandra grabs the handle of her bag and begins down the short hallway. "I'll see you in a few weeks," she calls back to me.

Then, moments later, I hear the door click shut after she exits the apartment.

Exams wrapped up yesterday, and we're both leaving for the winter break between quarters. She'll be visiting her family in India for the first time in three years. I, too, will be spending the holiday with my family, but unlike Chandra, I plan to return well before the New Year since my father is heading promptly to Europe on business, with my mother accompanying him. They will then be celebrating the turn of the year with family friends in Madrid, and I'd rather ring in the New Year on my own terms instead of being a part of the charade I'm required to play in their presence.

I finish packing the rest of my things for the trip on the Caribbean Sea. Then, I zip up my suitcase and roll it to rest near the front door, in anticipation of being picked up by the driver my mother arranged to arrive in about an hour.

Just enough time to run a quick errand.

Slipping my arms into my jacket, I scurry back to my room to retrieve the two sixteen-by-twenty-inch frames wrapped in brown paper that are resting just inside my closet. I shuffle out my door and down the steps, and then I begin the six-block walk toward Foster's apartment.

While I've seen him at work this past week, we haven't spent any social time together due to exams. Yes, we've progressed to booty-call buddies, but neither of us has made the gesture to get together like that for a few days, both being so busy.

The past weeks with Foster have been…interesting. When I first met him, never would I have imagined in my wildest and craziest dreams—and there are many—that he and I would morph into hook-up partners. But that's what we are, and somehow, we've managed to remain cordial coworkers as well. In our off hours, we get naked for a roll in the sheets, and it's had no effect on our friendship. The sex is just that—sex.

Foster has made it clear to me that he has no interest in dating anyone, which is fine by me. In my mind, I'm calling our sexual trysts nothing more than a good dose of banging therapy. *What girl wouldn't want to fuck out all her frustrations with a guy who looks great with no clothes on?*

Added bonus—Foster is really great in bed, possibly the best sex I've ever had. And there's no need to impress him with any crazy erotic moves, like if I were his girlfriend. Of course, it pleases me that he seems to enjoy it as much as I do, but I'm in it for me, and he's in it for him. No pressure.

But it's hot. Fucking hell is the sex ever hot.

No wonder I keep going back for more.

The way he bent me over the other day, pulled my hair, and made me come twice, almost back-to-back, really got my attention. The spanking turned me on more than I'd expected. Then, there was another time on his couch. Okay, so it was multiple times spanning into the wee hours of the morning. He should probably just burn the thing from all the sins we committed on the cushions. The kitchen is a whole other story. I'll never look at the countertop the same way ever again. Eating out doesn't always have to take place outside of one's residence.

Damn, his tongue is something special.

It will be missed while I'm away.

Now that the quarter has ended, I likely won't see him again until returning to work at the beginning of the next school term. The items in my arms aren't pressing, but I got them back from the framer just yesterday and thought they would make a nice gesture as a Christmas present. Part of me was hesitant at first about giving him anything at all, wondering if it might be crossing some line in our friendship and arrangement, but I decided to push that aside. I gave one to Chandra and Wolfgang yesterday, and they're friends, so I perceive no problem with giving something to him as well—as friends.

Turning the corner at the bottom of the hill, I spot Foster's building near the middle of the block. I had considered calling, but I figured a drop-by would be more casual. When I spoke with him the other night at work, he mentioned he wasn't going out of town for the holidays, and his only plans were to spend Christmas at his grandmother's farm. If he's not home, I'll just leave the gift outside his apartment.

Knocking lightly on his door, I promise myself to only count to thirty before deciding he's not home and leaving. When I mentally reach the number nineteen, the wooden entrance opens to reveal my comrade between the sheets and coworker of superior intelligence in a pair of dark denim jeans and a white T-shirt underneath an unzipped hoodie. He's wearing his glasses, shielding his tired red eyes. I'm sure exams have been rough on him. I look like hell myself.

"EJ." He squints. "Hey, I thought you were leaving today."

"I am." I tighten my grip around the frames under my arm. "Can I come in for a minute?"

"Sure." He steps back, allowing me to enter the apartment. "You got a new hair color. Are you going for au naturel this time?"

"Yeah. I need to look good for holiday pictures with the family. Thought it might be best to avoid any freak-show comments from the 'rents."

Shutting the door, he asks, "So, did you come by to get one for the road? It's a little early for a booty call, but I can accommodate, if need be."

"Good to know." I laugh. "But not this time. Can I take a rain check?"

"Sure." He steps in closer. "Can I get you something to drink?"

"No, I'm not staying long. I have a flight to catch." I pull the frames out from between my arm and body, holding them outward in his direction. "I wanted to give you these."

He cocks his head. "Did we say we were giving each other gifts?"

"No, we didn't." I push the items in question closer to him.

Transferring the gifts into his hands, he says, "I didn't get you anything."

"That's okay. It doesn't need to be reciprocal."

He stares at the paper-covered squares and then peeks at me a few times, shifting his gaze between the items in his hand and me.

"Go on," I urge. "Open them."

Foster carries the gifts to the granite island in the center of the kitchen and begins to tear the wrapping from the top frame, revealing an image from the first shoot I did in his presence at the fountain a few months ago. Without him, the project would have been a catastrophe and I never would have received the high mark.

"I just wanted to say thank you," I stagger, "for helping me. And I thought maybe your walls could use a little color."

"Thank me? For what?" He taps his fingers on the glass. "All the sex?"

I lean my hip on the counter. "Do you usually have girls thanking you for that?"

"No, but there's a first for everything."

"Well, today isn't it."

"Damn," he whispers. "So close."

He stares at the image matted behind the glass, one of my favorite shots from the series—a silhouette of fountain water rising from the pool below. The lighting catches the spray in such a way that, in contrast to the surrounding darkness, it appears almost angelic. It's a moment caught in time, humanizing the flowing substance in a spiritual way.

"It's more than water," he utters quietly after staring at the image for some time.

"What?"

"More than water. That's what you said when you were taking these that night, that there was a story beyond the simple elements of hydrogen and oxygen, and I just needed to look deeper."

"You were listening," I say, surprised he recalled the details of our conversation.

"Yeah." He turns his attention to me, a smirk playing along the edges of his mouth. "Plus, this big brain of mine remembers everything."

"Shit, I'd better start watching what I say around you."

"It's a little too late for that. Your mouth is a ticking time bomb." He sets the frame on the counter. "Thank you, but you really didn't need to give me anything. I was happy to help."

"Well," I say mischievously, "I didn't want you to think all the sex we've been having was payment for the assistance."

He lifts a brow. "Well, if it were, you've overpaid."

"True." I edge the other frame closer to him. "Don't forget this one."

Like with the first gift, his hands pull at the brown covering to reveal the next picture—an image of vibrant color, bubbles, and illumination surrounded by mystery and temptation. It's warm and striking, and it displays a life of its own.

Fire in water. Fire with water. Together.

"It's my favorite," I say quietly over his shoulder. "The way the fire overpowers the water, but at the same time, allows it to have its own way. It's like they aren't fighting. They're dancing."

"Dancing," he repeats, tilting the frame closer.

"Yeah, like a waltz. There's harmony in their battle."

"It's…it's really wonderful, Evelyn."

"You like it?"

"I do." He sets it down next to the other. "Thank you again."

"No, thank you. Without your help, these images never would have been possible." My fingers trace the shapes of the image, and my arm brushes his. "Because of that, I figure, in some ways, they're yours as much as mine."

"That's giving me more credit than I deserve," he states, his voice in a low tone.

"I don't care."

A small silence enters the room with neither of us saying anything more about the images or our time together that brought about the art before us.

I withdraw my hand back into my own space. "Well, I guess I should get going," I announce, adjusting my coat zipper. "I don't want to miss my flight."

"Right."

Stuffing my hands into my jacket pockets, I walk back toward the entrance with Foster on my heels. He grabs the brass knob attached to the wooden entry to open the door a quarter of the way.

"Have a safe trip to New York," he says.

"Actually, we're going down south to see family friends. We get together every year. It's kind of a pain in the ass, but it should be nice to get out of the cold for a little bit."

"Oh, well then, enjoy the sunshine. Get a tan for me."

"I will." I play with the ends of my hair. "You have a merry Christmas, Foster."

"Thanks." He tightens his mouth and then slides an arm around my shoulders, pulling me in for an unexpected hug. "Merry Christmas," he says next to my ear, squeezing me a little tighter.

Unsure of what else to do, I slip my hands around his waist, embracing him as well, and nod my head.

He releases me from his arms. I take a step back.

Foster widens the door. I exit into the hallway.

I turn, facing the awkward moment created between us.

Was a line just crossed in our arrangement? A hug?

"See you later," I say nonchalantly, hoping the moment passes quickly.

"Sounds good."

I descend the steps.

Halfway down, just before the first landing, Foster calls, "Hey, EJ?"

Gravity halts in my stomach.

I pivot on my heel, peering up at the man whose body I've gotten to know intimately over the past few weeks. "Yeah?"

He clomps down the steps, meeting me where I stand. His hand balls into a fist, resting in the space between us. "You forgot something."

I smile.

I shake my head.

I bump my fist with his.

"See you later, Fozzie."

"Okay, Evelyn."

Seventeen

Four peaceful days at sea in the Caribbean aboard my family's boat have been more pleasant than I expected. Unlike years in the past, my sister has not joined us for this voyage. Being newly married, she's spending the holiday skiing with her husband at his parents' vacation home in Vermont. Her lacking presence has taken the constant pressure off of me since my parents are enjoying their time alone. I'm more like a tag along on this excursion, which is fine by me. I've been spending most of my days enjoying the sun from the seacraft's deck while only meeting up with my mother and father for evening meals.

However, our time floating over the crystal turquoise waters is coming to an end. It's Christmas Eve, and we've pulled into port where a small island houses a private hotel owned by longtime friends. Here, we will meet up with the Beauchamps, like we do every year for the holidays, at one of their most exclusive properties.

The Beauchamps and my parents have been close friends since their days at college, meeting while attending Yale for graduate studies. My father was a business major, as was my mother, and the Beauchamps—Guy and Sophia—were all in the same program. It was a college romance as well as a partnership made for a lifetime. They were married within two months of each other, stood for each other at the other's wedding, and have been tied together by friendship and business for years.

The Beauchamps have a lucrative, large global hotel business. My parents' advertising company, The Boyce Agency—founded by my grandfather on my mother's side—has handled their advertising and marketing account for almost three decades.

The importance of this family to mine has been ingrained into my being since birth. Their only son, Gerard, is three years my senior, and it's no secret that it has always been the hope of both of our parents that we wed one day, joining our families as one in a more permanent fashion. If there's such a thing as being betrothed in this modern society, Gerard and I are it.

The boat has been docked for the past hour, and I'm dressing for the impending festivities with our lifelong family friends.

There's a light rap at my door.

"Evelyn," my mother's voice calls.

"Come in," I answer, attaching the emerald earring to my left lobe, completing the set. Along with the matching necklace around my neck, they were gifts from my grandmother on my sixteenth birthday.

My mother, dressed smartly in an ethereal cream ensemble, enters my quarters. "I thought you were going to wear the green dress," she states, observing my festive red outfit.

"I thought this would be more seasonal."

"They're both nice," she offers innocently, "but the green has a little more flair. There's still time to change."

"Would you like me to change?" I ask her reflection in the vanity mirror.

"I think the green one is more suited for the occasion, and it would match your earrings."

I cringe internally.

The blonde matriarch hasn't asked much of me this entire trip, and an outfit change isn't a great deal to argue over, but I hate that she is always trying to micromanage me in these situations. It's annoying.

However, to make the evening run smoother and without any added tension, I acquiesce by saying, "You're right. I'll change."

"Good. It shows off your beautiful figure better, too." She reaches for the door handle to give me some privacy. "Gerard's favorite color is green."

She exits my room, and I grunt, feeling tricked into being her lap dog once again. Her ability to control me is so seductive and cunning. When it comes to me, she only has one thing in mind—finding the perfect husband. Scratch that. Making about ten-thousand babies with Gerard, so she can finally call the Beauchamps family is at the top of her list.

With reluctance, I change out of my red dress and into the green one, and then I meet my parents on deck where they are watching the sun set over the pristine waters, glimmering where the light meets the quiet waves lapping at the surface.

"There she is," my father states with a smile, bringing youth to his face. "You look wonderful. Absolutely stunning."

"Thank you," I respond, grasping the matching designer clutch tighter with both hands.

My mother gives me an approving look as her keen blue eyes trace my form up and down, clearly satisfied with my entire ensemble.

I'm a fucking prop. I wonder if she actually sees strings sewn to my limbs like a marionette.

"We should get going," she says to my father, rubbing her delicate fingers along the shoulder of his suit.

"Of course."

My mother leads the way across the bow of the ship, and a staff member assists my family onto the dock. My parents walk arm in arm down the wooden planks toward the parking area where a car is waiting for us. We shuffle into the vehicle and travel twenty minutes up the hill to the secluded hotel.

When the luxury vehicle comes to a halt, I straighten my posture in preparation for an evening of smiles and formalities. The Beauchamps are wonderful people, but being under their watchful gaze, as well as my parents', always has me feeling like a guppy in a fish bowl.

We exit the cocoon of leather seats into the warm night air. A humid breeze skates across my shoulders, so I adjust my shawl to keep off any chill from the nearby ocean. A finger, my mother's, lightly grazes my hairline to place a small flyaway strand of light-brown hair back into place. She smiles at me, warm and approving, before my father offers her an arm to enter the lavish building. Our driver begins to unload our luggage for the evening's stay as we head up the steps to meet our family friends.

Within view, visible before I've even reached the top, stand Guy, Sophia, and their son, Gerard, waiting for us. This moment is such a foregone conclusion, like I'm walking into some strange dating game. With my sister out of the picture, it's obvious who I will be expected to spend most of my conversation time with while here—Gerard.

"Thomas," Guy greets my father, opening his arms when we reach the summit of the staircase, "Nora, welcome. So good to see you again."

"You, too." My father grasps the hand of his longtime friend and kindly pats him on the shoulder. "We wouldn't have missed it."

"Nora." Guy leans in and kisses my mother on both cheeks while my father makes his salutations with Sophia. "You haven't changed one bit."

"Neither have you," she replies with delight in her voice. "But we just saw you a month ago, so I should hope not."

They all laugh, polite and clearly happy to be in each other's presence.

"Evelyn," Sophia greets me, placing her manicured hands on my shoulders, "you are more beautiful every time we see you. And I just adore this color on you."

I steal a glance at my mother, who appears more than gratified by the compliment.

Sophia kisses me on both cheeks and then asks, "Gerard, doesn't Evelyn look stunning?"

"Like a goddess in the moonlight," he states, stepping toward me, his hazel eyes more alive than I remember. "Merry Christmas, Evelyn." He kisses me on my cheek.

"Merry Christmas," I respond, polite. Then, I kiss his newly shaven face.

"Shall we head in?" Sophia states as more of a suggestion than a question, opening her stance toward the entrance. "Drinks are waiting on the veranda."

"Absolutely," my father responds for the group.

"May I escort you?" Guy asks my mother, offering her an arm.

She takes his gesture, looping her elbow with his, and my father follows suit, asking for Sophia's arm in his. With Guy and my mother leading the way, my father and Sophia walk toward the grand entrance, shrouded in golden light.

"May I?" Gerard asks me, holding out his arm.

"Of course."

I circle my arm through his, and we enter the hotel, about fifteen feet behind our parents. We've been coming here for the past five years since Gerard's family bought the place. The hallway is grand, accented in greens and yellows with opulence at every turn. Fine woods line the walls displaying local art, luxurious white-and-cream marble stone make up the floors, plush furnishings fill the space, and sculptures of glass hang from the ceiling, bringing a mystical twinkle to the overall ambiance. This place is almost like a dream.

We turn a corner toward the back of the building, showcasing my favorite view of all—the ocean. The sun has set, and framed by the white-trimmed doors, the ebony waters cascade splinters of silver under the oyster-colored moon.

My feet slow, and I stand in awe at the stunning view before us.

"You always were a sucker for the ocean at night," Gerard murmurs into my ear. "Like a goddess in the moonlight."

I laugh. "I still can't believe you said that." I elbow him. "You likely gave both of our mothers an orgasm with those words."

"They might have quivered with pleasure."

"How could you tell through all the Botox?"

"I have a keen sense about women."

"Ew. That's just gross. These are the women who gave birth to us."

"You're the one who brought it up."

The relationship between Gerard and me is definitely a friendly one.

When we were kids, I hated everything about him—what he stood for and the fact that he was my parents' choice for me. The concrete detail, that he was a part of the overbearing control of my family's plans, irked me to no end.

Then, when I was about fifteen, all of that changed.

We were out at sea together, and our parents docked for the evening, going to dinner and leaving the children aboard the boat to fend for themselves. It was my fault that we had been told to stay on board.

Earlier in the day, I'd had an argument with my mother about my recent studies, and she'd found one of my art pads full of sketches. She'd then found four more. While most parents would have likely been proud of their child's creativity, my mother always saw mine as a distraction, and she'd tossed the booklet along with all my drawing supplies overboard. I had been completely distraught, crying and throwing a tantrum like a four-year-old. Surely, the teenage hormones hadn't helped with my irrational and ill-tempered disposition, but my mother hadn't tolerated outbursts of any kind. Crying was not an option in our family because it showed weakness. She'd told me that I was not a proper lady and couldn't be seen in public.

After that moment, all the children had been punished and told to stay aboard the docked craft while the adults went to dinner. My sister shunned me for the evening, calling me spiteful names—adding a blow to my ego— before locking herself in her room. As the sun set, I found myself choking down tears at the ship's edge, mourning my lost treasures at sea and wondering how I could possibly feel so out of place among the people who were my family.

About an hour later, when the tears had dried, I felt another body sitting next to me—Gerard.

"You know," he said quietly in the foreign accent I so hated at the time, "there's a saying that those who never cry suffer far more than any others."

I sniffed, drained of tears, the ache and longing still weighing in my belly. "I doubt that."

"I don't." He handed my exhausted hands a small artist's pad with textured paper and a pack of drawing pencils. "I had the steward pick them up in town."

He took his index finger to his mouth in a gesture of silence, indicating a secret between us. My worn and spent emotionless body was able to muster a grin. I nodded and concealed the items from view under my leg. In comfortable silence, we sat side by side for some time until the sun rested under the water's edge.

"So, who said that?" I finally asked when the darkness surrounded us.

"Said what?" Gerard asked.

"Something about those who never cry suffer more?"

"Hans Christian Andersen. It's from *The Little Mermaid*. Mermaids can't shed tears, and thereby, they bottle all their pain."

I exhaled, immersed in the view of the gently lapping sea. "Then, I must strive to be a mermaid. Living in those depths is likely better than trying to survive up here."

He nudged his shoulder with mine. "I'll go with you."

From that day on, Gerard and I merged a friendship based on our mutual understanding of expectations that neither of us fully desired. While we both knew our parents loved us, we also knew freedom was something we would never fully have. Unlike so many others, our birthright was a blessing of opportunities and a curse to the wanderlust of our souls.

Over the years, our relationship has grown into an agreement. We play the charade for our families, knowing that peace is the best course of action. We're friends and like siblings in arms.

While his companionship is pleasant at these reunions, there are always the underlying expectations from our parents. We try to portray enough interest to keep them at bay but not enough for them to be overly hopeful. It's a chess match of us versus them, and each movement needs to be precise.

A small breeze blows the drapes, creating a flowing wave of fabric, outlining the entryway into the grand room. I push my shawl back up and over my shoulders, preparing for the cooler air at the water's edge. We step out onto the veranda, and to celebrate our annual union, we each take a drink from the server coming around with champagne.

My father raises his glass. "I just want to say how thankful I am for my family and friends. After all these years, we still remain close."

"And hopefully for many years to come," my mother adds, glancing at Gerard and me where we are paired at the balcony railing.

"Yes, agreed." My father smiles. "I love you all and feel blessed for our continued fortune."

"I couldn't have said it better," Guy adds. "Thank you everyone."

We lift our flutes higher, and following my father's lead, we say in unison, "Cheers!"

The crisp fizzy liquid sluices across my tongue, and I drink to the living facade.

Eighteen

With dinner service complete and our dessert plates being cleared, the servers offer us coffees and fine whiskeys to end the evening meal. My father and Gerard's both order scotches, and our mothers decide on another glass of champagne each, in lieu of the traditional after-dinner drinks, like they're celebrating.

When asked if I desire anything else, Gerard interjects by saying, "A bottle of the reserve, if you don't mind. And two glasses."

"Certainly," the server of short stature responds, nodding approvingly, before leaving the table.

"A bottle of wine?" I ask Gerard, amused since I'm already slightly tipsy from the two glasses I consumed at dinner.

"Are you saying no?"

"Of course not. Never."

The friendly conversation continues around the table, everyone joyous with the season and company. A few moments later, my parents are being served their after-dinner cocktails, and the sommelier uncorks the wine at Gerard's side. The wine expert pours enough of the grape liquid into Gerard's glass for him to aerate, sip, and ultimately approve. Our glasses are filled, and the remainder of the bottle is set between my friend and me.

"So, what's the occasion?" I ask, lifting my glass.

"It is Christmas." He clinks his glass with mine, and we both drink. Then, Gerard grabs the bottle in his other hand and rises from his seat. "Take a walk with me?"

"And leave this lively party?"

"I thought you might approve of the suggestion."

He offers me an arm, and I empty myself from my chair, locking my elbow with his.

"And where are you two off to?" his mother asks, bringing the entire table's attention to us.

"I'm just taking Evelyn for an evening stroll. Would you all mind if we left your company?" he asks coyly, knowing full well that none of them would care one bit.

They just want to call attention to any time he and I spend together—alone.

His mother gives a knowing look to mine while our fathers both smile broadly.

"Of course we don't mind," my mother answers for all of them. "You two enjoy your walk."

Gerard pivots on his heel, leading me away from the table and out of the private dining area, down the long hall toward a part of the hotel I've yet to see, despite coming here for years. We tend to only stay on one end, and this section is generally used for resident staff.

"So, where are we going?" I ask, squeezing his arm.

"It's a surprise."

Intrigued, I allow him to escort me farther down the hall and into an ultra private room that resembles a small aquarium with fish tanks lining the lower half of the walls. At the end of the space, a large floor-to-ceiling window opens up to the dark foliage below the summit.

"What's this room?" I question, peeking at the colored fish swimming in the illuminated waters.

"Just a sitting room," he says.

I peer over my shoulder, finding Gerard resting the wine on a nearby table along with his glass.

"It was the one room I had a say over when we acquired the place—design-wise, that is."

"I like the fish."

He steps toward the entrance, brightening the lights slightly, allowing me to see the details of the walls more clearly. "Do you like the decor?"

I scan the framed artwork—approximately a dozen masterful reproductions of Van Gogh's work. His more noted and popular works are represented, but I'm pleased to see some of my favorites and lesser-acknowledged masterpieces, including *Wheatfield with Crows* and *The Red Vineyard*. Near the window, overlooking the water, is a print of *Starry Night Over the Rhone*.

"They're all Van Gogh," I say.

"Every last one." He leads me toward the window. Pointing down at the sand, he asks, "Do you recognize that spot? Near the rock where the water meets its edge?"

I smile. "That's where you kissed me. Of course, I remember. We were practicing, just in case."

"Yes." He laughs. "Just in case."

"That was such a long time ago."

"Five years. Do you remember our pact?"

"Yes." My gut flips, sour with anticipation of what he's leading toward. "We made it the same time in that very same spot, agreeing to wed when I turned thirty."

"Yes."

"We still have a lot of years left before then."

"Come," he requests, taking my hand and leading back to where the bottle of wine rests.

I take a seat and allow him to fill my glass to the brim, and then I take a long drink, nervous as to why he could possibly be bringing this up so soon. He sips his wine, calm and practiced. My palms become clammy as the seconds and then minutes perpetually tick by.

Finally, he rests his glass on the table between us, staring at the plum-colored liquid trapped by the fine crystal.

"Do you know why I agreed to such an arrangement with you?" he asks, his question firm and steady.

I take a moment, sorting the words in my head before replying, "Because…we were being stupid? Because…some things are inevitable? I don't know. It was all so silly at the time. I almost thought it was a—"

"A joke?" He raises his brows.

"No," I say, backpedaling, realizing that I might have insinuated something hurtful. "No, of course not. But I wasn't really sure it was serious. I mean, we were tipsy on champagne, and I was only seventeen."

"Yes, you were, but you were fearless. You still are."

"I don't feel fearless."

He covers my hand with his own. "You are though. The fact that you even dreamed of and still constantly fight for something more than living underneath your parents' thumb is one of the most admirable acts I've ever witnessed." His eyes shift to his glass. "And because of that determination, I fell in love with you." He returns his gaze to me, focused and sincere. "That's why I agreed to the pact that day."

My muscles tense. "Gerard…I never knew."

He grins. "I know. It's my fault. I never told you." He rises from his seat, pacing toward the large print of *The Red Vineyard*, pondering over the brush strokes.

Staring at his back, I ask, "Why didn't you ever say anything?"

"Because I could see that the way you looked at me never mirrored the way I felt inside. I was afraid it would put a divide in our friendship."

I set my glass of wine on the table and join him, resting a hand on his shoulder. "Gerard…I do love you but not—"

"Not like that." He smiles to himself and then pats my hand. "Don't worry about it."

"I'm so sorry."

"You shouldn't be."

I remove my hand, feeling the wall of emotional separation being erected between us, as we stand side by side, gazing aimlessly at the artwork before us.

"Do you think they're happy?" Gerard asks into the silence.

"Who?" I question, confused.

"The workers in the painting."

I've been looking at paintings all my life for my own enjoyment and, in the later years, as study. His question is a simple one, and part of me wants to reply with a formulated answer, one that would make a scholar proud.

But I don't.

Art is all about feelings, emotions, and the human connection. As I ponder the people in the painting, I see them, and I see myself.

Focused on the figure in shades of blue and green with a basket on her hip, I say, "I think they're as happy as they can be for people put to work at a task they never desired."

He nods his head. "I used to think that, too. But do you know what I think now?"

"No. What's that?"

"That happiness is waiting for everyone." He faces me. "I love you, Evelyn, but it's much like the way you describe the happiness of these workers in the painting. I loved you as much as I could, given something I never desired, but there's more to be gained outside of what we were born into."

My head tilts as I try to understand his words.

"I'm sorry," he continues, "but I'm breaking our pact."

"You're confusing me."

"I can tell." He glows and somehow seems to become inches taller in a matter of moments. "I'm just going to say it. I've met someone."

"You meet a lot of people."

"Yes, but never anyone like her."

"Oh," I say. "Her?"

"Yes." He smiles so bright that he gleams. "I think I was waiting to find her, and that's why I never told you about my feelings for you. There was someone else waiting for me."

Then, I comprehend the truth of what he's telling me. It's all over his persona, his aura, and his entire being. It's so obvious, and I was blind until he shoved it directly at me, like a bullet to the head.

"You're in love?"

"Yes."

"Who is she?"

"She's a public attorney who lives in the States—in New York City, of all places."

"Huh?" I blink a few times. "How did you two meet?"

He grins widely. "I was in New York on business, went out one night, saw her at a bar, showed her my undeniable charm, and she called me an asshole."

"Sounds like love at first sight," I comment sarcastically.

"It was," he counters, serious. "The spark in her eyes. The way that she flung her dark hair over her shoulder. The quirk of her lip, teasing me. And then, the moment she spoke, I knew."

"You knew what?"

"That she's the one."

My heart races. His emotions are so palpable.

"What do you mean, the one?"

He grips my shoulders, ensuring that my focus is on him. "Evelyn, you're my closest friend in this crazy journey, and you should be the first to know." Gerard inhales. "I'm going to propose. I'm going to ask Caroline to be my wife."

"Marriage?" I state, flabbergasted. "Gerard, you're only twenty-five. You have your whole life ahead of you."

"And I want to spend it with her."

"What do your parents think?"

He laughs, like a giddy child in a candy store. "It doesn't matter. For the first time, it truly doesn't matter. I don't care about what they think. Since meeting her, everything is so simple."

"Simple," I repeat, saying the word, trying to understand how he feels.

"Like breathing air and taking that first step, all at the same time."

He's taking a bigger-than-life leap with someone else, going beyond the expectations of his breeding. I beam, unable to be anything but ecstatic for him in this moment.

"I'm so happy for you," I say, throwing my arms around him.

Circling his hands around my waist, he breathes, "Thank you, Evelyn. I was hoping you would be. I'm going to need someone to lean on if she actually says yes. My parents won't likely be pleased. She's not you."

"Of course, she isn't. No one could be as fabulous as me."

"You're so modest."

"We both know that's a lie." I giggle. "Even though she's not as remarkable as me, I'm sure no one could be better for you than her. I've never seen you look the way you do right now. You're freaking glowing."

"I appreciate that."

"And she'd better say yes, or else I'll kick her law-knowing ass the next time I'm in New York."

"I'd expect nothing else. Thank you."

Squeezing him tightly, I cherish his happiness. The kind of love he projects is something I'll never be able to enjoy. It's beyond stipulations, expectations, and all the rules we have both come to abide by through the years.

With Gerard's arms wrapped around my waist, I spy a figure peeking through the doorway. She doesn't budge, only allowing the pleased look to grow upon her face as she continues to watch Gerard and me in an embrace.

Nineteen

There's an anticipated knock at my apartment door, only four minutes past Foster's estimated arrival. He never disappoints when it comes to punctuality.

I've been back in town for almost three whole days, and I don't miss the sunshine, the boat, or all that comes in the expectant package of spending a holiday with my parents.

After the formal Christmas with our longtime friends, we all parted ways. The Beauchamps headed back to France, Gerard took a flight north to New York for what he'd claimed to be a business trip, and my parents began the next part of their journey to Madrid. I packed my bags and flew home to the quiet campus where many of the students were still on break with their loved ones, including all of my friends.

The silence was a welcome friend when I first returned from the angst surrounding my family. While the trip on the surface was easy, it left a bad taste in my mouth. Gerard's sudden news about his upcoming engagement and the unsettling knowledge that our parents will not likely embrace it has left me feeling a little…funky and flustered.

So, when Foster texted me earlier today, inquiring if I was back in town, I was thrilled by the idea of having some company, a distraction. Foster is a good one. My fingers dialed his number, and he answered on the first ring. As a formality, he and I exchanged a few words in greeting, got down to the nitty-gritty, decided we were both losers with no friends in town—other than each other—and now have plans to watch a movie this evening. Of course, I asked if that was code for ripping off my clothes and sticking it in. He sarcastically replied that he had no idea what I was talking about.

As the sound of a second knock echoes through the walls, I pick up the play prop from the counter and proceed toward the door.

I call out, "Just a second."

With my heart racing, I'm excited to actually have human contact after days of solitude.

I hold the fake mustache on a stick to my upper lip and open the door.

Foster is dressed in a canvas jacket and a beanie due to the snow, and his glasses are fogged from the balminess of the apartment building's air.

He gazes upon me with confusion when he notices my prop. "What is that?" he asks.

The sound of his familiar voice steadies my pounding heart.

"I mustache you a question," I state in a serious machismo voice.

"Okay…"

"Are you ready for the greatest night of your life?"

"I'm not so sure. Are you going to be wearing that?"

"Maybe. I've been told that men like a curly mustache."

"I'm pretty sure that's not the kind of lip hair that's being referenced."

"Are you saying it might be something else?"

He tightens his mouth, trying not to laugh. "Think about it."

My mind goes over what he's trying to insinuate. It only takes me a few moments before it clicks that he's made a joke about cunnilingus.

"Damn, you're naughty sometimes." I shake my head and lower the mustache.

"Just trying to stay ahead of the game with you."

"Good luck with that. Come on in."

"Thanks."

Stepping aside, I allow Foster to enter my apartment. He sets down a small bag at his feet, and then he proceeds to take off his coat and hat. Like any good hostess, I hang his things and then show him in. This is the first time he's ever been here, seeing that we usually go to his place. I just thought it was safer to avoid confrontation and questions from Chandra. It's not that I'm ashamed of Foster or what we have going on, but it's easier not to put a label on it for others. Plus, he lives alone, so his apartment makes more sense for our trysts. There, we're less likely to disturb anyone while doing the bump and grind.

"Drink?" I ask, leading him through the living area toward the kitchen.

"Yeah," he responds absently, his eyes wandering over the walls of the apartment. "Nice place. It's…colorful."

"Thanks." Opening the fridge, I say, "We have beer, soda, beer, chick wine, wine coolers—who the hell brought those over? Beer, water, prune juice…" I peek over the door, chuckling at his inquisitive look. "Don't ask. Beer…and—"

"Let me guess. Beer?"

"You got it."

"A beer would be great."

Pulling two off the shelf, I shut the door, pop the caps from both of them, and then join Foster at the small bar space in the kitchen where he's patiently waiting.

"Here you are," I say, handing the cool brown glass bottle into his hand.

"Thanks." He offers a gift bag in my direction. "And this is for you. It's good manners to bring a gift for the hostess."

"I didn't realize I was having a formal dinner party." I set my beer on the counter. "What is it?"

"Most people do something called *open it* to find out."

Widening the mouth of the bag, I mutter, "Smart-ass," and then dig into the package. I pull out a solid cylinder object wrapped in tissue paper and begin to tear the delicate covering from the gift, revealing two stacked clear pint glasses. Separating them from one another, I turn them within my hands to have a better look at the printed design.

I laugh. "Is that Sir Isaac Newton?" I ask, referring to the image of a man in a wig, holding an apple in one hand while making a rock-and-roll hand gesture with the other. Underneath the bust of the ancient-looking gentleman, the words *My Laws Rule* are scrolled across the glass.

"The one and only. The other is a cheat sheet in case you ever play the elements drinking game again," he adds, pointing to the pint with the periodic table of elements.

"These are perfect." I wash them quickly at the sink and then place them on the counter, one in front of him and the other next to my beer, for immediate use. "I love them. Thanks."

We empty our bottles into the new glasses and each take a drink. I then invite him into the living room in preparation to watch a movie. He takes a seat on the overstuffed tan sofa across from the television.

"So, how was your Christmas?" I ask, crouching down to shuffle through the film collection Chandra and I have acquired through the years.

"It was nice." He places his glass on the coffee table. "We all went to my grandmother's farm. She doesn't like to travel much, ever since my granddad passed away."

"Oh, I'm so sorry."

"It's okay. It was a few years ago. But it makes the most sense anyhow. Her place is really the only one big enough for all of us."

"All of you?" I ask somewhat absently, trying to weed through the large amount of chick flicks that he would have no desire to watch.

"Yeah. My aunts, uncles, and all the cousins."

"Sounds like you have a pretty big family."

"Kind of."

Still sorting, I ask, "Do you have any brothers or sisters?"

"Two older sisters and a younger brother." He sips his beer. "Both of my sisters are married and live out of town. One lives in Texas and the other in Georgia. They usually come back for the holiday, but Camille couldn't make the flight from Georgia this year. She's expecting a baby, and her doctor said she's passed the flying window—whatever that means. My brother is still in high school and will graduate this year."

"Sounds like a lot of people. Are you guys a clan or something? Do you have Team Blake T-shirts, too?"

"Yes. We wear them whenever we get together and go out to dinner. That way, the whole world knows we're coming."

I peek over my shoulder, smiling at him. It's good to see Foster again. While away with my family, my entire life was all about the show and the facade. This, our friendship, is easy—low maintenance and without any expectations, comfortable and free.

"So, what do you think?" I ask, holding up three movies. "*Twilight*, *The Hunger Games*, or *Star Wars* marathon? The originals, of course."

His fingertips touch his brow. "The Force is leaning me toward the dark side."

"I knew you would pick *Star Wars*. All guys have a thing for watching Princess Leia run with no bra."

"One can't deny the beauty of breasts and gravity."

"I'm in it for the clothes and Hans Solo's ass."

I pop the disc into the player and join Foster on the couch. Pressing play from the remote, the familiar intro music cues through the speakers, and the long prologue scrolls up the screen.

Foster sits back, settling into the cushions. "I always thought this movie was some psychological experiment about the profound way all of the universe's problems really just come down to daddy issues."

"What?" I guffaw. "How many times have you seen this?"

"Likely too many."

"I would say so if you're going all philosophical on Obi-Wan and the Rebel Alliance."

"How many times have you watched this?"

"Enough."

The movie begins, and we're both immediately engrossed in the opening scene.

"I can't believe you own *Star Wars*," Foster comments. "You don't really seem the type."

"Why? Because I don't go around speaking Yoda all day?"

"No." He looks me up and down. "You just don't strike me as a Jedi fan."

"Well, I'm not, truth be told. These actually belong to my roommate. She has a thing for costumes and bought the entire set for research. I've watched so many movies with her for just the clothes that it's kind of ridiculous. I could probably tell you every outfit in every scene for this entire series. And that's a lot."

"So, you really are in it for the clothes."

"I told you."

"What about the hairstyles? Do you know all of those, too?"

"Yes, those are easy," I state, mocking his simple question. "The men all have the same shag-o-rific hair, including Chewie, and all the girls look like some form of Kabuki. The end."

Foster smiles, takes another sip of his beer, and then edges a little closer to me. Getting comfy, I draw my feet onto the cushions, tucking them at my side. Our bodies aren't touching, but the natural heat builds in the minute space between us. As the movie continues, I take in his unique and familiar scent. It's pleasant, comforting...Foster. Sitting next to him right now is like crawling into bed and smelling the sheets after a long trip away. You know you're home.

"So, how was your Christmas?" Foster asks about thirty minutes into the movie.

"Pretty much the same as every year. Lots of sun and water."

"Must have been nice to see your family though?"

"Sort of." I crinkle my nose. "It's always good to see my dad. My mom is my mom, but she wasn't that bad. My sister ditched us this year, spending the holiday with her new husband's family in Vermont."

"What is it about your mom? I know you said you two have issues, but you never said what they were."

"Typical mother-daughter crap, I guess." I bite my lip and focus on the television screen. "She just doesn't know me."

"Have you tried talking to her?"

I laugh at how absurdly simple his question is. "There's no talking to that woman when it comes to certain things. And yes, I've tried talking to her on several occasions. She's like the Hoover Dam when it comes to outside thought—somewhat impenetrable." Then, without any thought or pause, I say, "And something tells me when she finds out about Gerard, I'll never hear the end of it."

"Gerard?"

Realizing I've said too much, I reply, "Sorry. Never mind."

He tilts his head. "Who's Gerard?"

"A friend of the family." I shrug. "We've known each other since we were kids."

"So, did something happen between you two?"

I squirm, feeling like I'm being interrogated, but the softness of Foster's face has me forging on.

"Actually," I say, leaning into the taupe cushion at my shoulder, "nothing happened between us, and that's why she'll be upset."

He squints. "Wait, so your mom would be mad because nothing happened? Now, I'm really confused."

"No." I sit up. "She's going to be upset because he's getting married...and it's not to me."

He furrows his brow. "Are you secret royalty or something? You weren't betrothed to each other, were you?"

I sputter a guffaw. "No, but my mother makes great efforts at ensuring that life turns out the way she's planned. She's a very adamant person."

Foster rests his elbows on his knees. "Plans are for fools who are naive and selfish. No one can predict anyone's life, no matter how hard they might try. At the end of the day, everyone was gifted with something called free will. If she loves you, she'll respect your choice."

"Then, I don't know if she loves me that much."

"That's really fucked up."

"Tell me about it."

Twenty

A muffled sound vibrates across my eardrums as my body is swayed, nudged, and poked repeatedly. I swat at the annoyance, like a pesky fly at a picnic, hoping it will go away.

"EJ," a warm voice whispers in my ear. "EJ…"

"What?" I lazily huff, shifting my shoulder toward the warmth at my side.

"You fell asleep," he says quietly, grasping me by the arm. "The movie's over."

Inhaling deeply, I attempt to pull myself out of my slumber. It's no use.

"C'mon," Foster's voice says, soft and gentle. "Let's get you to bed."

Before I'm aware of all that's happening or can even object, I'm in Foster's arms and being lifted from the sofa. Peeking through my lids, I focus on his jawline as he carries me down the short hallway toward my room.

"My knight in shining armor," I mumble, nuzzling closer into his chest, too sleepy to protest about being coddled in such a way.

"Yes. I'm saving you from a dreaded sore neck in the morning by not letting you sleep on the couch." He stops in the middle of the hall. "Which one is yours?"

"The last door."

He continues down the hallway and enters my room with me in his arms. Setting me on the bed, Foster takes off my shoes and then reaches for the button on my pants.

"Are you trying to take advantage of me in my state of delirium?" I ask, teasing him.

"You would like that too much," he replies, sliding my jeans down my thighs. Tossing them aside, he then pulls back the covers and guides my legs underneath. "I'll let myself out. Get some sleep."

I'm not sure why, but I reach out and grab his forearm as he's turning to leave.

"Don't go," I say, a hint of desperation in my voice. "Stay."

His silhouette relaxes as he stares down at me in my half-awake and half-asleep state. The seconds of silence lurk and expand in the air as my request lingers into the hazily dim light of my room. Taking his non-reply as an answer or realizing that I might be so tired that I'm making up conversations in my head, I roll over, burrowing down into my pillow.

I allow my mind to float to the subconscious, the impending deep slumber, when the bed sinks behind me. An arm slinks around my waist, a man's heat warming my back, and I fall fast asleep, like it's nothing more than a dream.

~~~~~~

A soft wind blows along the treetops, rustling their newly green leaves into a harmonic opus. Glorious and beaming, the sun shines through the cottony clouds above, magnifying the bold-colored flowers lining the arbor ahead where a man with auburn hair waits next to an officiate on this momentous day. Classical music strums through the air, lulling the guests into a state of pristine joy.

The tune shifts into processional music, inviting bridesmaids outfitted in fine luxury gowns down the aisle. Each one with perfect coifs, makeup, and stature walk like obediently trained specimens along the white runner and take their designated space near the arbor. When all six are aligned and smiling, like the props they are meant to be, the melody morphs into the "Wedding March."

On cue, the guests stand in honor of the bride.

I rise with them, facing the aisle.

A woman in soft white fabric, escorted by a gentleman with silver hair, makes her way toward the groom. She glows brightly under the veil of tulle and lace, tears streaming down her cheeks, and she ascends the steps to meet her soon-to-be husband. When she's at his side, Gerard turns to face her, and his entire aura lights up so bright that the sun above is nothing in comparison.

We all sit in awe of the splendor about to take place between these two people. A few words are said, the bride's father gives her hand to Gerard, and the ceremony commences.

As the father of the bride takes his seat, a blonde woman at my side exhales heavily.

My mother.

A chill runs up my spine, turning the cordiality of the moment into an iceberg of dread.

A low growl rumbles from her chest, announcing her displeasure. She turns her steely cold eyes in my direction. With obvious disgust, her features become hard as she fidgets with the bag on her lap.

She says nothing.

Neither do I, avoiding her awful glare.

Lifting her chin, my mother turns her attention back to the couple at the altar, relieving me of her focused anger.

Listening to the sermon, I try to enjoy the momentous occasion centered on my childhood friend. He deserves happiness. Everyone does.

A large palm covers my own, warming the cold feelings inflicted upon me. I peer at the person next to me, his face full of mischief and sarcasm—a dangerous combination for anyone.

"Fancy wedding," Foster states, *low and mocking for only my ears. "Shitty crowd though. Who invited the evil witch?"*

"Better question is, who forgot to drop a house on her?"

He squeezes my hand as we grin at one another, amused in our own world beyond the wedding.

"Foster"—I lean into him—*"thank you so much for coming with me."*

"Of course. That's what friends do for each other."

~~~~~~

Lazily, my heavy lids open to the early rising sun peeking through my bedroom windows. Stiff with sleep, I slowly adjust my head on the pillow toward my nightstand to check the hour.

At my side, with his head resting on the pillow, Foster, still and awake, watches me with his deep sea-blue eyes as I come out of my slumber.

I blink.

My lips part.

He edges himself closer, the warmth of his body engulfing me under the purple duvet. Grazing his lips with mine ever so lightly, like flirting butterfly wings, he softly breathes his heat into me. My fingers walk their way to his chin covered in stubble, dancing along the shape of his face, as my mind still rests somewhere between a dream state and reality.

Teasing and tempting, our mouths dust over one another, never fully connecting. Foster's hand hesitantly floats along the shape of my hip and underneath the thin cotton fabric of my shirt, caressing and memorizing the curves of my form. I thread my fingers through his warm caramel–colored hair as my mind and body become more alive. He proceeds to tempt me with his mouth as he draws his palm along my skin in an act of foreplay and questions.

"Kiss me," I beg, the desire building.

Our mouths connect at my request, and a moan of relief rises from my chest. Grabbing me by the backside, he pulls me tight to his body and sucks on my tongue.

With a firm arm wrapped around my hips, Foster rolls onto his back, taking me with him. I position my legs across his waist, grinding my exceedingly horny-as-hell pelvis against his equally aroused erection.

"Good morning," he says between sucking on my lower lip.

"It certainly is."

Foster lifts the cotton top over my head, dropping it to the floor, and then he unsnaps my bra, freeing my breasts, and tosses it to the side. I help him out of his shirt and savor his inviting flesh under my palms. His mouth is instantly at my nipple, sucking and gently nibbling, sending erotic messages to the space between my legs in sudden need of stimulation. I release my head over my shoulder, giving him full rein to my chest, as I grind over his length.

His hands slide down my bare back and underneath my panties, grabbing my ass, pulling me harder over him, while his mouth seductively slays my own. I raise my body to aid his wanting fingers in removing the rest of my clothes and then slip his boxers from his legs as well. Reaching over his naked form, I open the nightstand drawer, finding a condom.

No words are said. No words are needed.

He takes the contraceptive into his hand and prepares himself for an act that we have done several times before. When ready, I reposition myself over him with my hands propped on either side of his head, sliding his cock between my slick folds.

"Sit up," he requests.

I smile, knowing. "You want to watch, don't you?"

"Yeah."

Licking my lower lip, I push myself upward and straddle him, my entrance teasingly kissing the tip of his length. With him focused on my sex, I sink myself over him. His breathing hitches as I inch my way further down, fully taking him inside me, and then I rise back up. I do this slowly, several times, taking gratification from his obvious enjoyment.

He loves it.

Foster lightly taps my ass cheek.

Then, he does it again, causing me to ride him harder, searching for deeper penetration. He circles his thumb around my clit, and I arch my back, grasping his thighs for dear life, as a flame of heat sparks pleasurable vibrations through my fast-pumping blood.

I whimper softly.

"Evelyn," he breathes.

At the sound of my name, a blazing fire erupts under my skin, and I quiver uncontrollably for what feels like an eternity.

When my breathing slows, I lean forward and kiss his lips in gratitude for the unbelievable orgasm. He kisses me twice, rolls us so that I'm on my back, and then positions his arms under my own, propping himself up on his elbows.

Foster thrusts into me—hard, heavy, intentional, and with extreme ferocity. I grip his shoulders and dig my fingers into his skin, in the midst of our primal act. It doesn't take too long before his body takes on a familiar pace. He pants in a distinguishable tempo, his muscles tense. Then, he enters me a final time with a guttural force, releasing a satisfactory long grunt.

Relaxing my body while Foster rests in a satiated stupor, I savor the feel of his nakedness over my own, covered in perspiration and fulfillment. He lifts his head from the crook of my neck, and I place my hand in his line of sight for a high five, which has become somewhat customary after we finish our bang-o-thons.

Between labored rasps, he presses his warm lips into my waiting palm and then collapses over me once again.

I tentatively slide my hands around his back.

He returns the gesture, narrowing his embrace, until the only sound remaining is our hearts beating in unison against each other's chests.

We remain still.

We breathe.

We hold each other.

Then, the phone blares my mother's ringtone into the comfortable moment.

It's early, too early for anyone to be calling, so it must be important.

"I should get that," I mutter, squirming underneath Foster's weight.

He releases me from his grasp, rolling over and off of me. Sitting up, I reach toward the bedside table and grab my cell.

"Hello?" I say groggily, faking as if her call awoke me.

"Evelyn," she says firmly, "it's your mother."

"Yes, I gathered that from the caller ID."

Foster rises from the mattress, points into the hall, and mouths, *I'm going to use the bathroom.*

I nod my head and pull the sheet up over my breasts as he exits the room.

"Evelyn…" my mother summons. "Did you hear me?"

"Sorry." I wipe my palm across my brow, trying to get into the character of a sleepy college student, not one that just had her brains fucked out for breakfast. "I'm not really awake."

"Typical. Well, I was calling because I heard some news this morning, and I thought you would like to know."

"What's that?"

"Sophia Beauchamp called, announcing that her son just got engaged. You could imagine my excitement when I heard this."

I clamp my lids tight, exhaling the building tension. "I know."

"You know what?"

"About Gerard. At Christmas, he told me he was going to propose."

Foster reenters my room.

"Evelyn," she growls, "that should be you, not some...some attorney from Nebraska."

"She lives in New York."

"Whatever. She's just a poser from the Midwest. He should be marrying you."

Foster slips into his boxers and then pulls his T-shirt over his head while my mother mumbles a slew of gibberish.

"I don't know if I'll ever be able to forgive you for this," she says, finally finding comprehendible words.

Foster takes a seat at my side, placing his glasses over his face.

"He loves her," I respond factually, "not me."

"And why not?" she asks, like she really has no clue whatsoever.

"Because I wasn't the one."

"Well, you should have done a better job at trying to convince him otherwise. Have I taught you nothing?"

Angered, I sit up taller, gritting my teeth. "I'm sorry I failed you...again."

She then quietly says the same words she has said to me weekly since I was a child, "The world is a cruel place, Evelyn. Your decisions will haunt you if you aren't careful and you don't choose wisely. We make our own lives, and you aren't in control of yours."

"I know what I want to do with my life."

"What we want and what is best aren't always the same thing."

I squirm and reply as I've been taught, "You've been telling me this for years. I've gotten the gist."

"Then, start acting like the smart young lady I raised," she huffs, air vibrating through the connection. "I'm going to tell your father about this. He's not going to be happy."

"I know."

"You should," she says, her voice hard and full of daggers. "I'm going to go now. I will send your congratulations along with ours to Gerard and his new fiancée."

"Thank you," I say, my mouth tight. At my side, Foster patiently sits as I continue with this extremely uncomfortable but not unexpected conversation, "That's very thoughtful."

"It's the right thing to do," she says like it's a lesson I need to learn. "And don't forget to call us as soon as you hear about grad school. Surely, you won't make a mess of that as well, will you?"

"Of course not."

"Take care, Evelyn," she says shortly before ending the call.

I lower the phone from my ear, set it on the nearby table, and then slink under the covers, resting my head on the pillow. Foster expectantly stares down at me as I try to mentally wash away the conversation with my mother.

"Should I go?" he asks.

"If you want." I shrug.

"Are you all right?"

"Yeah. Just had a lovely chat with my mother about how I'm the child she always dreamed of and I'm living up to all of her expectations."

"I see." He scratches behind his ear, releasing a few tufts of hair. "Do you want to go and get some breakfast?"

"We can do that."

Twenty-One

My hand dabs the brush across hues of umber and vermilion, combining them, resulting in a brilliant color of sunlight at dawn. I paint a sensual curve along the rib of my human canvas, depicting his molecular composition with shades of reality. The image of the hydrogen element, a nucleus surrounded by a singular circling proton, comes to life with the stroke of my hand. I strategically position it next to the rendering of the carbon particle on Foster's pectoral muscle.

Over the last couple of days, Foster and I have spent a fair amount of time together since neither of us have any school or work obligations—or family ones, for that matter. His company has been easy and fun. It's almost like having a girlfriend over for a long visit while we do nothing, other than eat and hang out.

Well, there's the sex, too. That's one thing I don't tend to partake in with girlfriends.

Today started out no different than any other. We lunched at a local Indian restaurant where we dined on curry and naan bread, and then we headed back to my place to explore each other's bodies more intimately.

Actually, we fucked each other hard and fast and then fell asleep, exhausted.

After awaking from a short nap, an impulsion took over, and Foster became my study. I began drawing a number of profiles of him in my sketchpad while he slumbered next to me.

My hands worked furiously—depicting the shape of his nose, cheeks, chin, mouth, and body—over and over again with graphite, shading the tiny details making up the uniqueness that is him. It was somewhat strange, drawing him for the first time. There was something almost second nature about it. His face was one I'd come to know in a private way over the past several weeks, and my hands were channeling that knowledge.

When Foster finally awoke, he caught me in the act of taking advantage of him as an unknown model. He wasn't upset by my interest to use him as a study. We then got into a discussion about the human form, and Foster—being the science-drawn person that he is—went on a tangent about what really made up a person from a chemical standpoint. He discussed the more elemental aspects of human life, explaining that all people were essentially made up of the same thing, a scientific balance of elements. He taught me that oxygen made up about sixty-five percent of our bodies.

No surprise to me that we are all made of air.

Of course, I went the philosophical route, pinpointing that we were all made up of moments of our pasts and our environments.

At first, I let him jabber on about all the technical and mechanical parts of the world—like he often does—but the more I listened, the more fascinated I became. He was so fierce in his diatribe that I got swept up in his energetic storytelling and how he viewed life through the details of science. Foster then went one step further, showing me images from the Internet of what each element looked like in its raw form and how combining all those things with the right chemistry were able to make the person sitting in front of me.

Him.

The same chemistry that made me.

As he continued to talk, I grabbed the sketchpad and began to draw what he was describing. My hand couldn't move fast enough as he raced through his knowledge, fueled by my interest. When I filled the last blank page in my art book, I handed it over to him and dug through my closet for a set of stored-away watercolors. I requested him to take off his shirt, which he did without question, and I began to paint his flesh with the transferred knowledge I had received in combination with my imagination. He continued to answer questions as I asked them while I attempted to create the masterpiece of what he was made of on the inside.

The elements of him.

Of life.

Of all of us.

Foster's chest is now completely covered in watercolors, a collage of the many periodic elements that make a human being, streaming and connected together in a fluid symphony of color and design. I dip my brush into the ocher tint and begin to create another circle, one to depict sulfur, on his shoulder.

"You're really into this," Foster comments, remaining as still as possible.

"Shh…" I hush him. "I'm working."

With the arm opposite of where the fresh paint is being applied, he places his glasses over his face and then turns the page in the sketchpad full of my previously created images, studying them. "I still can't believe this is how you see science."

"Why not?" I ask absently while creating the nucleus detail in a shade of purple.

"It's all so…vivid."

"Well, you made it sound very exciting. It's your fault."

"This can't be from me," he insists, showing me an orange-and-blue image of a carbon molecule drowning in darkness. "It's too…exotic."

"You doubt your passion. And it's safe to say that you're the driving force behind that one. All I did was channel it onto the page."

He lays the pad back on the bed. "They're really amazing. I've never seen anything like this, and I've been looking at the elements in many variations for most of my life. What you've done is beyond what my mind has seen, yet it is still so accurate."

"Keep it then," I say, blotting my brush on a nearby cloth. "You can have it."

"I don't want to take your things. These are too good for you to just give away."

I lift my head, so my clear blue eyes meet his cobalt ones behind dark frames. "I have no use for those. Plus, you would love them more than me. They're yours."

I concentrate on the human mural, defining a few lines, while Foster sits patiently. He never complains about the coolness of the paint, the air, or any position I request for him to hold.

"How long have you been doing this?" he asks out of nowhere.

"For a little over an hour." I chuckle. "Don't you remember the last hour?"

"Not this." He points to his abs. "Drawing, painting, taking pictures—the art stuff."

"Hmm…" I twist my mouth, adding a thin line of detail to the composition. "Not sure. I've been drawing pictures in my mind and seeing the world differently than reality long before conveying the images to paper. But I never defined it as art back then." I laugh. "My mother called it daydreaming. She was right. I was constantly wandering in the made-up world in my own head. But to answer your question, it likely started the moment my...sitter took me to a museum. She helped me focus my imagination to the page, using art as a medium. She was a musician and saw things a little differently, too."

"So, you were born an artist."

"Unfortunately," I say, adding a small scarlet detail near his collarbone. "It's not exactly a blessing."

"I don't know about that." Foster's index finger lightly traces over the dried connecting swirls and circles near his waistline. "I admire your creativity."

"You're one of the few." Lifting my brush from his skin, I sit back on my heels, observing the product. "I think it's done."

"Yeah? How does it look?"

"Hang on." Shuffling backward off the bed, I move the art supplies to the floor and then retrieve my camera from its nearby case. "Do you mind if I shoot you?"

His mouth gapes in mock shock. "You aren't going to post these online, are you?"

"Absolutely not. I plan to use them for blackmail later in life."

He narrows his gaze in warning.

"Why don't you take off your shorts?" I bite my lower lip, amused. "It will make the pictures more valuable."

Foster shakes his head. "Take the pictures, you hedonist. I'm keeping my shorts on."

"You're no fun." I raise the camera and focus on his chest through the lens. "You look fabulous, darling."

"Oh, shut up," he retorts sarcastically. "Just do it before I change my mind."

Clicking the shutter, I capture the painting on his skin—the weaving of science, humanity, and imagination—from a number of angles. Foster lies still on the bed as I snap him from the side, over his body, and head-on when he sits up at my request. When more than enough shots have been taken, I take a step back for one last look through the shots to ensure it's all been collected on digital film.

"Can you lie back down?" I ask, stepping up onto the bed. "I want to get a few more from this position."

"Sure," he complies, easily resting both hands behind his head. "I think you like it on top."

"All girls do. They're just too afraid to admit it."

"But not you?"

"Have you met me?"

"We've been acquainted."

With a foot placed on each side of his waist, I take a few more images of his torso, focusing on the area at his neck where the paint ends and Foster begins. Then, without any thought, like my hands are guiding my subconscious mind, the lens travels along the length of his face, focusing on the fine details of his features. It finds the crease between his chin and his mouth, the indentation at the center of his upper lip, the often underrated area where his hairline meets his cheekbones, and the softness of his ears. My camera encapsulates them all.

"Can you take off your glasses?" I ask, still behind the lens.

"I thought the paint was lower?"

"Humor me."

He obliges, revealing his deep blue orbs, soft and open. Zooming in, I observe their sensitivity, vulnerability, and the layers of his humanity often shielded by the reflective glass barrier. There's lightness, darkness, hunger, and—dare I even say—fear lurking within them as the sound of the clicking shutter memorizes their shape and unspoken story.

"Got it?" he asks.

I nod, waking myself out of the mesmerizing moment. "I think so."

Lowering the camera, I take a seat with my legs crossed, next to Foster. He sits up and leans over my shoulder, so we can view the frames together. One by one,

I flip through the images of colors and shapes, including the more intimate ones of his face.

Foster makes no comment.

"What do you think?" I ask hesitantly, knowing that he might see what's evident to me in the latter images.

"You did…it's beyond anything I imagined. I'm almost afraid to shower."

"I hope you aren't serious." I rest the camera in my lap. "I'll send you a few copies."

"I would like that." He gazes down at the artwork on his chest. "So, is this what all art history majors do? Obsessively paint their friends?"

I laugh. "No, it's just me."

"So, you're special?"

"Haven't you noticed?"

"It's come to my attention." Foster traces a plum swirl on his lower ribs. "I'm curious though. What does an art history major do after graduating from college?"

Reaching over his legs, I place the camera back in its bag. "Most of them get jobs at museums or go on to grad school to again get a job at a museum, as a curator, or go into teaching and research. I don't know. There are a few other things, too, but those are the most popular options."

"Which one of those are you doing?"

"None."

"Oh?" He grabs his black frames from the nearby side table and returns them to his face. "So, you're one of the others?"

"I guess you could say that. I'll be going to grad school and getting my MBA."

"Really?" He sits up straighter, turning his full attention toward me. "Do you plan to run an art business or something?"

"Hardly," I sputter. "I'll be going to Yale most likely. It's my duty to take part in the family tradition."

"Wow. Yale, huh?"

"Yeah, I'm a double legacy. They have to take me." I stare at my lap. "You know, you're the first person I've ever told that to."

"About getting an MBA?"

"Yeah…well, Chandra knows but not about Yale."

"Is it a secret?"

"I guess not." I lift a shoulder. "It's just not something I'm shouting from the rooftops."

"Do you not want to go?" he questions, his voice low and steady.

Grazing my fingers along the colorful dots, circles, and waves on his chest, I ask, "Do I seem like the MBA type?"

"Not really." He wraps his fingers around my wandering hand. "If I'm being honest, you don't seem like the art history type either. I don't see you working in a museum or sitting in some office, doing research."

Our gazes slowly connect.

"Sometimes, what we want to do and what we have to do aren't always the same," I say, like it's a script that my mother has burned into my soul.

"It sucks, doesn't it?"

"Like you wouldn't believe."

He releases my hand, and I join it with the other on my lap.

"What about you? What are your plans after graduation?" I ask.

"MBA, likely Stanford or Duke. My grandparents are alumni at both."

"Ah, you're a legacy, too," I tease, bumping his shoulder. "Who knew we had so much in common?"

"I never would have imagined."

171

Twenty-Two

Foster parks his vehicle in front of a small Victorian home on the hill that overlooks the city. I peer up at the quaint house, highlighted by a streetlamp in the black sky. The light illuminates the house's palette of bright colors, accents of green and purple against the yellow facade.

"Is this it?" I ask, unbuckling my seat belt, preparing to exit the car.

"Yep. We're here." He kills the ignition and opens the car door. "Let's go in."

I step onto the sidewalk as Foster rounds his well-loved more-than-ten-years-old Honda Accord. With a six-pack of beer in my hand, I follow his lead and ascend the steps to the front door of his friend's house where he rings the doorbell. We wait under the tiny covered alcove, listening to the sounds of voices in cheerful spirits reverberating from within the walls.

"Thanks again for inviting me," I say, tucking a sun-kissed strand of hair behind my ear, highlighted from my recent time at sea. "And for reminding me how lame it is to spend New Year's Eve alone. It was by choice, you know."

"You were going to be a total loser, and I can't be associated with someone like that. What would people say?"

"Yes, we wouldn't want anyone to insult your judgment. We both know what a blow that would be to your intelligence."

"Exactly."

The door opens, and the golden light from within floods the porch, framing a tall man's silhouette.

"Hey, man," Graham, Foster's light-blond friend, says, widening the entrance. "You made it."

"All in one piece. And I brought a friend, too," he adds, placing a hand at the middle of my back. "You remember EJ, right?"

"How could I forget?" he asks rhetorically. "You're the girl who likes lots of tongue in her bets."

"I'm glad I made an impression. I'm not sure if being known as tongue-girl is a good thing or a bad thing, but I'll go with it." I lift the six-pack in his direction, and he takes it in his free hand. "Thanks for having me."

"Sure thing. C'mon in."

Graham steps aside, allowing Foster and me to enter the warm house fragrant with pine and the remnants of pizza. He shows us a chair near the steps where we can leave our jackets and then leads us through a short hallway to the kitchen where a stream of voices in conversation billows out.

In the tight space of white-and-green tiles, three men—two I recognize as Peter and James from that fateful night when I won my bet at the bar—are gathered around a small table, playing a card game, while three girls are in the midst of a conversation at the counter. A fourth girl, a fit brunette with angular features, enters the room from a side hallway at the same time as us and makes her way past the group of women.

"Hi, Foster," she says in a cold tone.

"Hey, Fiona," he responds easily.

Fiona openly evaluates me and then joins the men at the table, resting an arm on James's shoulder. Graham shakes his head and then proceeds toward the refrigerator, placing my beer inside.

"Foster!" Peter shouts, rising from his seat to greet him. "Good to see you."

"You, too," Foster says in return. "How was your Christmas?"

"Boring as hell. I couldn't wait to get back."

"Understood." He points an index finger in my direction. "You remember EJ, right?"

"Of course. Her views on Newton's laws are unforgettable." He pauses, staring at me in deep thought. "Speaking of, do you think you could do me a favor?"

"Possibly?" I say, unsure.

He leans in closer and points a thumb over his shoulder. "Do you see the guy over there with the red shirt and dark hair?"

I peek at the gathering of men seated at the circular table, identifying the person in question. "Yeah. What about him?"

"I would give my left nut if you could show him your scientific knowledge. That Newton's law bit is epic."

"Lance?" Foster questions.

"Yes, the asshole," Peter answers. "He just took fifty bucks from me, and I'd like to bring his ego down a bit."

"Consider it done," I say, amused. "What kind of wager are you thinking?"

"Shit, I don't know. Just make it good."

"How about I get your money back?"

"I was kind of hoping for a little more than that."

"Like what? Should I have him try to lick his own dick?" I ask, totally kidding.

Foster chuckles.

"That could work." Peter nods his head while rubbing his chin, seriously contemplating the wager.

I laugh. "I'll think about it."

Graham joins us with a plastic cup in hand. "You two help yourself to whatever you like. Beer's in the fridge, and liquor is on the counter next to whatever food Lilliana and her friends brought."

"Thanks." Foster turns to me. "Do you want anything?"

"A beer would be great."

We all disperse. Graham joins the group of girls and hooks an arm around the average-height strawberry-blonde with curly hair, Peter takes a seat at the table next to James, and Foster and I step toward the fridge to get a beer. Once we both have our drinks, I follow his lead and gather around the ongoing card game.

It's a little after ten in the evening, less than two hours until the New Year, and it's easy to ascertain that this will likely be a low-key evening of friends, libations, and fun.

"Thanks again," I utter at Foster's shoulder.

James deals the cards to everyone at the table.

"For what?" Foster asks.

"The invite."

"Don't thank me yet. There's no guarantee it will be anything memorable."

I scan the tame playing of cards, observing the content faces of all the guests. "The night is young."

Over the next hour and a half, I become acquainted with mostly everyone, learning that Graham, Lance, and Peter live in the house together. All of the men, including Foster and James, are chemical engineering majors and have known each other since freshman year. Apparently, it's a tight-knit class since they spend so much time in labs and doing group projects.

As promised to Peter, I attempt to finagle the fifty dollars back from Lance. I add a bet for him to dip his balls in his own beer and drink it. The latter is not my idea. It's Peter's, but I go with it. Thankfully, James, Foster, and Graham silently play their part well, knowing all along that I have the upper hand. The table goes wild when I reveal my knowledge of Newton's law once again, and it instantly befriends me to everyone. This also helps to open conversation with the group of girls—Lilliana, Graham's girlfriend of the past three years, and her two friends, who are pleasant, sweet, and getting drunker by the hour.

At fifteen minutes until midnight, Lilliana suggests we all go outside to ring in the New Year. We arm ourselves in our coats, and with drinks in hand, we huddle onto the back porch overshadowed by the faint stars and moon above.

"So, how long have you and Foster been an item?" Lilliana questions me.

Foster is chatting with his friends on the other side of the wooden deck.

"Oh, we aren't a couple." I take a sip of my drink. "Just friends. He and I work together."

"Really? Sorry, I just assumed. He hasn't brought a girl around in a while. I just figured…"

"Well, there's nothing to figure." I gaze up at the stars, dull and almost unnoticeable. This is clearly not the night Van Gogh envisioned when he looked at the sky. I lean in closer to Lilliana and say, "But if you are worried that he might be gay, I assure you that he isn't."

"No, I knew he wasn't gay." Her focus shifts away from me and toward James and Fiona, who is obviously his girlfriend based on the way they haven't left one another's side all evening. "We all know that." She checks the time on her watch. "Less than five minutes left until we get to start again. I'm going to go and find Graham. It was nice taking with you, EJ."

"You, too."

She leaves me, so I'm alone on one side of the porch while everyone congregates at the other end. I take the moment of solitude to gaze above, imagining the painted sky of *The Starry Night* with myself swimming among its brushstrokes.

Every year at this time, people across the world make resolutions and promises of grandeur to themselves for their betterment. A New Year is literally minutes away, and my wishes remain the same—to live in a world outside of my reality, in a dream of my own making. As graduation draws near, hope for such a dream gradually plunders. Determination can take a person only so far when the visceral truth of reality keeps rearing its ugly head.

Escaping into a dream is just that—a dream.

"Hey, there," Foster says as he approaches. "It's almost midnight."

"So I've heard."

"Do you think you're ready for the New Year?"

"Probably not, but this one is basically over, so onto the next."

"Thirty more seconds!" Lilliana shouts with Graham's arms around her waist.

"C'mon," Foster says, tugging me toward the group. "Let's go and join them."

Surrounded by Foster's inebriated friends, we count down the remaining seconds until midnight.

When the moment comes where everyone shouts, "One," in unison, cheers erupt, and people scream, "Happy New Year!" throughout the neighborhood.

We all clink our cups and beer bottles before embracing one another. Whirling around in the crowd, I take in the excitement as couples kiss to celebrate the start of another three hundred sixty-five days.

Time has been reset for everyone.

"Happy New Year, Evelyn," Foster says close to my ear. Then, he chastely kisses me on my cheekbone.

I tilt my head, connecting my lips with his, and I forget the noise, if only for a second. "Happy New Year, Fozzie."

Foster's friends make the rounds, wishing each other well for the impending year. I stay by his side, welcoming hugs from each of them, some even kissing me on the cheek.

James is one of the last of his friends to pull Foster into a hug, laughing about the previous year and some of their many mishaps. When they release each other from their embrace, Foster reaches toward Fiona, James's girlfriend, with his arms open wide, but he pauses the moment she steps back.

"Happy New Year, Foster," she says, stiff and cold.

Nodding, Foster lowers his arms. "You, too, Fiona."

"I've decided I'm not going to be angry with you anymore," she says, James resting an arm over her shoulder. "That's my resolution—to forgive you."

"I appreciate that. I hope you know I never meant to hurt you."

She harrumphs. "Yeah, well, I should have known better. It's obvious you were using me."

"We should get a drink," James interjects, tightening his hold on her.

"Did you even care about me at all?" she asks Foster, ignoring James's suggestion.

Foster's jaw goes tight.

"That's what I thought," she says. "I really was an idiot." She spares a look at me as I stand at Foster's side. "Good luck with him. Just don't expect much. He's not exactly emotionally available. Corpses have more feelings."

Fiona turns within James's arm to leave, but then she pauses in her tracks, glancing over her shoulder at Foster. "By the way, tell Sasha I said hi. I'm sure she's happier without you." Fiona lowers her voice as she says, "I certainly am."

She then leaves our company with James at her side. Foster remains still, his gaze following after them.

"Ignore her," Graham says to Foster, coming forth once James and Fiona are out of sight. "She's had way too much to drink, and we all know her motives for...well, what happened between you two, weren't really the right ones."

"She's a vulture," Lilliana adds. "An opportunist. She's nothing but a—"

Bitch? That's the first word that comes to my mind, but what do I know?

"No," Foster says, giving Lilliana a stern look, shaking his head. "It's fine."

"Forget about it," Graham continues as convincingly as possible. "Let's get a drink."

Foster removes the glasses from his face, mindlessly wiping the lenses clean with the bottom of his shirt. "Maybe it's best that I go."

"Because of Fiona? No, dude. Stay. The night is still young."

"Nah." He returns the frames to his face. "It's for the best." Foster peers at me. "Are you ready to go?"

"Sure." I nod my head, understanding that his need to leave is not to be questioned. Pivoting toward Graham, I say, "Thank you so much for having me. It was great."

"Anytime, EJ," Graham replies. "Come by anytime. And you two drive safe."

"We will," Foster answers for both of us. "I'll see you in class in a few days."

The men nod to one another, and then Foster turns on his heel, creating a path among the remaining guests with me following close behind. We wordlessly make our way through the house and out the front door to where Foster's car is parked at the curb. I let myself into the passenger side as he rounds the hood and then takes a seat behind the wheel before starting the ignition.

It's a silent drive along the vacant streets on the early morning of this New Year's Day. Foster, completely in his own mind and understandably so, keeps his head forward and on the road ahead, never even sparing me a sideways glance.

I don't ask any questions. I don't say a word. There's a time to be quiet, and this is one of them because all sound is just white noise when inner thoughts are the only language one can comprehend.

When he pulls up to the front of my apartment building with the car running, not finding a place to park, it's clear that we will not be spending the rest of the evening together.

I unfasten my seat belt, gather my purse, and grab the handle to exit.

"EJ?" Foster says as I'm about to open the door. "I'm sorry about tonight."

"Don't worry about it. I had a nice time, and your friends are great." I release my hold on the lever and settle back into my seat. "Are you okay though? I kind of got the hint that something was going on between you and Fiona."

"It was that obvious?" he asks rhetorically.

"That you two used to go out? Yeah, it's pretty clear. She wasn't too thrilled about the way things ended, was she?"

"It was just bad timing." He stares ahead, out the windshield. "Me and relationships don't mix. She's proof of that. I was very…unavailable for her."

"Well, you're really busy," I remind him, thinking of all his extracurricular activities and studies. "I still don't know how you manage to do it all."

He laughs softly to himself. "My busyness is a more recent thing. I took up all those activities, including the library job, so I wouldn't have time to think about *her* anymore."

"Fiona?"

Foster shuts his lids. "No. Sasha, my ex."

I wait for him to say something more. The hum of the running car is the only sound filling the silence. Leaning my head against the warm fabric seat, I observe his features while the stillness echoes. They aren't tortured or even overly hurt but muted, like the name Sasha somehow resonates a form of emotions vetted so deep into his being that a scar remains.

"How long ago did you two break up?" I finally ask, realizing he might need a little nudging.

Men aren't known for spilling their guts. It's like their penises block some forms of speech.

"A little more than a year." He smiles to himself, contemplating. "You don't want to hear about this."

"I don't mind." I adjust my positioning so that I'm facing him a little better. "You listen to my crap all the time. You can certainly tell me some of yours. And if you'd like, we could slam our exes together, calling them nasty names while eating ice cream."

He chuckles. "And paint each other's toenails?"

"Yes, and watch really crappy romance movies."

"Sounds like one hell of an evening."

"Or we could just get hammered and blame it on the New Year."

"True. There's always that."

I palm his forearm. "So, tell me about Sasha, the bitch. I need to know more before I hunt her down and peel back her fingernails, one by one."

He gives me a you-are-crazy-and-I-really-hope-you're-kidding look. "That's really sweet of you."

"And completely out of character. So, you'd better start talking before my sugary goodness wears off."

A smile, a genuine one that actually shows some semblance of humor, spreads across his face. "Okay. We were high school sweethearts, and…it sounds pathetic even to say it."

"Go on," I encourage, hoping he gathers some momentum.

"I was supposed to go to Duke, but she didn't get in. So, I came here with her."

"Wait, hold the phone." I sit up straighter, intrigued. "You gave up Duke to come here with her? Duke for this place?"

"Yeah. It wasn't the best decision, but back then, I would have done anything for her."

"Wow, Foster, you had it bad."

"No kidding." He shakes his head. "It was really kind of pathetic."

"So, what happened?"

"About a year and a half ago, she went to England to study abroad and never came back. She met someone else, and that was that. I came to find out that she had been cheating on me for six months before she decided to tell me about him."

I blink—a lot. "That's awful. She really is a bitch."

"You're not the first one to tell me that."

"That's probably because it's the truth. What she did was not cool at all."

"I guess it happens." He taps the steering wheel a few times with his fingertips. "I didn't take it very well either. I even flew to England to try to convince her to come back, but she still stayed."

"Geez," I mutter. "I don't even know what to say."

"There isn't much to say."

"Do you still talk to her?"

"No. I talk to her brother often though. Our families are close. Parker was my roommate, but he moved out last year when he graduated."

"Oh." I bite my lip, registering and connecting the dots between his ex and his old roommate. "How does Fiona play into all of this?"

"Fiona was a mistake." He shakes his head, shutting his lids. "After all of that went down with Sasha, I was a mess, but everyone encouraged me to try to get back out there.

"Fiona's part of the science department, and we've all known each other for some time. She showed interest, and one thing led to another. Before I knew it, we were a couple. But I wasn't ready. She wanted more in the relationship, and when I couldn't give it to her, she tried even harder. Eventually, it got ugly, and I said a lot of not-so-nice things, so she would get the hint. It didn't end well. Between what I went through with Sasha and then with Fiona in the mix, our group all had a rough time. People took sides, and there was a lot of yelling. We're all friends again now, but it wasn't like that until recently. I was happy when Fiona moved on with James. It's a better fit anyhow, but apparently, she still harbors some resentment."

"Yeah, I caught on to that."

He positions his torso toward me. "So, there you have it. That's me. I'm *that* guy—the one who had his heart broken and now sucks when it comes to relationships. What do you girls call it? Walls? Emotionally broken? Oh, wait, Fiona called it emotionally unavailable."

I giggle. "Something like that. And you don't suck when it comes to girls or relationships, Fozzie. You just had a bad string of luck with them." I cover his hand resting on his thigh with my own. "When you're ready, the right person will come along."

"Now, you sound like you're reciting a line from a movie."

"Maybe it is a line, but it's one I truly believe in."

Twenty-Three

The first week back to school has gone as expected—full of syllabi, reading lists, assignments, meetings, and picking up various supplies. Not to mention, it's been filled with boring speeches and lectures from professors with a side of homework. I've already gone through the chore of checking in with my advisor in regard to my thesis and confirming that I'm on track to graduate come spring. Everything is set and in motion.

Walking into my art theory class, I'm overcome with a sense of pride. This is an upper-level class, usually only taken by fine art majors, and I worked my way here by following an aggressive track since my freshman year. It's not typical for an art minor and not unheard of either, but it's something I aspired to accomplish.

I spy Wolfgang seated at the back table, going through his phone while waiting for the professor to arrive. Meandering through the maze of workspaces and students, I take a seat next to him, setting my bag at my feet.

"Well, well, well," Wolfgang says, shoving his phone into his pocket. "I was starting to wonder if you were alive."

"What are you talking about?" I remove the beanie hat from my head and shake out my recently cinnamon-tinted locks. "I texted you last night, confirming that we were in the same class."

"Yeah, after I haven't heard from you for almost two weeks."

"It was Christmas break."

"So? A guy needs to know if his muse is breathing or not."

"Now, I'm your muse?" I shrug out of my jacket.

"I might have been inspired by you in the past. It's some of my best work."

"Of course it is. Nothing but phenomenal things comes from me. You are lucky to have a goddess like me in your presence."

"And there she is." He reaches toward his feet, bringing up a cardboard carrier with two coffee drinks. Pulling the smaller cup from the pairing, he places it in front of me and says, "Small nonfat latte."

My hands circle around the drink. "You really are the best."

"That's what they all say."

A tall man with lemon hair falling to his shoulders enters the room with false panache, banging his shin on the small garbage can near the door. All the students grow silent as the infamous Professor Turner takes his place at the front of the room, muttering a few obscenities under his breath.

The man is a genius in his own right, having consulted on and been commissioned for numerous sculptures on campus, in the city, and worldwide. He's known for his eccentric attitude and lifestyle full of women, men, and lively parties. One thing he's also known for is pushing students to their breaking points, actually causing a few in the past to have episodes of madness. The man finds boundaries and wants to break them.

He frightens, intrigues, and inspires me, all at once. I hope to learn a great deal while in his classroom.

"Good afternoon, people," Professor Turner addresses the class, shuffling through his bag and pulling out a stack of papers. He hands them to a student sitting at the table nearest him and then begins to pace the room as a copy of the syllabus is divvied up to each person.

Pausing at the front of the room, he shoves his hands in his front denim pockets and then leers at each and every one of us. He then speaks, "For those of you who don't know, I'm Professor Turner. You can see my credentials and accolades as well as how you can reach me on the paper before you. If you're in this class, congratulations. This is your moment of glory as an artist. Savor it because this is nothing like the real world where you will learn what it feels like to starve and have people spit on your work and your spirit. This is the pretty before the ugly. Don't get used to it."

He steps between the tables, making his way down the middle of the classroom toward the back of the room. "In this class, my job is not only to make you reach beyond your comfort zones, but to also teach you how to rise from rejection and objection. If you don't think you can handle being called a peon and a moron on a daily basis, I suggest you leave now."

The professor pivots on his heel, and every student follows his path as he slowly proceeds to the front of the class.

"I will be both objective and subjective in my critiques, and I promise, I won't be nice. If you need flowers and unicorns, the preschool is down the street. Pack your teddy bears for the trip."

Turning to the group of attentive students, he spreads his arms wide with an all-knowing schmuckish grin playing across his face. "So, are you in, or are you out?"

The classroom becomes silent, and I swear, dust motes can be heard as they float around us.

"Well?" Professor Turner probes everyone. "You had better answer. Without conviction, your work is nothing."

"In," a few students mutter near the center of the room.

"That was pathetic."

"In!" the entire class, myself included, says with confidence.

He shakes his head, pacing toward the window. "You all need to work on your decision-making skills—pronto. Growing a few balls would help, too. This is going to be a long quarter. The world is becoming soft."

Leaning his backside on the register under the window, he crosses his arms over his chest, letting an uneasy silence rain down, like a black cloud of time ticking away with every pump of our beating hearts. We all hold still, waiting for a bomb to go off, only to be detonated by the yellow-haired man in control of our artistic destinies.

Next to me, Wolfgang raises his hand. "Excuse me, Professor?"

"Did you find your balls?" Professor Turner inquires, brows raised.

"Yes. I generally keep them next to my dick."

Everyone in the room audibly pulls air into their mouths.

"Finally," the professor proclaims, approval lacing his tone. "Someone with gumption and worth talking to. What was your question?"

"Is the syllabus supposed to be blank?"

Like everyone else in the room, I scan the handout. The front is a printout of information about the professor and pertinent information like office hours, a phone number, and an email address are listed. I turn over the page to find it empty, excluding the word *Syllabus* at the top.

"Yes." Professor Turner pushes himself off his haphazard seat and begins to roam about the room. "You only have one assignment in here, but I'm not going to tell you what that is. That's for you to decide. This is an upper-level class, and it's up to you to find your own path. I will only be here to advise you. For this class, you will choose and work on one project of your liking. It can be whatever you want and with any medium. You have freedom to choose. Let your mind and talents guide you. The only stipulation is that it has to make a statement of some kind—whether that is about you, the world, poverty, hunger, the universe, or iced tea. I don't care. Just show me your passion. I need to see it and feel it. Make me cry."

He pauses, picking up one of the handouts from a nearby student, and he shows us the empty page. "This," he states, "is like a blank canvas. Tell me a story, one that intrigues me."

Giving the paper back to the student, he takes a place at the front of the room once again. "Also, for those of you who pass this term with sufficient work, you will be eligible to install your project at the student show in my gallery downtown for display during the spring term. The final call about who has their work on display and who doesn't will be at my discretion. Passing is not an automatic in. As many of you might already know, my gallery only does this once a year, and it's considered to be a great privilege. Not only will many of my colleagues be there, but also buyers, sellers, and fellow artists will be present. For many students, this one show has been the springboard of their careers. In other words, if you want to make it, you'd better be in this show."

Hums and sighs fill the room as the gravity of our work in this class begins to set in.

While I am on the art history path, which is engraved into my core, the thought of showing my work to others at a venue like Professor Turner's gallery might be just what I need to prove to my family that there are opportunities for me outside of my father's firm.

"That's all for today," the professor announces, taking a seat behind the desk and shuffling through his bag. "Use your studio time wisely. I will be here during the designated class hours to answer questions, should you have any. Also, I will need you all to email me your proposal within the next week. Really think about what you want to present to the world, your message. You know how to reach me." He waves his hand like he's shooing a fly. "Class dismissed."

A few students speak quietly to one another as they're gathering their things to leave while others line up to have a word with Professor Turner. Not giving it much thought, I collect my items, including my barely sipped coffee, and I silently head toward the door with Wolfgang by my side.

When we are outside the classroom, I playfully backhand my friend across the bicep. "Wolfie! Next to your dick? Seriously, when did you get so ballsy? And I'm not trying to be cute."

"You liked that, didn't you?" He grins like the conniving wolf he can be.

"I'm not so sure, but I think I'm Full of Myself Turner got a mini hard-on."

"Probably," he says proudly. "But another student actually gave me a tip."

"To what? To talk about your schlong?"

"No." He guffaws. "To just say whatever the hell you want. I guess he likes it when students lose the filter."

"Well, there's no doubt yours was missing."

"Truth."

Together, Wolfgang and I tread toward the building's exit, making idle conversation about the holiday break, our class schedules, and the ludicrous weather because it's uncharacteristically as cold as a witch's bitch of a left tit today.

Bundling up to brave the outdoors, I pull my beanie over my head and slip on my gloves. Wolfgang opens the door, and the chill hits my exposed skin like tiny razor blades on coarse hair. With my arms wrapped around my middle, I accompany my friend to the end of campus where we generally part ways to head back to our respective apartments.

At the corner, waiting for the crosswalk signal to change, he asks, "So, any idea what you are going to do for your art theory project?"

"Not really. He made it sound like it needed to be epic. I don't know if I have epic in me."

"Sure you do. We all do."

"Oh, yeah? What do you think you're going to do?"

He chuckles. "I don't know. I'm sure it will come to me when I least expect it."

I shake my head, slightly annoyed by his ability to take so many things in stride. "You make it sound so easy."

"Well, there's no reason to make it complicated." He faces me. "The professor said it should be something you're passionate about while making a statement. That feeling comes from deep within. It's already in you."

"Yeah, but finding that one thing…"

"Just take a mental step back, and let it happen. It will come. Here…" He drops his bag to the ground and places both hands on my shoulders.

"What the fuck are you doing?" I laugh.

"Go with it." He squeezes my arms. "Now, close your eyes."

"This is so corny," I object. But I do as he asked, allowing blackness to take over my vision.

"Now, relax."

I exhale and release some tension from my muscles. "Done."

"Now, let go of all thoughts. Clear your mind."

"You've been going to too many yoga classes," I tease.

"Shut it."

"Fine. Meditation, on."

"Good. Now, think of warmth."

"I'll do my best even though my tits could cut glass because it's so cold."

"Well, that's a vision," he says coyly. "Not that kind of warmth though. The kind that makes your heart feel excited, like it's racing. The kind that heats you from the inside."

I lick my lips, relax my brain, and listen to Wolfgang's words, letting the feeling of passion overwhelm me, wrapping it around the blank vision in my mind.

"Are you there?" he asks.

"It feels like it."

"Okay. Now, slowly let the thoughts come in while resting in that warm space."

Under the darkness of my lids, a slew of colors—fiery and wet, purples and greens, yellows and pinks—all morph and swirl around one another. My hand slides along the formed and heated canvas of tones and shades, and then it's gone, taking the more rigid shape of elements and molecules, like the ones I drew and painted not long ago in my bedroom.

Then…

A mouth…

His mouth.

Eyes…

His eyes.

A face…

His face.

Foster's face, bright and endearing—surrounded by hexagons and octagons, representing different molecules—holds its place in my mind's thoughts.

"Did anything come?" Wolfgang asks, pulling me from my trance.

My lids flutter open, refocusing to the light of day. "I'm not sure."

Twenty-Four

Shoving my keys into my jacket pocket, I slug my bag over my shoulder. I head through the length of the apartment, ready to leave. As I'm rounding the sofa in the living room, the entrance door opens, and Chandra appears at the threshold, her cheeks red with exertion. Clumsily, she adjusts her arms in an attempt not to fumble the bolts of fabric, her bag, and what looks like the mail. She's having a hot-mess moment, if I've ever seen one.

I drop my belongings to the ground and scurry over to assist her. "Let me help," I say, reaching for a collection of fabrics.

"Thanks," she huffs, gratefully handing over a few items into my aiding arms.

We carry her supplies further inside, sloughing them all on the couch. She steps back and regains her composure after blowing a ridiculous amount of coal hair from her face.

"You should have told me it was supply pickup day," I remark, staring down at the enormous amount of materials now strewed across the cushions. "I would have helped you."

"Jeremy was supposed to," she says, plopping down on the red chair since all of her new belongings are taking up the rest of the seating. "He got sidetracked in the studio and forgot. I don't know."

I raise a brow. "Trouble in paradise?"

"No, not at all. He's great...when we actually do see one another. It's just the beginning of the term. You know how it is." She drops her hands to her thighs. "I've been swamped with classes, and so has he. I swear, senior year is sucking away my social life."

"Tell me about it," I agree, thinking of how I've done nothing for the past week, other than go to class, do homework, research, and study.

The cumulative teaching staff has been slamming the entire student body from the beginning of the term, and there's no letting up in sight. I've even had to reduce my hours at the library, down to one day a week, to compensate.

"I've barely even seen you since you got back," I say.

"It's been really bad, and it looks like you are heading out now."

"Yeah." I step around the sofa and pick up my bag from the floor. "I've got to go to work."

"Well, have fun."

"Thanks." I position the strap of my bag higher on my shoulder and make my way toward the door.

"You got some mail, by the way," Chandra states.

My hand lands on the knob. "Oh, yeah?"

She rises from her seat, collects a large envelope from the couch, and holds it in my direction. I give it a cursory glance, noting the Yale emblem in the corner. Based on its size and thickness, it's safe to assume that the contents include an early acceptance letter. It's arrived way ahead of schedule, and it makes me wonder if applying was even necessary, as if the institution is begging me to attend with such a blatantly advance reply.

My parents will be pleased that their clout has won me a place they so desperately desire.

"Can you just leave it on the counter?" I open the entrance, uninterested in dealing with that reality. "I'm going to be late."

"Sure thing," she replies.

"Thanks."

I exit the apartment and hurry down the steps.

It's been almost a week since I emailed my project proposal to Professor Turner for my art theory class.

After speaking with Wolfgang that initial day after class, I had been unable to think about anything other than the impromptu human art project between Foster and me that had occurred over the holiday break. As much as I'd tried, I couldn't shake the visions of molecules and his face from my mind. Soon, those images had morphed into something else, further expanding upon the idea. So, instead of trying to fight it, I'd decided to surrender and accept that a project focusing on the science of man was what I was going to depict.

I've already begun research, and I have a plan of how to accomplish my artistic statement, but I would really like to get Foster involved, if possible. He's the reason, the inspiration, and the holder of more elemental, chemical, and scientific knowledge than I could likely ever find on my own.

This piece wouldn't exist, even in theory, without him.

Somehow, somewhere, and someway, Foster has become my muse, and I've learned over the years that it's best not to fight profoundly speaking passion.

Approaching the glass entrance of the engineering library, I spot Foster helping a student at the front desk. It's been a few days since we saw one another—the last time being when I stopped by his apartment after a long day in the studio. I was beyond exhausted, yet I was drawn to his place, longing for his company. Despite waking him, he greeted me with a smile and invited me to his bed where we partook in what we usually do—sex. I stayed the night, sleeping surprisingly well at his side. It was like the restless part of my brain that always found him could be at ease from knowing he was close.

I'm blaming it on my recent art-project obsession.

Making a good impression with my work for Professor Turner is key to winning a spot in the student art show. Because of this, Foster now consumes many of my thoughts, day and night…and in the early morning hours.

Setting the bag near my feet, I log in to the computer and begin the process of checking in the returns. There aren't many, but the night is young.

When Foster finishes helping out one last student, he rotates in his chair. "How was your day, dear?" he asks, teasing.

"It was fine, sweet stuff," I respond, turning in my seat toward him. "Busy as hell, as usual. And yours?"

"The same." He rests his elbows on his knees. "Why does it seem like I haven't seen you in forever?"

"It's all your fault. I told you that you needed to give up some of your activities if you wanted to have a social life."

"Are you schooling me?" he asks, adjusting his dark frames.

"Possibly."

"Do you want to maybe…get social with me tonight?"

I purse my lips. "Possibly." I grin. "Maybe." My smile widens. "Highly likely."

"I'll take that as a yes."

"Fair enough."

I scoot my chair under the desk and open up the application to check in the pile of books to my right.

"I was hoping to talk to you about something," I say, pulling over the top volume from the stack.

"What's that?" he asks, back to work and clicking his mouse.

"It's about a project I'm doing. It's kind of a big one."

"Need help with more explosions?"

"No. Actually…" I pause, trying to formulate the right way to phrase what I'm about to say without sounding too needy. "Do you remember when I…painted you?"

His hand stills, and so does the rest of his body. "Sure," he responds in a low tone. "I don't think it's something I'll ever forget."

"Yeah." I chew on my bottom lip. "Um…well, there's this assignment for my art theory class, and I was planning on doing something like that."

Foster drops his hands to his thighs. "Okay…so, you're planning to paint someone for an art assignment. Interesting."

"No, not that part." I rest an elbow on the desk, adjusting my posture to give him my full attention. "I want to show the inner beauty of man through the vision of science. Kind of like what you and I were talking about but as an installation, and I was hoping that you would help me with it—if you have time, of course."

"What do you need from me? More time with my shirt off?"

"Shirts can be optional." I smirk. "But I was hoping you could answer some questions for me—"

"Of course. No problem."

"And…I was hoping, maybe you would model for me, too?"

He gives me a you're-pushing-the-envelope-but-I'm-going-to-say-yes-anyhow look. "Don't you think that skirts over the line of our friendship a little?"

"And your dick in me doesn't?"

"Yeah…" he drawls, running a hand through his bronzed hair. "That bit of insertion might be, uh…testing some boundaries. We do have sort of a special friendship."

"Exactly. So, why not do me this favor as a special kind of friend and model for me?" I bat my eyes like one of those idiots with pouty ruby lips in the movies. "Pretty please? I'll give you a cock smooch."

"Who am I to say no to an offer like that?" Foster tightens his mouth, unsuccessfully trying not to show his enjoyment. "Fine, I'll model for you. And just so you know, I would have said yes, even without the cock smooch."

"Maybe that's more for me."

"Well, I wouldn't want to be the guy who takes away from your enjoyment."

Twenty-Five

A little more than two weeks have passed since the day I asked Foster to assist me in my art theory project. Today, he's stopping by my apartment for me to make a mold of his chest and shoulders as part of the installment to later be casted and painted.

Due to his ridiculously busy schedule and my own, most of our conversations of science, human anatomy, and simplistic elemental theories have been through texts and emails with minimal face-to-face time between his classes and activities. We've also had a few late-night sessions, but those were more of the social nature. Sometimes, it's best to let the body rather than the mind lead toward one's needs.

Noticing the time, I close a fictional telling of Van Gogh's childhood, a book that I've been combing through for minute details to finalize my art history thesis. My advisor suggested I give it a look before turning in my paper for another round of critiques. I've found a few obscure details about the man's life to add to my paper but nothing profound, and I plan to turn in my final findings within the next month.

Crossing the threshold of my bedroom, I enter into the kitchen where Chandra and Jeremy are reading silently next to one another at the bar. Now that the hustle and bustle of the start of the term has settled, he's been over more often, and my roommate has never been so content.

"Hey," Chandra says, placing her book on the counter. "I didn't know you were here. I thought it was your studio time now."

"It is," I respond, filling a glass with water. "Foster is coming by though for mold-making. I thought it would be best to do it here rather than in a space with tons of people."

"That makes sense. He might not be comfortable with standing half-naked in front of a bunch of strangers."

I smile to myself at the thought of Foster without his shirt on. There certainly is something enjoyable about the image. "My thoughts exactly."

She straightens in her seat, giving a sidelong glance to Jeremy, who appears to be consumed in his book, not paying attention to us. "Do you need any help?"

"Nah." I sip the water. "I'm doing a simple one-step plaster. It should go pretty smoothly and only take about forty-five minutes. Easy-peasy."

She disengages herself from the stool, rounds the small countertop dividing us, and joins me within the small kitchen space. Gently grabbing my elbow, she leads me toward the other side of the room, out of Jeremy's earshot.

"What's going on?" Chandra asks, her voice hushed.

"Huh?" I question, resting my drink on the counter.

"Are you two dating?"

"Who?"

"You and this Foster guy. I get that he's helping you with your work, but you two have been spending a lot of time together lately."

"Is that a problem?" I ask, feeling defensive and caught off guard.

"Of course it isn't. You've just been so vague about him, and he's not in any of your classes, so it's a little odd to me that he would be modeling for you. I was just wondering if something was going on."

"I work with the guy. We're friends. He's helping me out as a friend. That's all."

"Okay…" She gives me a look of surrender. "But I know you're sleeping with him. You aren't as sneaky as you think."

I exhale, dropping my hands to my thighs. "Go ahead and give me the lecture. I know you want to."

"No lecture. You can sleep with whomever you want. I'm just wondering if there's a reason you aren't telling me about what's going on."

I peek in Jeremy's direction, confirming that he's paying us no mind. "We're fucking, all right? Happy?"

"Do you even like him?"

"Of course I do, but…we're just…"

"Just what?"

"It's…I don't know. He's my friend. It's not the kind of relationship you're trying to insinuate. I didn't want to put a label on it. Plus, it's crude to call him my fuck buddy."

"Why? That's what you two are, right? Fuck buddies?"

"I guess." I shrug, averting my focus to the top of the glass where the non-rippling water lies still in the perfect shape of a circle, constricted and in control.

Chandra takes a step back, examining me for more than a comfortable moment, drilling me with uninhibited judgment. "I know that look."

"What look?"

"I've seen this before. You bottle your shit up so tight that it's like no one can see it, not even you, but I can. You're in denial, and you like him way more than you're letting on—or maybe even more than you realize. You're trying so hard to fool yourself that you don't even see it."

"Are you kidding?" I pull her out of the kitchen and into the hallway to ensure our conversation is way out of the relative hearing space of Jeremy. "Have you seen him? He's *so* not my type. The guy lives and breathes formulas and science. He likely even has a pocket protector. He's neatly contained in a square box, and I'm a glop of grape jelly, splattered all over the floor on a good day. We aren't exactly compatible."

"Then, why have you been spending so much time with him?" She crosses her arms and raises her brow. "And don't tell me it's for your project. I'm not stupid. This all started before break, and there was no art theory class last quarter."

"Maybe it's the sex."

"Must be really great then."

"Shit yeah, it is. The best I've ever had."

"The best you've ever had?" she challenges.

"Shut up," I say in an attempt to halt the conversation.

"Maybe it is the sex, but I'd be willing to bet that it's a little more than that."

"You've been reading too many women's magazines and self-help articles."

"Or maybe I see something between you two that you don't."

Bringing my hand to my head, I press my fingertips into my temple. "Why are you giving me such a hard time about this?"

"Honestly? Because I'm afraid you're going to get hurt. This whole thing just reeks of a mess. Friends with benefits? Someone is always on the losing end of these things. They never end well."

"Yeah, well, not with me. I've got it covered."

"Then, maybe he'll be the one to get hurt."

"I won't let that happen," I tell her with the utmost conviction.

She laughs silently to herself, shaking her head. "Complete denial."

Twenty-Six

After my little discussion with Chandra, she and Jeremy retreated to her room, and I corralled myself in the living area, waiting for Foster to arrive.

Her words did nothing but frustrated the hell out of me. She has no idea about the relationship, or lack thereof, that Foster and I have grown into. Sure, we might have become closer over the past few months, but we're still nothing more than friends. Well, there is a little more, but he and I have an understanding.

Screw her and her stupid probing. She's making a mountain out of a molehill.

There's a light knock at the door.

That's Foster.

Shaking out my hands, I step toward the dark wooden entrance and dispose of Chandra's ludicrous suggestions in order to concentrate on the task at hand. Foster is here to help me, and I don't need her illogical ideas flooding my mind. Those are her opinions and not mine.

Opening the door, I greet the man whose form is exceedingly familiar. I've been sketching him for weeks now. It's almost like my hands have some semblance of muscle memory to all his angles.

"Hey, thanks for coming." I step back to allow him to enter, noticing a surge of cold sweat erupting on my palms.

"No problem," Foster says, joining me inside.

I close the door and wipe the uncalled for embarrassing moisture from my hands. Then, I proceed through the apartment with Foster on my heels, and we head toward my bedroom where all the supplies have been set up and arranged. Crossing the threshold, I pick up the apron from a nearby chair, loop it over my head, and tie the straps around my waist.

"This isn't really what I was expecting," Foster remarks, slowly shutting the door behind him. "Are you planning on killing me?"

My mouth slacks. "What? No!"

"This place looks like a kill room. There's enough plastic in here to bag a body—or ten."

"Funny." I turn up the heat, adjusting the thermostat over his shoulder to make the room more comfortable for his soon-to-be lacking attire. "There will be no killing. I promise. Now, take off your shirt."

"You're so commanding."

"At times."

Foster drops his bag to the floor and unzips the main compartment. He shifts through the contents, finds what he's looking for, and holds out his arm, presenting me with a small bundle of art brushes wrapped in a red ribbon.

"What is this for?" I ask, taking the offering.

"I saw these at a supply store the other day when I was…getting something for a lab assignment, and I thought you might like them," he says, stuffing his hands into his pockets.

"Thanks," I utter, confused. "That's considerate."

"You're welcome. You go through them all the time. I just figured…you could use more."

My thumb grazes the tips of the soft bristles, fanning them one by one, as Foster and I both stare at the unexpected gift in my hand. The tips have a velvety smooth texture that is pliable to my touch. I revel in their untainted newness. There's something special about the clean fibers, like they hold future memories waiting in my dreams. *Who knows what these will create?*

"So, should we get started?" Foster questions, refocusing our attention to the task at hand. "I have a class and need to leave in about an hour."

"Yeah, of course." I set the gift on the desk. "I don't want you to be late. Thank you again so much for doing this."

"Sorry to rush you, and you're more than welcome," he says, removing his glasses and resting them next to the gift on the desk.

"I hope you aren't missing anything to be here."

"Just a club meeting, but it's not a big deal."

"You didn't need to do that. We could have arranged to meet another time."

"I don't mind."

Foster pulls the blue knit sweater and gray T-shirt with a comic book character print over his head and then shoves them into his bag. When he rises, a sudden sense of discomfort whips through me from the sight of his skin, and I avert my attention toward the stack of supplies laid out for the mold.

Don't let Chandra get into your head.

Foster proceeds to strip off his pants, leaving on only a pair of form-fitting underwear that I requested he wear for this moment.

"Do I need to take these off, too?" he asks, pointing to the gray cotton covering very little of his body.

"No," I barely squeak. "You can leave those on. I only plan to plaster to your hip bones. We can roll them down a little if needed."

"K. Where do you want me?"

Pointing toward the center of the room, in the middle of the plastic sheeting on the floor, I tell him, "Right here."

Foster takes his place, standing where directed. Crouching down, I sift through my stack of supplies, pilfering a small jar of petroleum jelly.

Holding the lubricant in his direction, I ask, "Did you want to put it on or have me do it?"

"You should." He pauses, humor dancing along the edge of his features. "Lube is more your specialty."

"Right," I state plainly, surprising even myself. This is banter 101, and I'm failing miserably.

Popping off the lid, I submerge my forefinger and middle finger into the gelatinous substance and extract a heaping glob.

"This might be a little cold." I show him the thick pile of goop. "Sorry in advance."

He nods.

Foster flinches slightly when I dab the cool jelly onto the warm area of his body just above his pectoral, but he soon relaxes to my touch as I draw tiny circles over a two-inch diameter. When he appears to be used to the temperature, I gently begin to spread the protective barrier over the rest of his recently shaven skin.

I had advised him to remove the hair from every place the plaster would touch, and I'm glad he took my suggestion. Otherwise, the disengaging process could be painful.

It doesn't take much time for me to cover his shoulders, arms, chest, ribs, and abs in the jelly substance until I reach just below his hip bones. I make sure not to neglect a single cell of skin.

He says nothing during the process.

Neither do I.

"There," I utter just above the quiet as I cover the last few inches below his navel. "All set." Reattaching the cap to the small tub of lubricant, I ask, "Do you want to take a minute to move around before we start? I'll need you to be still for about half an hour."

Foster shakes his arms, shifts the weight between his feet, and then cocks his head from side to side a few times. "I think I'm good."

"Right."

One-word sentences? What is wrong with me?

I move the tray of water along with the prepared strips of plaster cloth to the center of the room. I circle my fingers around his hand and place it directly over his heart, and then I arrange his other arm at his side, but I leave some space between it and his torso.

"I'll only be doing your shoulder on this one," I comment, referring to his vertically resting arm. "Are you comfortable?"

"I'll be fine," he reassures me.

"Okay, I'll be as fast as possible."

"Like a quickie?"

I faintly titter. "Not quite. I doubt you'll enjoy this as much as you would a quickie."

"I guess we'll find out."

I soak the first cloth in the tub of water, lightly squeeze off the excess liquid, and then gently apply the tiny sheet across the length of his shoulder, smoothing out all the wrinkles so that it takes on the shape of his body.

"Have you done many of these?" he asks quietly, his exhale fluttering along my cheekbone.

"No," I reply, my voice soft and airy. "You're my second. I did one on Chandra years ago, but that's it."

"So, you're a novice?"

"A little." I reach down, repeating the wetting process of a new cloth. "Why? Are you nervous about my skills?"

"Not really. I'm sure I'm in good hands."

"Thanks for the confidence." My fingertips gently draw the wet white plaster sheet along the form of his bicep. "I just hope it turns out the way I've envisioned it in my head."

"I'm sure it will be great."

"We shall see."

Over the next twenty minutes, I apply the tiny slivers of plaster cloth, one by one, to Foster's naked body, covering every inch of the front portion of his upper torso. He's an exorbitantly tolerant model, never complaining about the coolness or pressure of my touch or the fact that he's unable to move, even minutely. During the entire process of transforming his skin from tender flesh to a thickening white mold, he keeps his lung movement in control so not to expand the hardening sculpture as it sets.

"This is the last one," I tell him while on my knees, applying the final cloth to his lower abdomen. "You just need to hold still for about another ten to fifteen minutes, and then we can remove the finished product."

"What do you plan to do while I remain here like your human statue?"

"I don't know." I rise, running my palm over the front of his body to ensure that every piece is as it should be. "Probably sit on my bed and stare at you while eating popcorn."

"Will you share some with me?"

"Maybe…" I lightly stroke the shape of his collarbone with my fingers toward his neck, lost in the space where the plaster ends and Foster begins.

The pads of my fingers crawl their way up and over the artificial barrier of the hardening cloth, landing on the man underneath, exploring the shape of his chin and jaw. Unmoving, Foster remains still as I dance my touch higher to his cheekbones and along his nose, as if my fingers are searching for what my brain registers in the drawings and sketches. However, my talent could never truly capture the work of beauty standing before me. It's one of a kind, and I doubt that anyone could ever be so gifted to truly re-create something like Foster.

Moist lips press to the delicate skin inside my wrist, jolting me back to reality and out of the dream space of the moment I've submerged myself into.

"Sorry," I mumble, disconnecting my touch from his face. "I got caught up a little…"

He releases the faintest grin. "I do, too, sometimes."

"Yeah." My eyes dart all over his set features, noting the white splotches. "Um…and I got plaster on your face."

"Occupational hazard?"

"Unfortunately." Wiping my hands on my apron, I back away from him and step toward the door. "I'm going to get a washcloth to wipe that off before it sets."

"I'll be right here, not going anywhere."

"Yeah."

I grunt to myself. *A one-word sentence again?*

I empty myself into the hallway and shut the door at my back, giving him some privacy and myself a moment to gather my scattered brain.

Where the hell did I go?

It's not uncommon for me to get lost in my work, but it almost felt like I was getting lost in him.

Are the two worlds colliding, meshing, morphing, blurring, and breaking past the spoken and unspoken lines of what we claim to be?

Am I that oblivious to what's happening between Foster and me?

No. This is just my imagination grasping on to Chandra's words, nothing more.

I fill a bowl with soapy water, grab a washcloth from the kitchen, and reenter my room to find Foster exactly where I left him—half-naked and partially covered in plaster. Approaching him, I wring out the water from the rag, set the bowl aside, and then lightly begin to blot away the drying plaster on his face.

"Sorry about this—again," I say, having to rub his cheekbone a little harder than might be considered gentle.

"Don't worry about it." He twinges slightly when I add pressure to remove the substance from the delicate space under his eye. "It was an accident."

With a few more blots, all the white markings are removed, leaving his face as pristine as it was when he arrived. I then take the opportunity to clean up the rest of his body, wiping anyplace where the plaster accidentally touched unintended skin. Within the time it takes to remove the unwanted splatters, the cast has set to Foster's body and is beginning to warm from the chemical process.

"It's time," I tell him, setting the cleansing wet cloth into the bowl. "Are you ready to get that thing off?"

"You have no idea," he says, relief filtering through his voice.

"Was it really that bad?"

"No, but I'm starting to sweat—and not in a good way."

"That doesn't sound sexy." I giggle, slowly slipping my fingers under the edges of the hardened mold to begin the process of breaking it away from his body.

"Yes. *Sexy* is not the adjective I would use."

Finding a good grip, I wiggle and pry the cast from his chest, popping it off like a bottle cap, in one solid piece. Foster, still in his model position, gazes almost proudly at the finished product.

"You can see the details of my fingers," he remarks, slowly lowering his hand away from his chest.

"Pretty cool, huh?" I question, holding out the replica for him to inspect.

He gently runs his palm along the inside of the mold. "More than cool."

I smile, amused by his childlike fascination with such a simple process. Setting the hardened plaster mold in a safe place near my closet, I collect a towel from the clean laundry supply and hand it over to Foster, so he can wipe off the remaining layer of petroleum jelly from his skin.

"At least you're moisturized," I say as an offering in regard to the goopy substance.

"That's an understatement."

Foster wipes off the gooey mess the best he can, hands the towel back to me, and then crosses my bedroom toward where his things lie on the floor next to my desk.

"I need to get going," he says, unzipping his bag and pulling out his clothes.

"Sure. I hope I didn't make you late."

He glances at the time on his phone, sets it on the desk next to his glasses, and then stands up with denim in his hands.

"It'll be close, but I should be able to make it to class on time," he says as he dresses, rapidly pushing his legs into his jeans. "No worries."

Foster slips the T-shirt over his head and then his sweater, straightening them both out as he turns toward my desk to retrieve his other items. He places his signature dark frames over his face and then grabs his phone. His hand stills for a moment over the screen, and then he shoves it into his back pocket. Reaching back toward the desk, he grabs two sheets of paper.

"Are these what I think they are?" he asks, spinning toward me.

I step forward and peek at the early acceptance letters between his fingertips—one from Yale and the latest from Dartmouth that arrived just yesterday. Both are for their MBA programs.

"They aren't recipes for apple pie," I say, thumbing the top of one of the letters.

"You got into two really great programs at two amazing schools."

"They must not have had enough art history majors as applicants and needed to fill a quota."

"I wasn't doubting why you got in." He sets the papers back from where they came. "You have the grades, and I'm sure you're…eclectic enough for their needs. I'm just really surprised you applied. You made it sound like you didn't even want to go."

"I don't. Not really."

"Then, why even go through the application process?"

"I told you." I shrug. "Family tradition. Some things are inevitable."

Foster steps tightly into my space, our chests nearly touching. It's like there's a thin barrier between us made of a delicate bubble just waiting to pop.

"It's plain as day that you don't belong in some corporate world designed by an Ivy League education. I'm not saying that as an insult, but it's not who you are. I'm sure your family would understand if you traveled down a different road."

"No, they wouldn't," I say, resolved. "I wish they would, but unfortunately, they never will. I've tried to convince them otherwise."

"But if they care about you, they would know how unhappy you would be living like that." The tips of his fingers flutter with my own. "*I* know how *miserable* you would be."

Our hands fold together, clasping as one. His other palm drifts along the length of my arm, resting just above the elbow.

I'm speechless, unsure and—dare I even say—scared.

He *knows* me.

"Fozzie," I say barely above a whisper.

He leans in, and I close my lids in anticipation of feeling his lips on mine.

Our breaths meet.

I can almost taste him.

There's a light rap on the bedroom door.

"EJ?" Chandra calls, her voice tentative.

My eyes fly open, finding Foster seductively close.

"Yeah?" I call back, feeling caught.

"Can I come in for a sec?"

Foster and I exchange a glance, acknowledging the lost moment.

I back out of our magical bubble and then open my door, revealing a few inches of my dark-haired roommate's face.

"What?" I question, trying not to sound annoyed.

She peeks over my head toward Foster and then lowers her voice to say, "Cal's here."

Twenty-Seven

"What?" I half-shout, unsure I heard Chandra correctly. *Did she say—*

"Cal's here," my roommate repeats, her voice much lower than mine. "He's waiting for you in the living room."

"Why in the hell did you even let him in?"

"He said it was important, some legal matter, and he wasn't going to leave until he saw you."

My lip curls. "What the fuck?"

Foster clears his throat, reminding us of his presence.

"I need to get going," he announces to both of us in the midst of our not-so-hushed conversation. "I'm going to be late."

"Right. Of course," I say almost in a daze, widening the door.

Chandra steps down the hall toward where Cal is waiting.

"I'll walk you out," I say to Foster.

This all feels so surreal.

Leading the way, I escort Foster to the main part of the apartment where Cal is casually sitting on the sofa with a motherfucking bouquet of flowers in his hand.

213

Roses.

Red ones.

The color of love.

I want to poke his eyes out.

What is he doing here?

I hope he pricks his finger—or his penis would suffice.

"EJ," Cal says, rising from the couch to greet me. The collection of blazing crimson floral at the center of his chest is like a target of destruction.

I audibly grunt and give him an I'm-going-to-freaking-scratch-your-eyes-out look. He takes the hint and sits his ass back down, shifting his focus between Foster, who is close on my heels, and me.

Grabbing the knob to the front entrance, I face Foster, whose attention is clearly not on me but on Cal in all his rocker glory as he's dressed in a leather jacket with bright blue hair. He's wearing eyeliner, too.

Keeping it classy.

This is a disaster of epic proportions.

My ex is unexpectedly sitting on my couch with a romantic-looking bouquet of flowers and the guy…Foster…who I'm sleeping with, will likely—

What does it matter? We are just friends. That's the deal.

"Thanks again for doing this," I say to Foster, trying to focus him away from the train wreck on my couch. "I really appreciate it."

"No problem," he states, reaching for the door and opening it like he can't leave fast enough. He gives another glance in Cal's direction. "I hope it works out the way you want."

"I think it will," I reply, trying so hard to keep my shit together right now.

What in the ever-loving fuck is Cal doing here?

"I'll see you at work," he quickly adds as he walks out the door.

With little desire, I shut the door. Slowly, I spin around and cross my arms in preparation to battle the punk asshole who so boldly decided to show up at my apartment without an announcement or invitation.

Like a guard dog, Chandra busies herself in the kitchen area with Jeremy at her side, patiently waiting for the medieval shitstorm that's about to go down in our living room. She and I exchange a look, and she acknowledges that she should stay right where she is. I turn my attention to a man who only possesses one brain cell because a smart person would have known better than to come near me after fucking around behind my back.

"Cal," I sternly say, rounding the arm of the couch. I glare down at him. "What are you doing here?"

He rises from his seat, holding out the bouquet in my direction. "I brought you something."

I raise my brows, giving him the are-you-serious look.

He pushes them further into my personal space, insistent.

"That's so sweet of you." I swipe the flowers from his hand and march my ass straight into the kitchen, slipping past Chandra and Jeremy. I open the cabinet below the sink and shove the bouquet into the trash. It might be a little dramatic, but fuck him.

Fake-dusting off my hands, I casually join Cal back in the living room.

"Sorry." I smirk. "I wanted to put those in some water before they dried out. Now, would you mind telling me what in the hell you're doing here?"

"Do you think we could speak in private?" Cal questions, gesturing toward our kitchen audience.

"Absolutely not. You don't get to spend time alone with me ever again. Now, you have exactly sixty seconds to explain to me why you're here."

He presents me with a large envelope.

"What's this?" I ask.

"A proposal."

"Cut the shit. Our romantic days ended the moment you started poking the groupies," I sneer.

"I wasn't screwing the groupies. It's not like we even had any."

"So, what? She was just some random whore you picked up in a drive-through?"

He growls. "Are we really going to do this?"

"That's up to you. You can spend the remaining thirty seconds however you like. I suggest you start by telling me you're sorry for being an asshole."

"Oh, c'mon!" he exclaims, tossing up his hands. "Like you really cared about me in the first place."

"Who are you to judge how I felt about you, you…you penis muncher? I gave you almost a year of my life. I was planning my future with you, for you."

"Sure you were," he says full of sarcasm. "We both know that's a lie."

"You're such a prick. And why would you even think that the way I felt about you was a lie? I never cheated on you. I supported you throughout our entire relationship— going to all your shows, loaning you money when you needed equipment, or that time your gig fell apart and I called in a favor to a friend to get you a new one. There's more than enough proof in my actions. I gave you everything I was, everything, and you shit on it. You shit on us by sticking your dick in someone else when I went home for the summer."

"Yeah, I heard all about your summer."

"What is that supposed to mean? I was working at a museum. That was all."

He shakes his head, holding the envelope in my direction once again. "Will you just take this?"

With aggression, I snatch the envelope from his hands, tear through the top flap, and withdraw the sheets of paper. I scan through the pages, gathering very quickly that it's a copyright release request.

"Copyright of what?" I ask, confused.

"It should be on the first page."

I shuffle back to the front sheet and examine the words more closely, discovering that a small record company wants the license to distribute the branding logo I did for Cal's band when he and I first met.

"You guys were signed," I utter unbelieving, still flipping through the pages.

"Yeah, a few months ago. They want to put us on tour soon, too."

I stack the papers together, shove them into the envelope, and hand it back to Cal. "Congratulations, but I'm not signing this."

He reaches into his rear pocket and offers me a small gray-shaded square. "Here. They sent me with this. It's only half to show good faith because they can't legally give you the rest until the contract is signed."

I reluctantly take it into my hand and assess the check from the record company. It's not a sizable amount even though it's only a portion, but it's likely fair.

"I don't need this," I say, waving the monetary offer through the air.

"Oh, I know you don't." He laughs. "Your family has you set for life. You don't need anything from anyone."

My hands drop to my sides. "What do you know about my family?"

"Not too much, in all honesty, which is kind of weird, seeing how we were together for so long."

"It's not like I ever met your parents," I respond in defense. "So, what's the big deal?"

"Well, when you come from a family like yours, I kind of get the feeling it is a big deal."

"Why do you say that?"

"You don't know, do you?"

"Obviously not. I have zero clue what you're talking about."

"Your mother pulled me aside when she came to visit you last spring."

"She did?" I ask, incredulous.

"Yep." He hooks his thumbs through his belt loops. "Told me about how you couldn't possibly be in love with me because…how did she put it? I'm not from the right breeding. That a guy like me and a young lady like her daughter would never have a future. That I would likely never be able to support you, let alone myself, and that I was low-class and not worthy of someone like you."

"She said those things to you?"

"Yes." He nods in affirmative for emphasis. "Of course, I might be paraphrasing a little, but you get the idea."

"She doesn't know what she's talking about."

"Maybe, maybe not, but in any case, she was sure to let me know that anything between you and me would never last, that I was likely just a fling before you settled down with some hotel heir."

I shut my lids, shielding the world from my frustration due to my family's oppressive ways. I'm just a cog in a master plan not of my making.

When will it stop?

"Why didn't you tell me this?" I question, feeling blindsided.

"I don't know." He shoves his hands into his jacket pockets. "Maybe because I believed her."

"Why would you?" I question, shocked by his statement.

"Honestly?"

"Yes, honestly. Tell me."

"Because the reality is, I never really felt that close to you. When we were together, it was like you were never able to truly open yourself up. And after meeting your mother that wonderful Sunday afternoon, I realized that there was a lot more to you than you'd ever let on. Way more."

"Are you talking about my family's money?"

"Yeah, that and"—Cal gestures a hand up and down the length of my body—"this is all a facade."

"Then, I guess you really never did know me, did you?" I cross my arms over my chest. "Because what you see is what you get."

"If you say so," he replies sarcastically.

I open my mouth to say more in my defense, to try to convince him otherwise, but I close it quickly, no longer having the desire.

He's not worth it.

I don't care if he does know me.

He doesn't need to.

It's over between us.

Suddenly, the sight of Cal is no longer disgusting. It's like I've gained some semblance of closure, fully understanding where we went wrong. Sure, he's a complete dickwad, and his actions certainly do prove that, but we somehow lacked the connection needed for us to survive as a couple. As close as I might have thought we once were, it wasn't meant to be.

Maybe I really didn't give him my heart, like I once thought. If I had, he would never have doubted my affection, no matter my mother's words.

Maybe I'm not capable of giving my heart to anyone.

Maybe it will never be available, stunted somewhere in time.

Is it because no one has ever fully given their heart to me?

Maybe some mysteries of the heart will never be solved, including mine.

Not wanting to dwell in some pathetic pity party, I focus on the check in my hand.

A decision is looming.

I fold the monetary promise in half and tuck it into my pocket. "I'm calling this Dickhead Severance Pay."

He let's out a sigh of relief. "If it helps you sleep at night."

"It will. Now, give me the damn release forms."

Cal hands over the envelope containing the formal papers.

"Do I need to sign it with blood?" I ask, trying to push his buttons a little.

He pulls out a ballpoint pen. "Use this."

I sign the document, granting permission for his band to use the logo I created on any of their merchandise. I flip through the pages just to confirm that I agree to all the terms. When I come across the part about future royalties, I cross out and initial that section, indicating that I desire no further moneys from them, including the other half due from the initial purchase.

I don't want to see Cal ever again.

I'm cutting all ties to this part of my life.

I'm letting go of any stored away anger, resentment, or regret.

I'm releasing.

Twenty-Eight

After almost five days of Foster not answering my calls, not returning my voice mails, and only replying to my texts with nothing more than one-worded answers to my questions, I knew something was wrong between us. There's been a noted disconnect in our communication since the moment the man of my past, Cal, showed up at my door, and Foster walked out of it.

This thing between Foster and me has changed into something more than we originally agreed upon that fateful day in his kitchen. They aren't conscious thoughts—at least not on my part—but there are always unspoken assumptions in any relationship between a man and a woman when orgasms are involved. We had all the right intentions, but one can't fight the chemistry of the human body. It has a tendency to oppress the mind with all those hormones running through it. I blame science.

However, Foster's days of ignoring me are coming to an end. It's Sunday afternoon, and he should be home. I'm not a stalker, but the past few weeks, he and I had routine sexfests and pizza on this day. So, I'm going to pop by and see if he wants to continue the weekend tradition, and while I'm at it, I'll ask him what the hell is going on because nobody likes to be ignored, especially me.

In front of his apartment, I put on my game face and give his door a sturdy knock, so there's no way it couldn't be heard. Almost immediately, the sounds of footsteps carry through his place, getting louder until they're just on the other side of the divide. When the wooden entrance swings open, a svelte blonde woman I've never seen before catches me off guard. She's undeniably attractive.

Gravity drops heavily in my gut, and a surge of uncontrollable fury zings through my body.

I don't like that she's here.

I'm jealous, and I shouldn't be…but I am.

"Hi," she says, confused. "You're not the pizza guy, are you?"

So, he is continuing the pizza Sundays—just not with me.

"Um, no," I reply, fiddling with the buttons on the bottom of my jacket. I remind myself that there's no reason to be jealous or upset even though those feelings are creeping up fast and furious. "Sorry. Is Foster here?"

"Is that the pizza guy, Hills?" a male voice calls.

"No," she responds, her corn-colored hair sweeping across her shoulder, as she turns to face the guy approaching. "Tell Foster he has company."

A man with dark hair and warm eyes the color of teak, comes into my view. A curious smile crosses his lips.

"Oh, well, come on in," he says, waving me inside. "I'll let him know you're here."

I hesitantly step inside. "Thanks."

"Foster!" the male shouts to the back of the apartment. "Someone's here to see you."

The sound of a door clicking open from the rear alerts my ears.

"I'm not falling for that," Foster calls in response, his voice warming me in ways that it shouldn't. "It's your turn to buy."

"It's not the pizza guy," the man retorts, obviously delighted.

"You can't pull that shit on me. My IQ is still higher than yours, even after killing all those brain cells last night. Just pay the man."

The dark-haired man laughs a little and shakes his head. "He always thinks he's got one up on me. Why don't you have a seat? I'm sure he'll be out in a minute."

"Right," I say, stepping into the main living area, unbuttoning my coat and taking a seat in a nearby chair.

The man and the woman, whose names I still do not know, sit next to one another on the sofa.

"I hope I'm not interrupting anything," I say.

"You certainly aren't," the man confirms. "We were just hanging out."

The blonde woman, the polite gentleman, and I all veer our focus toward the hallway when heavy footfalls ring through the apartment. Foster comes into view, his hair slightly damp, and he slows when he spots me seated in his living space.

"Hey," Foster says, his voice hitching slightly. He shoves his hands into the front pockets of his denim pants. "EJ, I wasn't expecting to see you today."

Thanks for the warm greeting.

"I know. I just haven't heard from you in a few days, and I wanted to stop by." I rise from my seat. "Sorry. I can tell it's a bad time and all. You have company."

"No…" He fingers through the strands of hair just over his ear. "It's fine. You can stop by. Did you need something?"

Ah, man, this was a bad idea.

"Foster?" the girl that first greeted me speaks. "Aren't you going to introduce us to your friend?"

"Sorry. Where are my manners? Of course." He gestures to the couple on the couch. "EJ, this is Parker and Hillary. Parker and I used to be roommates until he decided to graduate last year."

"And move on to better things," Parker adds, rubbing Hillary's back.

Hillary stands, holding out her hand in greeting. I take it briefly and cordially.

"It's nice to meet you, EJ." She smiles in Foster's direction. "Foster has told us absolutely nothing about you."

"Likewise." I glance at Parker, catching myself in a lie. Foster already told me about him in regard to his sister, Sasha, who is also Foster's ex.

"But you know how he is."

"We sure do." She laughs.

"All right," Foster interjects, "enough taking jabs at me. And I did tell you about EJ. She's the one who took the pictures you were admiring earlier."

Hillary points to the framed images on the wall. "These are yours?"

"Yes, I took those, but they're Foster's." I share a look with the stone cold man at my side.

"I thought you said a person named Evelyn took these?" she questions him.

"That's me," I answer for him, "but besides my mother, only Fozzie calls me that."

"Fozzie?" Hillary says, amusement spreading across her face like a child in a candy store. "Are we going by Fozzie now?"

"No," he states sternly. "EJ's being funny." Foster gives me his full attention, his head cocked slightly to the side. "I didn't know that's what your mother called you. You never mentioned it before."

"Yeah. I must really like you because hearing that name usually has me wanting to tear my hair out," I say, covering the truth with a sarcastic tone.

"Does it bother you—when I call you that?"

I shake my head.

"This one is my favorite," Hillary says, pointing to the large sparkler image of orange and gold, pulling Foster and me out of our moment of peacemaking.

"Foster helped to make that happen," I tell her. "The orange one you see there was all his idea."

"Really?"

"She gives me too much credit," Foster states. "It's just a sparkler in water."

"That party trick?" Parker guffaws. "This is how you're getting girls now?"

"Don't underestimate the seductive power of fireworks," I say in Foster's defense. "I couldn't wait to get him out of his clothes after we did the experiment."

All of their eyes widen, including Foster's, as they gaze at me like deer in headlights.

Shit, I really need to look into thickening my filter before I speak.

"I'm just kidding," I lie through my teeth, playing it off, even though I really was ripping the clothes from his body afterward.

Parker raises his brows.

With a question in my voice, I add, "The truth is, he couldn't wait to take off mine?"

Hillary stifles a giggle.

"I don't know if you're joking or not," Parker states, rising from the couch, "but you certainly do make a memorable first impression."

"She has that effect," Foster says plainly. "EJ is memorable for most."

"I can see why."

There's a knock at the door.

"Delivery," a male voice announces from the hallway.

"I'll get it," Hillary says, walking toward the entrance. She makes the exchange of money for two large cardboard boxes with the deliveryman and then carries them into the kitchen.

"I should get going," I state.

Hillary sets the food on the bar in the kitchen. "No," she insists. "Stay. There's plenty for everyone. Plus, Parker and I are just going to eat and run. We need to get on the road before it gets too late."

I look to Foster to see if he has any objection—or desire—to me remaining here with them. It's still his place, and I hate to intrude, especially since there's obviously a slight disconnect between us.

He mouths, *Stay*, and gestures for me to follow Parker into the small eating area.

Accepting the hospitality, I nod and take a seat on one of the stools next to Foster and across from his friends.

Over a meal on paper plates, I get to know Foster's friends. I learn little tidbits about his days growing up and some of the shenanigans that Parker and Foster got into as children and teenagers since their families are close. I also learn that Parker and Hillary met their freshman year, here at this university, and have been together ever since. Parker is now attending grad school in New York. Hillary lives with him in a quaint studio apartment and is working for a small magazine as a junior copy editor.

"EJ's from New York," Foster adds to the conversation. "She grew up there."

"Oh, really?" Hillary lights up. "What part?"

I audibly swallow. "Manhattan," I offer, knowing it's vague.

"That's so exciting. I love Manhattan. What was it like, growing up in the city?"

"I assure you, it's different than growing up around here."

Oblivious to my redirecting, Hillary continues, "The people can be so brutal. That must have been tough to grow up with—the way they judge you so quickly. Everything is a competition—from getting on the subway to ordering coffee. Hell, even buying groceries can be cutthroat some days. I never believed it until we moved there, but the saying really is true. If you can make it there, you can make it anywhere."

"Yeah, it's pretty fast-paced, and the rivalry is real. You do gain a decent survival instinct though, if nothing else."

"Do you plan to go back after you graduate?" Parker questions me.

I adjust my body in my seat. "Maybe. I'm not sure. I don't really think New York is my scene anymore."

"Well, I just love it there," Hillary states, glowing from the conversation about the city that never sleeps. "The hustle and bustle. The excitement. The competition is always buzzing in the air, and the nightlife is like no other. I can't imagine being anywhere else."

"Then, it's perfect for you," I tell her reassuringly. "New York will always be exciting. That never changes. It can be stressful, too. The expectations are ridiculous."

"Tell me about it, but I love the challenge. I find myself feeding on it sometimes."

"I do, too, but it's good to know your limitations." I finger through the ends of my hair. "It's a cruel place that can chew you up and spit you out whole before you even realize what happened."

"You sound like you know this from experience," Parker states.

"Yeah." I chuckle, glancing at Foster, who is hanging on my every word. "Nobody does failure quite like me."

"Well, what doesn't kill you makes you stronger," Hillary offers, like there's a silver lining to everything.

"Are you reciting lines from fortune cookies again?" Parker teases her.

"So what? Is that a problem?" She giggles, bumping her elbow against his. "I like Chinese food, and those cookies are good. Don't doubt the wisdom of their knowledge, especially when there's a sparkly ring inside."

I quirk my head in confusion, and Parker takes note.

"I proposed to her over takeout," he clarifies, taking her hand in his. "The ring was inside the cookie."

"That sounds so...romantic."

"Or corny," Hillary suggests. "I loved it though. It showed how well he knew me and my affection for wontons."

Right then, I decide I like Parker and Hillary and wish I had met them sooner. There's something just so genuine about them as a couple. It's too bad they're only here to visit.

"So, are you planning on going back to New York tonight?" I ask, engaging them in further conversation. "It's a really long drive from here."

"No," Hillary states, wiping her mouth with a napkin. "We're driving to my parents' house. They live about three hours away. We need to start getting ready for the big celebration."

I raise my brows, not following.

"They're getting married next weekend," Foster explains, stacking my empty plate with his. "They just stopped by last night to...check up on me."

"Somebody needs to," Parker mumbles as I say at the same time, "Oh, wow. Congratulations."

"Thanks," Hillary responds directly to me, ignoring the side conversation between Parker and Foster. "Let's just hope we make it through the week. There's so much to do until then, and my mother is about to lose her mind, but it's her own fault. She insisted that we get married in my hometown."

"Don't act like you didn't want to get married in the same church that your parents did," Parker chides. "We wouldn't be here otherwise."

"True." She smiles. "Plus, this way, all of our family and friends can come."

"And Foster has no excuse not to be there," Parker states, giving Foster a knowing look. "I already let you off the hook about being a groomsman."

"I told you that I'd be there," Foster reassures him, dumping the paper plates into the trash. "I promised."

"You'd better be."

"Are you threatening me?"

"If that's what it takes, then yes."

"It's not needed. I'll be there. I wouldn't miss it."

Twenty-Nine

No more than thirty minutes later, Hillary and Parker slug their overnight bags over their shoulders and are exiting Foster's apartment for a long three-hour drive north to the bride-to-be's hometown. They say their cordial good-byes to Foster, and once again, Parker adds a comment about seeing Foster next weekend for the wedding.

When the couple is finally gone and the door is shut, only Foster, silence, and I remain.

He joins me next to the small kitchen island, gazing at the intricate granite details—specks of gold, black, blue, and green spattered across the surface like droplets of paint.

"Your friends are really nice," I comment while creating an imaginary figure eight on the cool stone.

"They're good people." He rests his palms on the counter. "Parker's like my brother in a lot of ways."

"I bet that must be hard with everything that happened between you and Sasha."

"It's had its ups and downs, but we're still close—well, as close as we can be now that he's living in another state."

"And about to get married," I remind him.

"Yes, well, that was a foregone conclusion. Everyone knew they would eventually tie the knot. They've been together for so long. It was a matter of time."

"Ah, you must be happy for them."

"Sure I am. Who wouldn't be?"

"Fools. Only fools." I tap my nail against the hard surface. I came here for a reason, and the idle chitchat isn't it. "So, where have you been lately?"

"What are you talking about?"

"Don't play dumb guy with me, Foster. It doesn't suit you."

I cross my arms over my chest, and he straightens, mirroring my stance.

"I don't know what you're trying to say," he adds.

"Really? Do I need to spell it out?"

"Apparently."

I huff, "You haven't returned my phone calls in almost a week. I'm lucky to get an answer to my texts. It's like I don't even exist to you anymore, like you've cut me off."

Foster blinks. He holds my gaze.

"Are you mad at me?" I ask, probing. "'Cause if you are, you should just tell me rather than play this hide-and-seek game. I thought…" I shake my head, unable to continue. "I thought…" I groan.

Foster holds his position, stiff as a board. He removes the dark frames and sets them upside down on the counter between us. Then, he presses two fingers to the center of his forehead.

"Are you going all possessive girlfriend on me right now?" he finally says, not even looking at me. "Because I'm not interested in that kind of conversation."

My heart stops.

Breathing ceases.

Did he say girlfriend?

"No," I stress. "I'm asking you straight up if there's a reason you're ignoring me. And don't say that you haven't been. Something's wrong."

He doesn't reply.

Releasing his fingers from his head, he lifts his deep blue eyes to reach my clear ones.

He remains speechless.

He appears stoic.

"This is about the other day, isn't it?" I ask, trying to fill in the unvoiced words. "When we did the mold-casting at my place?"

He stares absently.

"Foster!" I shout. "Tell me what's going on in that head of yours."

"Are you fucking him?" he asks, cold and serious.

"What? Who? Cal?"

"The guy at your place with the flowers. Mr. Rocker with the blue hair dye. He's your type, I assume, and he was there to see you."

"Yeah, he was, but it's not what you're thinking."

"Are you two sleeping together?"

"God, no!" I exclaim, taken aback. "And fuck no. That piece of shit was my ex. I wouldn't touch him with a ten-foot pole."

"Oh, so you used to fuck him?"

"Yes, I did, but I'm not now. I'm fucking you—or at least I was until about a week ago." My chest cavity rises and falls.

Foster and I are somehow in the midst of an argument.

"Are you going all jealous boyfriend on me?"

He covers his eyes, growling. "Shit, Evelyn. No."

No. He said no.

Why does it feel like the real answer is yes?

"Then, what is going on?" I ask, the timbre of my voice considerably lower than it was moments ago. "Why aren't you talking to me?"

He places his palms on the counter. "I don't know. I just thought you were…with that guy. I thought I was making it easier."

"Easier? How would not talking to me make it easier?"

He grunts. "This"—Foster gestures between the two of us—"is getting complicated."

"So, this *is* about the other day, isn't it?"

"I was pissed, all right?" he concedes. "I didn't like seeing that guy at your place. I shouldn't be mad about it, but I am." He ponders out the kitchen window. "That's it. Are you happy now?"

"Yes, I am," I enunciate. "Thank you for finally just saying it. Your verbal constipation was getting really annoying."

There's a pause in the air.

He chuckles.

Every muscle in my body relaxes.

"I hope you know," I continue sincerely, "that I would never do that to you. I would never start seeing anyone without telling you first. I know what it feels like to be cheated on, too."

His mouth tightens. "You don't owe me anything like that. We aren't a couple."

His statement is nothing but the truth.

We aren't a couple.

We're two people who made an agreement.

That's all.

"True," I retort. "But…we are friends, and out of respect for that, I would never hurt you in that way. I would be up front and tell you if I was seeing someone, which I'm not."

"I appreciate that."

I quickly add, trying to level the playing field, "And if you ever feel like seeing someone, I hope you would tell me, too."

"Well, you don't have to worry about that with me." Foster steps away from the kitchen island and opens the fridge. "I have no intentions of dating anyone."

"Right."

My heart sinks completely, bottoming out near my toes and spreading along the floor.

There it is.

Reality unveils itself completely, hitting me with the velocity of an angry gunshot. My heart stings, punctured emotionally by the unintentional biting words released from the man before me.

I'm wounded by facts.

It's not his truth. It's mine.

His words have hollowed me.

I hadn't realized how hopeful I was for something more committal between Foster and me until it was taken away from me just now. In the very beginning, he'd stated he wasn't interested in dating. I had known that from the day I met him. He'd said girls were complicated, and he was right.

My thoughts are everywhere at once.

I'm complicated.

Watching Foster retrieve a soda, anger comes over me. I desperately want to direct it at him for making me feel something more romantic for him, but I can't. It's not his fault. It's mine. I let my foolish hormones convince my brain that our connection was beyond sex, despite knowing the rules all along. After all, we'd set them together.

My heart broke the rules.

I'm pissed at my betraying heart.

What I felt was one-sided.

What I feel is unrequited.

Typical.

"Do you want one?" Foster questions, offering me a cola.

"No, thanks." I blink away the slight prick of tears from the major onslaught of emotions. "I'm good."

"EJ, I'm sorry. I should have returned your calls this week." He sets the can on the counter. "That wasn't very friend-like of me."

"No, it was a pretty dick move."

"That's one way to put it." Bending at the waist, he rests his elbows on the ledge, staring at his unopened drink. "Maybe we should stop sleeping with each other before things get too…blurry. I'd hate to lose your friendship over a misunderstanding."

"Yeah," I barely whisper, letting the reality of his words sink in. "It's probably for the best."

We share a moment of remorse.

"It's too bad though," I state. "We were really good at it—the sex thing."

"We did seem to know what we were doing," he agrees solemnly.

"That's an understatement."

He lifts his palm from the counter, balling it into a fist. "It was fun though, right?"

"It was certainly a good run." I fake a smile, curl my own hand, and bump it with his.

Thirty

ONE MIGHT THEORIZE AS TO HOW A MAN WHO'S YOUTH WAS SELF-DESCRIBED AS "GLOOMY AND COLD AND STERILE" CAME TO CREATE SUCH VIVID CREATIONS IN THE LATTER YEARS OF HIS LIFE. MANY SCHOLARS AND HISTORIANS LOOK UPON VAN GOGH'S MENTAL ILLNESS AS THE CATALYST TO MOMENTS OF GENIUS IN HIS WORKS, BUT IT COULD BE ARGUED THAT ANY PERSON FACED WITH UNREQUITED LOVE COULD SUCCUMB TO MADNESS.

LOVE IS A DRIVING FORCE FOR A PERSON'S DECISIONS, MOTIVES, AND PURPOSE IN LIFE, AS IS EVIDENCED BY MANY STORIES TOLD THROUGHOUT HISTORY. IT HAS CAUSED HAPPINESS, JOY, WAR, AND DECEIT. WITHOUT LOVE, ONE CANNOT FUNCTION AND THRIVE AMONG THEIR PEERS OR HUMANITY AS A WHOLE. ITS ABSENCE CAN CAUSE

IRREPARABLE HARM TO THOUGHT
PROCESSES AND LOGIC—OR IN VAN
GOGH'S CASE, MAKE ONE CRAZED.

THOSE WHO CANNOT SURVIVE IN THE
WORLD DUE TO THE LACK OF THE
INHERENT HUMAN NEED FOR LOVE
SEARCH FOR ANOTHER PLACE TO
RESIDE. VAN GOGH CREATED A SAFE
SPACE TO ROAM WITHIN HIS
IMAGINATIONS AND BROUGHT THOSE
THOUGHTS TO LIFE THROUGH
GRAPHITE AND PAINTS. HE DEVISED A
PLACE WHERE HE COULD BE LOVED
AND ACCEPTED FOR WHO HE TRULY
WAS, CREATING HIS OWN KINGDOM OF
FREEDOM. THIS ACT MIGHT BE
CONSIDERED MADNESS, BUT IF THIS
WERE TRUE, THEN ALL DAYDREAMERS
EXHIBIT SOME BRAND OF PSYCHOSIS.

I pause my fingers on the keyboard, reading over the last sentence written for my thesis.

I sigh.

It's evident that my focus is overwhelmed by the recent events in my own life. While much of what I've written about Van Gogh's lifetime is true, there are assumptions being made that have been heavily influenced by my own story, and it's difficult to distinguish the line between his experiences and my own.

Maybe this isn't the right time to be working on my paper.

I save the document, close my laptop, and then shimmy it into the bag at my feet while manning the front desk of the engineering library. There are still a few weeks left in the quarter, and most of my paper has already been completed. It's probably a good idea to finish it when I'm in a better state of mind.

It's been a few days since Foster and I discussed the status of what we are now—friends without benefits. The sudden shift in our relationship was difficult to accept at first, but I've come to terms with the reality of our situation, finally coming down from the dreamlike world I was unknowingly building in my mind.

What else can I do?

I value his friendship too much and agree that ending our arrangement is for the best. There's no reason to muddy the waters between us even though my heart has already been taken to sea, looking for his. It's time to reel my emotions back to the safety of where they once resided.

It's currently the middle of my shift, and we're experiencing a major lull in activity at the library—so much so, that Foster excused himself to get a coffee more than twenty minutes ago, which was out of character. In all the time that we've worked together, I've never known him to be the java-indulging type, so I was a little caught off guard when he announced that he was heading out to get a cup after spending the previous forty minutes silently texting on his phone.

Communication between us during the first hour of working together had been slightly strained, but no more than had been expected. With our new arrangement, it's almost like we are starting over in some ways, and I find myself at a loss of how to act or what to say. I've been keeping quiet for the most part.

Since I'm unable to focus on my thesis, I lean back in my seat and peruse the Internet on my phone. I read an article about a koala stealing and driving a woman's car off her property, flip through images of celebrities at a recent red carpet event, and then take a test to see how bitchy I am. Apparently, I'm only twenty-nine percent bitchy. That result would be a shock to all of humankind.

As I'm about to click on another test to see what celebrity is my soul mate, Foster pauses just outside the glass entrance to the library, talking on his phone. In the unstealthiest manner possible, I stare at him as he shifts his weight from one foot to the other, and then he paces in a five-foot circle. Eventually, he stops in his tracks and makes eye contact with me through the clear divide. Caught in the act of gawking, I quickly shift back to my phone, moving my fingers along the screen.

A few moments later, Foster enters the library. He pulls out his chair, takes a seat, and then places a small white paper cup in front of my monitor.

"What's this?" I ask, referring to the unexpected treat.

"I brought you a hot cocoa with extra whipped cream."

But nothing for himself?

"Thanks," I say.

"If you don't want it, no worries. I should have asked before I left. I wasn't sure if you'd want coffee this late at night."

"No, this is great," I say, dropping the phone in my lap. I place my hands around the cup, flooding my skin with its heat. "I don't think I've had hot chocolate since I was about twelve. Is there a cherry on top, too?"

"Did you want a cherry?"

"I think my cherry days are more than long gone."

"I can easily attest to that."

His quick comeback surprises me.

A rising boil of emotions floods my veins, despite the imaginary wall drawn between us. My muscles release, deflating the small amount of tension I didn't realize they were grasping on to.

His smile widens, accentuating those adorable cheekbones.

I smile, too. *I can't help it.*

We smile together.

It's not just his mouth showing joy, and it's not just mine. It's ours combined, feeding off of each other to create that unidentifiable yet indescribable connection. It's a smile for both of us, made by both of us.

My happiness falters when the weight of our boundary creeps slyly between us. He's sitting less than three feet away, and I miss him. I miss us—the us we were, the us I want, and the us we're never meant to be.

The corners of Foster's mouth turn downward and a dimple forms in the middle of his brow. He leans back and pulls out the cell phone from his front pocket. It buzzes in his hand. Sighing, he swipes open the screen and then turns toward the desk where he commences to text.

Allowing him his privacy, I face my monitor and check for new holds. Sure, I just checked half an hour ago, but one can never predict the demand for volumes on petroleum refining, diesel engine mechanics, or centrifugation technology.

However, there are none. I'm zoning out at a blank screen.

Foster grunts, tossing his phone onto the desk with a heavy clunk.

Curious, I peek over my shoulder to where he's sitting with his glasses perched near the top of his hairline as he pinches the bridge of his nose.

"Is everything okay?" I ask, concerned.

"Yes. No." He exhales. "It'll be fine."

"You don't sound very convincing. Is there anything I can do to help?"

Foster laughs to himself.

He drops his hand to his lap and then laughs even more. The volume of his cackle rises, gaining the attention of two of the students in the nearby periodical section.

"Foster, what's going on?"

"Nothing." He shakes his head, humored. "Don't worry about it. Thank you though."

"Sure," I reply, confused. "No problem."

His phone buzzes on the desk, sending a vibration along the surface.

Foster once again grunts.

He doesn't move toward the call.

"Are you going to get that?" I question.

"No. There's no reason to."

After about another fifteen seconds, the phone stills.

I scoot my seat closer to the desk, and moments later, his cell alerts him to a call once again.

"Wow. You sure are popular tonight," I comment. "Did you start a dating hotline?"

"Like I need something like that."

It stops and then starts again.

Twice.

Becoming annoyed by the nonstop vibration, I grab his phone from the desk.

"What are you doing?" he asks, reaching for his property.

"I'm playing secretary," I remark. "Don't worry. I'll handle this."

"Evelyn…" he scolds.

Ignoring Foster and without any regard for who might be on the other line, I accept the call and say, "This is Foster Blake's answering service. He's not available at the moment." I swat at Foster's hand reaching for the device at my ear. "He's presently impersonating an annoying fly. Would you like to leave a message?"

"Who is this?" a confused male voice asks.

"Ms. Cunning. I'm Mr. Blake's new Secretary of Constant Callers. And who might you be?"

"This is Parker," his friend, who I met just a few days ago, says. "Can you put Foster on the phone?"

"Oh, hey, Parker. It's EJ. I was just kidding around." I swivel around in my chair. "Sure, he's right here."

"Actually, I'd rather talk to you."

"Of course you would. How might I help you?"

Foster holds out his hand, waiting for me to give him the phone. I shake my head and hold up my index finger, indicating for him to wait.

"Well," Parker begins, "you see, the thing is, I'm getting married this weekend."

"I remember. Congratulations. Hillary's great. You're very lucky."

"Thank you. I tend to agree," Parker states proudly. "So, here's the deal. Hillary's mother is down my fiancée's throat about this damn seating chart for the reception, and it's driving my bride-to-be absolutely insane, thereby making me extremely unhappy."

"Yes, planning any event can be quite a task. I don't envy that part one bit."

"No kidding. I'm starting to understand why people hire wedding planners, but her family insisted on doing everything, so we let them. Hillary said there would be no fighting her parents on this point." He pauses. "Anyhow, I've gotten off track. The problem is that, apparently, I mistakenly put down my dear old friend, Foster, as having a plus-one, assuming that no one in his right mind goes to a wedding event alone—and certainly not Foster. He wouldn't want to be that guy."

I swallow to contain the rise in emotions at the thought of Foster dating anyone. "No, he certainly wouldn't."

"But when I asked him about who he was bringing, he told me that he's coming solo. Now, this is something I don't understand, especially when he knows you."

"Oh..." My heart pounds a little harder.

"I take it, he hasn't mentioned it to you then?"

"Um..." I turn my back to my coworker, whose stone cold gaze is on me. "No, not at all."

"I told him to ask you, but he didn't think that you would want to come."

"It's kind of complicated," I whisper.

Over my shoulder, I glance at Foster. He's focused on his feet, intently listening to my side of the conversation.

"I'm going to put Foster on the line now. It was nice talking with you, Parker."

242

I quickly deliver the phone into Foster's waiting hand, rise from my seat, and then meander out from behind the desk. I begin to collect books and magazines from the tables to be returned to the shelves. I take my time, giving Foster the freedom to speak freely to his friend.

When the last magazine is filed into its place, I pick up the short pile of books and walk back toward the desk where Foster is thankfully off the phone, watching my every move.

"Hey," I say, resting the stack of volumes between us. "Sorry about that. I overstepped my boundaries."

"Don't worry about it." He grabs the top bound edition on molecular mechanics and scans it to be reshelved. "You didn't know."

"Still, it was inappropriate."

"I'm not mad," Foster states reassuringly while shortening the pile before him. "It's who you are."

In silence, I place the remaining books, one by one, into his hand, and he goes through the process of checking the bar code for their location. When the final volume has been scanned, I arrange the organized stacks onto a nearby cart to be filed later in the evening, and then I take a seat once again at Foster's side behind the desk.

"So, Parker's giving you a hard time?" I ask, edging into the topic that isn't being discussed.

"Per usual," he huffs, sitting up straighter. "Somehow, he's gotten it into his head that I won't be able to handle seeing Sasha at the wedding. Apparently, she's bringing her boyfriend from Europe with her."

I exhale sharply. "That's understandable."

"He's overreacting. I'm not that pathetic."

"Of course you aren't." I bite my lip. Knowing it's emotional suicide, I tell him, "But, if you were to ask, I'd go with you...to the wedding."

"I couldn't ask that of you. Things are awkward enough between us."

"I agree, but that doesn't change the fact that we're still friends. You've helped me so many times when I've needed it, and maybe it's time I return the favor."

"What are you saying?" he questions, his voice desperately low.

"I'd be more than happy to go as your plus-one." I pause. "Your wingman." I giggle. "Your arm candy." I grin. "Or your friend, if that's what you need."

Thirty-One

"I can't believe you're going away with him this weekend," Chandra comments, leaning into my bedroom doorframe with her arms casually crossed just below her chest. "And to a wedding. You know what that's going to be like, don't you?"

"It's going to be fine," I insist, stuffing a set of pajamas into an overnight bag filled with my other belongings. I then zip it closed. "It's just a wedding and just for one night. It's not like a romantic getaway or anything."

"Are you sure about that?"

"Yes. He and I discussed it. I'm going as his date but as his friend. Nothing more."

"Right." She titters. "His friend…with benefits."

"I told you, we stopped that. No more sex."

"So, you thought a night away, at a wedding, while sharing a hotel room would be a genius idea?"

"Are you playing some kind of mom card with me right now?" My fingers lightly comb through the soft highlights of my sideswept locks cascading in waves over my shoulder.

"No. But you do realize that this isn't the greatest idea. You're playing with fire, and the burn is going to hurt so bad."

"Yes. I do know there are potential consequences, but he's my friend, and whether he wants to admit it or not, he needs some support right now. Plus, weddings blow when you go alone. So, I'm making sure he's not."

"And you're the best person for the job?"

"Yes." I slip a modest yet classic set of sapphire earrings through my ears and then fasten the matching necklace at the back of my neck. "No one knows how to play a part better than me. I've been doing it my entire life."

Chandra sighs, dropping her hands to her sides. "It's not healthy."

"It's just one night." Pulling an elegant knee-length dress from my closet, I face my roommate with it draped across torso. "What do you think about this one?"

"It's stunning." She sighs. "Not too gaudy, unique enough to be noticed, and not too extravagant to detract from the bride."

"That's what I thought. Plus, it's blue—the color of peace, harmony, and tranquility."

I quickly slip off my yoga pants and tug the comfy T-shirt over my head, tossing them both into the laundry basket. Releasing the fine clothing from its hanger, I step into the garment and push my arms into the sleeves, opting to dress now in case there's nowhere to change when we arrive. The zipper on the back sits in an awkward spot, so I step over to Chandra and spin around, nonverbally asking her to help me dress. She does so willingly and then adjusts the fabric at my waist.

I circle around and ask her, "How do I look?"

"Way too pretty for just friends."

I frown.

"But," she continues, "you do look beautiful, and this color is perfect."

"Thank you."

"You're welcome. What shoes are you going to wear?" my fashion-loving roommate asks, her curiosity taking over.

"Nude strappy pumps with a modest heel."

"Perfection."

"I'm glad you approve." I return to my bed, pick up my bag, and then slip into a comfortable pair of shoes for the long three-hour ride to Hillary's hometown. "What about you? Anything fun planned for the weekend?"

"Just the usual with Jeremy—hanging out and homework."

"How are things going with him, by the way?"

"Really good." Chandra steps back from the doorway, out of the way, for me to leave the room. "He's starting to put in job applications for when he graduates."

"Oh, yeah?" I close my door, and then we both tread down the hallway toward the living room. "What about you? Are you applying as well?"

"A little here and there."

"In the same cities as him?"

"So far, yes."

"It's that serious, huh?"

"It could be."

I set my bag on the sofa and retrieve a wool three-quarter-length coat from the hall closet, placing it on top of my luggage. Chandra takes a seat in the red chair and begins to thumb through a fashion magazine. As I'm about to join her, there's a gentle knock at the door.

"I bet that's Foster," I say to Chandra.

"Nothing like stating the obvious," she quips back.

"Behave."

When I open the entrance, dressed handsomely in a well-tailored charcoal suit accentuated by a cobalt tie to match his eyes is Foster.

"Evelyn," he gasps. "You look…" His eyes roam over my body. "Nice."

"Thanks. You're looking dapper yourself." I rest a palm on my hip. "I clean up pretty good, don't I?"

"That is a complete and total understatement. You look amazing."

"It must be the shoes." I point the sneaker-clad foot in his direction. "They make the outfit."

He lowers his gaze, absent of his signature glasses, to the ground and laughs. "Those are something special. Unique."

"I thought so. I packed a fancy pair for later." Taking a step backward, I grab my coat, slip my arms into the sleeves, and then shrug the travel bag over my shoulder. "Are you ready to go?"

"I'm just waiting on you."

"Then, you are waiting on no one." I blow a kiss in Chandra's direction where she's still sitting in the chair. "I'll see you later."

"You two behave," she warns, masked in sarcasm.

"Yes, mom."

"Have a good weekend, Chandra," Foster says, waving to my roommate.

"You, too, Foster."

Exiting my apartment, I join Foster in the hallway, and we descend the steps together and head out the building. He takes the bag from my arm, leads me halfway down the block, and stops in front of a black Lexus. He pops the trunk.

"Did you get a new car?" I ask, wondering what happened to his well-loved Honda.

"Nope." He stows away my bag, closes the compartment, and then opens the passenger door for me to get in. "This is my grandmother's. I borrowed it for the drive since it's a bit of a hike."

"It's all fancy."

I slide into the beige leather interior, and Foster closes the door. He then circles around the rear, takes off his jacket, lays it on the backseat, and then joins me inside the car.

As he turns over the ignition, I ask, "Don't you need to wear your glasses to drive?"

"No. They're more for reading." He offers me a sidelong glance. "You look so different with your hair like that," he remarks, pulling away from the curb and into the street.

"Is that a good or a bad thing?"

"You know, I'm not sure yet."

Over approximately the next three hours, Foster and I enjoy the peaceful scenic drive to Hillary's hometown. Once we're outside the city limits and beyond the suburbs, there's not much to note since it's all the same—farms and fields with cows and horses. I wonder if the bride grew up doing hoedowns and wrestling cattle.

When we take the designated exit off the highway, I'm relieved to see some semblance of population the farther we travel into a small town center. Passing through the main business area and about a mile farther along the road, Foster banks a right down a long drive where a large stately white historic building comes into view. He pulls up and stops the car under the portico of the local resort and spa. The valets open our doors, and we exit the vehicle to check in to the hotel.

At the desk, we're told that our room isn't ready yet, but we can leave our bags with the bellman, and they will be delivered by the time we return after the wedding reception. Since the ceremony is set to start in less than half an hour, I head to the ladies' room to freshen up, change my shoes, and then meet Foster where he's lingering in the lobby.

Clicking my heels along the marble floor, I adjust the coat over my shoulders and then take Foster's waiting arm, looping mine through his.

We are already playing the part so easily.

Through the doors, he steers us past the parking area and down a sidewalk lining the driveway.

"Where are we going?" I ask, confused.

"The church is only two blocks from here. The concierge said we could easily walk there using..." He slows his steps and then turns us down a small paved path. "This walkway. It should take us straight there."

"Clever."

About five minutes later, we come to a clearing that opens to a simple Christian church constructed of brick. Pairings of people are filing in for the ceremony, and we follow their lead toward the open large wooden doors.

When we reach the base of the concrete steps, Foster pauses.

"What is it?" I ask, smoothing my fingers over the lapel of his jacket.

He captures my hand at his chest. "My parents are here. I just saw them go in."

"You mentioned they were coming."

"I'll introduce you to them at the reception."

"Sounds good. Is there anything I need to know?"

His brow crinkles. "No. They're easy people, but I didn't tell them anything about you."

"That's okay." I smile. "Parents aren't a problem for me. I find, the less they know, the better. They often make assumptions based on what they hope rather than what they are told anyhow."

"That's an interesting theory."

"Trust me. But when you introduce me, be sure to call me Evelyn. It will go over better than EJ."

"But that's not what you like to be called."

"By you, I do—well, I tolerate it," I add sarcastically. "Plus, it's just for one night, and it's just a name."

He tightens his grip around my digits and breathes, "Evelyn."

"You got it."

Lowering our joined hands, he says, "Let's do this," and he leads me into the church.

Inside, we're ushered into a pew on the groom's side toward the rear of the sanctuary. Muted violins play in the background as more guests take their seats for the upcoming ceremony. Not long after we've settled in, the groom, Parker, and his groomsmen appear near the altar. The music changes as the bridesmaids begin to make their way up the aisle. All of the guests turn to watch the procession, one by one, of women in gowns of slate and silver, their hair sparkling with gemstones.

Foster, like everyone else, follows the path of each one until they reach a point out of view. However, he pauses after the third girl passes, instead fixated on the pews near the front. I lean into his shoulder, trying to decipher what has caught his attention. There, in a dress of celery and adorned in pearls, is a woman with dark hair and eyes that mirror Parker's. Staring back at the man at my side, she releases an impish smile and then raises her hand, a gesture in greeting.

Foster returns her hello with a small wave.

"Is that Sasha?" I whisper, my words brushing against his ear.

He nods once in reply.

I lace my fingers with his and then press my lips to the corner of his mouth without any thought.

Slowly and with noted control, Foster tilts his head, connecting his soft orbs with my own, as I try to backpedal in my mind what made me kiss him just now.

The tune changes once again, and the audience begins to stand in preparation for the bride to make her way down the aisle. Foster plants his mouth on my forehead and then rises at my side. I do the same, lifting myself from the pew and holding myself high, hoping to catch my fluttering heart that is thumping steadily toward the sky.

Thirty-Two

The wedding was beautiful, romantic, and heartfelt. It was everything one would hope for in a ceremony where two people committed themselves to one another for the rest of their lives. The couple glowed with pride and an overwhelming amount of emotions.

Along with the other guests, Foster and I make our way to the reception hall located within the hotel where we will be staying at tonight. We're ushered into a large room for a social cocktail hour while the wedding party partakes in the picture-taking formalities.

We have a drink and nibble on some hors d'oeuvres as people mingle around the room in conversation, and I'm casually introduced to two of Foster's friends from childhood and their dates.

When our drinks are finished and his acquaintances have left us to socialize with others, Foster takes my empty glass and places it on the high table to our right.

"C'mon," he says, taking my hand and pulling me across the room of chatty people.

"Are we making an escape?"

"Hardly. I want to introduce you to my parents before they start muttering vile things about me for not saying hello yet."

"Would they really do that?"

"No. They're easygoing people. You'll see. I just don't want to be rude."

Hand in hand, Foster and I weave through the smattering of circular tables and meandering guests toward the center of the room while a gentleman begins to play a classic melody on the nearby piano. We come to a stop where two older couples are immersed in a lively conversation. The light-haired brunette and a man with hair of honeyed amber are unmistakably Foster's parents.

"Excuse me," Foster says, interrupting their conversation. "I just wanted to stop by and say hello."

His parents smile, gleaming with happiness, as they observe the sight of Foster...and then me standing close at his side.

"Foster," his father greets, approaching us, "we were wondering when you would come over and say hello."

"Does that mean I missed my nomination for Son of the Year?" he kids.

"Hush now," his mother says, closing the gap between us. She embraces Foster and then kisses him on the cheek—twice. "It's just good to see you."

"We were all together not too long ago. You're acting like it's been years."

"We weren't sure if you would come."

"Of course I came. It's Parker."

The couple his parents were speaking to excuse themselves, stating that they need to freshen up their beverages. I smile politely and then turn my attention back to the reason we walked across the room—his parents.

"Aren't you going to introduce us to your friend?" Foster's father questions.

Foster places his hand at my lower back and says, "Evelyn, this is my parents, Susan and Clayton. Mom, Dad, this is Evelyn. She's—"

"Delighted to meet you," I interject, offering my hand to his father and then his mother. "It was a beautiful ceremony, wouldn't you agree?"

"Oh, yes," Foster's mother states, flowing easily with my conversation direction. "They make a lovely couple."

"I've only met Hillary and Parker once, but I can tell, it was meant to be."

"We've known Parker for years," his father tells me. "He's fortunate to have found a girl who will put up with his shenanigans. He's had many. Foster can attest to that."

Releasing the charming smile I stow away for these occasions, I say, "That might be true, but something tells me that Hillary feels like she's the lucky one."

"I'm sure she does," his mother agrees, her smile widening in approval. "So, how do you and Foster know one another?"

"We go to school together."

"Oh? So, you're in the engineering program, too?"

"No, Mother," Fosters corrects her. "E—Evelyn and I work together at the library. She and I are just—"

"Getting to know one another," I finish for him. "He's been helping me with a project as well. I don't know how I would be doing it without him."

"That's...really nice to hear."

To seal the deal for any questions his parents might have, I thread Foster's fingers with my own. It's an innocent gesture but one people easily read into. His mother notices and smiles wider.

"If I can have your attention," an attendant announces over the microphone, "the bride and groom will be joining us shortly. At this time, we would like to move all guests into the dining hall."

The people around us begin to migrate to the area at my back where a set of doors opens to a large room draped in ethereal tones of cornflower and candlelight.

"Sounds like we are being beckoned into the next room," Foster's father says, taking his wife's arm in his own. "Shall we?"

At Foster's side, I walk with him and his parents to the room where the majority of festivities will be taking place for the rest of the evening. Near the entrance on one of four small tables, we find our names and table number, which is different than the one his mother and father have been assigned.

"Evelyn and I are going to take our seats," Foster says to them as we are about to part ways. "I'm sure we'll see you later."

"Of course," his mother says, filled with easiness just like her son described.

"Enjoy yourselves," his father says. "It was nice to meet you, Evelyn."

"You, too."

With our place cards in hand, Foster and I traverse through the crowd and tables, looking for our seating. He pauses momentarily at the sight of Sasha taking a chair at a table that is thankfully many over from our own.

Her presence in general makes my skin crawl.

Is it wrong to want to strangle her with the pearls around her neck?

Likely.

When we finally find our numbered table, Foster pulls out my linen-covered seat, allowing me to sit first, and then he takes the one next to me.

"Did you read some guidebook on dealing with parents?" he asks, a noticeable glow plastered across his face. "Or about going to weddings in general? Because that shit back there was textbook, all of it."

"I might have some experience on the subject."

"Ah, now, it all makes sense." He presses his tie against his chest. "Was this part of your training to become the daughter your mother always hoped you would be?"

"It could be. Let's just say, I did pay attention to some of the things I was taught—or maybe it's survival instincts."

"It shows."

Other guests begin to take their seats at our table, two of whom I recognize from the cocktail portion of the evening. We say our hellos briefly as the MC comes over the speakers, announcing the arrival of the bride and groom.

Over the course of the next hour or so, toasts are made, food is served, and the cake is cut. Now, all that remains is an evening of dancing and mingling.

At our table filled with two of Parker's cousins, a childhood friend, and their dates, conversation has been easy, kept to superficial topics about Parker's misgivings, school, and the bridesmaids' dresses. I play my part, offering polite comments at the appropriate pauses and bringing up new subjects when necessary to keep a steady flow of chatting while engaging everyone when possible.

My mother would be so proud that her chirping tidbits on manners are actually serving a purpose. I hate to admit it, but her lessons do have merit in certain situations, such as this one.

A couple from our table excuses themselves and takes to the dance floor as the bride and groom make their rounds, greeting each and every one of their guests. We're at the far end of the room from the start of their rounds.

"C'mon," Foster says, resting his napkin on the linen surface and rising from his seat.

"Are you asking me to dance?" I ask, taking his hand.

"Not yet. I could use a drink though. How about you?"

"Definitely."

Foster guides us around the table and across the dance floor toward the corner of the room where the bar is set up. Halfway there, the smiling and happy newlyweds stop us in our path.

"Congratulations," Foster and I say in unison.

"Thanks," Hillary says to me, gleaming.

The men start a small side conversation.

The bride admits to my ears, "I was so nervous."

"What for?" I question, in total awe of her beauty. "Everything was perfect."

She breathes a sigh of relief. "It was, wasn't it?"

"Absolutely. Seriously, one of the best weddings ever."

"Thank you. That means a lot. And I'm so happy you came with Foster. He's a really great guy."

"I agree. He's something special. I'm lucky to have met him at all."

Foster glances at me quickly—so fast in fact that it's quite possible I might have imagined it.

"I'm positive he feels the same about you," Hillary states, clasping my hand.

"We need to keep going," Parker tells his new bride. "More guests to greet."

"Yes, we don't want to keep them waiting," she says with her husband pulling her away. "It was nice talking to you, EJ."

"Likewise," I say, feeling Foster's arm slide around my waist.

"Are you ready for a drink?" he asks, his soft lips brushing the shell of my ear.

"Very."

Foster escorts me to the bar with his hand on my hip and then orders me a glass of white wine and himself a beer. Once our drinks are served, he leans his backside against the bar's edge, and we toast to the evening.

"Are you having a nice time?" I question after taking a generous sip of chardonnay.

"It's tolerable," he jokes. "You're making it even more tolerable."

"Is that a compliment?"

"Yes, it is." Foster shakes his head and leans an elbow on the ledge of the bar. "How about you? Are you having a good time?"

"It's more than tolerable," I tease back, stepping closer until the smell of his cologne occupies my senses. "And yes, I'm having a nice time."

"Well, somebody should."

A familiar sensation comes over me as we smile at one another, basking in each other's company.

There are moments with him, where it's only him.

This is one of them.

Taking the wine glass from my hand, Foster sets it on the bar next to his beer and then holds the tips of my fingers in his hand.

Concentrating on my recently manicured nails, rubbing his thumb along the length of my middle digit, he softly says, "You're really good at this."

"At what?"

"Pretending. When I asked you to come here with me, I wasn't expecting you to play a part. I just wanted you to come."

"Really?"

"Of course. You're my best friend, Evelyn. Everything is better with you."

"Fozzie," I quietly utter.

He lifts his gaze to join my own, and I'm sucked into the details of him. Lifting my palm and cupping his cheek, I study every part of his face, memorizing and imprinting into my mind his perfect imperfections, the minute characteristics that make up who he is—the small dimple between his brows when he's concentrating, the fine line at the corner of his mouth, and the two freckles at the crest of his cheekbone. His hand covers my own, and he slides it toward his mouth, pressing his lips deliberately into the sensitive area of where my lifeline is hidden.

"Foster?" a female voice interrupts at our side.

I quickly swipe my hand out from underneath his.

Sasha, whom I recognize from the ceremony, and a proper-looking man with dark wavy hair and of medium build tentatively wait for a reply.

"Sasha," Foster deadpans, straightening next to me while smoothing down his tie.

I lean in closer to him. He takes my palm in his, rubbing his thumb over the back of my hand.

"We saw you earlier and wanted to come over and say hello," Sasha says, reluctant.

"Hello."

She gestures to the man at her side. "You remember Elton, right?"

"Yes."

Elton offers a hand in Foster's direction, and with a prominent Welsh accent, he says, "It's good to see you again."

Foster regards his attempt at a formal greeting but doesn't budge. Elton lowers his palm, retreating, and then slides it around Sasha's waist.

"I'm Evelyn," I boldly state, taking control of this stupidly uncomfortable situation.

Sasha hesitantly shakes my offered hand. "It's nice to meet you."

"I can't say the same about you."

Her face goes slack, like someone has just stabbed her in the back, and a white state of shock takes over her pallor. I release her hand and then offer it to Elton, who takes it without any pause.

"So, are you the prickwad who was boning Sasha while these two were together?" I ask, my voice dripping with saccharine innocence.

He quickly pulls his grip from mine, shoving it into his pants pocket. "Well now, aren't you quite forward? And rude."

"I'll take that as a yes."

"That's him," Foster confirms. "Lord Elton Wellesley of Tool-ing-ham."

"Foster," Sasha pleads, "it was a long time ago. More than a year. Almost two. I was hoping that maybe we could move past all of that now."

"We have, Sasha," he states factually. "But no time in the world will make what you did ever be right."

"I'm sorry for what happened and for what I did and how I handled things. I've said it a million times. Why can't you just forgive me?"

"I do forgive you, but that doesn't mean I like you." He glances briefly at Elton. "Or what you're about. You're not the person I thought you were. Or maybe you've changed. Either way, you're just a status seeker now. Maybe you always were." Foster firmly grips my hand and begins to lead us onto the hardwood floor that makes up most of the room. "Enjoy the wedding. And the rest of your lives."

My steps quicken, trailing Foster away from his ex and to the far end of the dance floor. Without any words, he whirls us around, places my hand at his waist, rests a palm at my lower back, and claps my other hand at shoulder height. Then, to the steady beat of the music playing in the background, he easily leads me across the dance floor with noted grace.

"You can dance?" I ask, dumbfounded.

He laughs. "You seem surprised."

"That's because I am. What other talents do you possess?"

"None really."

He twirls me around, extending his arm, and then gracefully folds me back into an embrace.

"Where did you learn to do this?" I ask, blissful.

"After my grandfather passed away, I became my grandmother's dance partner. She taught me."

"That's kind of sweet. I take it, you two are close?"

"Somewhat. She's just partial to me because I was named after her husband."

As we continue to naturally sway to the rhythm of the tune blaring through the reception hall, I sink further into him, not realizing until this moment how much I've missed the feel of his body next to mine. Closing my eyes, I relish and savor my tiny fantasy—the one where he and I somehow have a happily ever after. It's a pleasant place for my thoughts to wander.

When the song ends, I come back to the reality of the dim lights and the harsh lines of the world.

Over Foster's shoulder, I spy Sasha and Elton still at the bar, having a drink. While part of me wants to stare daggers at Sasha for what she did to Foster in the past, my gaze keeps wandering to Elton. There's a certain properness to be noted about the way he holds himself, his glass, and the movement of his arms. His mannerisms and gestures are not that of many people I've come to know while attending college, and he appears to be no older than twenty-three. In some ways, he reminds me of Gerard. The way he's dressed and the way he carries himself tells me that he's been groomed in some way. It's somewhat unnatural—almost like me.

"Foster?"

"Yes, EJ?"

"Who is Elton?"

He halts and takes a step backward, distancing himself from me. "What are you asking?"

"He's just…different. And I'm not talking about the European thing. He has this air to him…and I was just wondering if I was missing something."

"Well, besides being a total asshole, he's also the son of a duke. Is that what you mean?"

"Like, as in royalty?" I question, shocked, recalling when Foster called Elton the Lord of Tool-ing-ham. I thought he was just kidding around.

He chuckles. "Yeah, he's considered a commoner, but he's around number six hundred in line for the crown."

"Is that what you meant when you called Sasha a status seeker?"

"You caught that?" Foster pulls me back into his arms, swaying us from side to side, matching the slow beat of a love song being serenaded throughout the room.

"I did." Savoring him, I rest my cheek on his solid shoulder. "Status is grossly overrated."

"I'm glad you think so."

Thirty-Three

When the MC announces that the bride and groom will be tossing the garter and bouquet, Foster indicates that it's time for us to go. We quickly say our cordial good-byes to his parents and a few of his friends, and then we hastily make our way out of the reception hall, stop by the front desk to get the key to our room, and then continue toward the guest room section of the resort.

The elevator opens on the third floor, and we bank two lefts around beige corners before coming to our room for the first time. Foster uses the key card to unlock the door and then opens it, allowing me to enter first. I flip on the light and see our luggage sitting on one of the beds, as promised. Also, as promised, our room has two double beds—one for Foster and one for myself.

I slip out of my jacket, hang it in the nearby hall closet, and then proceed to pick up my bag, moving it to the adjacent bed near the window.

"I guess I'll take this one," I proclaim, stepping out of my nude heels.

"That's fine," Foster says as he hangs his suit jacket in the closet. Then, he approaches me while loosening the cobalt tie. "Whatever makes you the most comfortable."

"Well, if this were a few weeks ago, I'd probably say that I'd be more comfortable if you were in bed with me," I tease with one hundred percent truth behind the sarcasm. "But this will do."

"Of course it will."

He slides the tie out from the confines of his shirt collar and sets it on his bed. Then, like I'm not even there, Foster begins to unbutton his pressed dress shirt from the neck down. When he releases the last one at the bottom of the white garment and is in the process of pulling his arms from the sleeves, I unzip my bag and hurriedly gather my pajamas.

"I'm going to clean up and change," I announce, heading toward the bathroom and away from temptation.

Seeing him with his clothes off is nothing new, but not to be able to touch him is something I'm not equipped for, and it's best to remove myself from the situation.

I shut the bathroom door at my back with my heart racing faster than it should be.

Chandra was right. Coming here with Foster for a wedding was a bad idea. It's not because of what might happen or what usually happens at weddings—a night laced with alcohol, bad decisions, and regrets—but because of what won't happen. There will not be any stolen kisses, gentle caresses, or any good old-fashioned sweat-rolling-off-the-back boinking.

I won't be that lucky.

At the vanity, I place my change of clothes on the counter and then begin to unpin my hair, allowing it to drape down the length of my back. I then wash my face, removing the superficial cover of beauty from my skin.

Reaching behind my back, I attempt to pull down the zipper of my dress, but I fail miserably, unable to get the proper leverage.

I try again.

And again.

Ugh.

Resolved to needing assistance, I quietly crack open the door and spy Foster pacing about the room in a T-shirt and boxers, staring at the floor and muttering to himself.

"Foster?"

His head quickly snaps in my direction, startled. "Yeah?"

"Do you think you could help me get out of my dress? Zipper issues."

"Sure."

I widen the door and turn around, sweeping the loose wavy locks over my shoulder so that he has better access to the problem area. Placing a firm but gentle hand on the bare skin of my neck, Foster traces the line of my back, pausing at the crest of my garment. With great restraint, I demand my body to remain still as he pulls the zipper down the length of my spine until it reaches its end just below the small of my back.

Peeking over my shoulder, I tell him, "Thanks."

He lifts his gaze from where his hands rest near my waist, meeting my own with an open vulnerability. I've seen that look before. It's usually fleeting, showing up during a few of the art sessions where he was my subject.

"You're welcome," he replies, stepping backward. He continues to hold me hostage with a myriad of sentiments fluxing in and out of his gaze.

I'm susceptible to all of them pulling me in.

I'm ill-prepared for this night.

I'm not in control of my emotions.

Finally, he says, "I'll let you finish getting dressed."

I close the door and then my own lids, stifling out the remnants of our small interaction. Changing out of my formal clothes and into my comfortable pajamas of a tank and shorts, I then exit the room, ready to crawl under the covers, praying that morning comes quickly so that this night can be behind us.

Breathe.

Two steps out the door.

Foster.

Unmoving.

I stop in my tracks.

He sits on my bed, next to my bag, focusing on the ground.

"Foster?"

"I can't do this anymore," he says low and steady. "I thought it would be easier this way, but it's not. It's worse."

My breath hitches, and the blood pulsing through my body drums loudly in my ears.

"Was any of it real?" Slowly, he connects his eyes with my own. "For you? Was it ever real?"

I gulp, unbelieving. "I don't know what you're asking me."

"The way you used to look at me sometimes, and even still, like you just did when I was helping you with your dress…I wonder if it was real or if you were just pretending."

"I…" is all my stunned vocal cords can muster.

"I'm not going to hide it anymore. It's real for me, even more so than I thought."

He stands, and I'm a statue glued to the floor.

"When your ex came to your apartment that day, I didn't like it one bit. I hated the way it made me feel. At first, I thought it was jealousy, which I played off as being normal since we were sleeping together, but then I realized it wasn't just that—the simple act of coveting something that wasn't mine. It was something else, something more."

Words.

So many words foreign to his mouth fly into the stillness and linger between us.

"The thing is, Evelyn…" Foster rubs his forehead. "Fuck, Evelyn! Do you know how hard it was for me to tell everyone that was your name tonight?"

"No," I reply, startled, not fully comprehending. "I had no idea."

"I guess you wouldn't, would you?" He shakes his head, muttering to himself, "It was all part of the show. The act. The deal. Our arrangement. But it wasn't for me. It meant more."

"Fozzie, I don't know what you're talking about."

"Fozzie." He laughs. "Every time you say that, I always think…"

"What do you think?"

"I'm tired of pretending, Evelyn—pretending that we're just friends, and tonight, pretending that we're a couple." He drags a palm across his face. "But most of all, I'm exhausted from pretending that I don't love you—not only to you, but to myself." Foster lowers his voice. "I've been falling in love with you from the moment I met you even though I've tried so hard not to." He takes three calm steps toward me so that we're an arm's length apart. "So, I'm asking, was it ever real for you?"

My world comes to a standstill. Silence ticks and tocks between us.

"Yeah. It was," I whisper tentatively and somewhat shakily. Releasing the pent-up emotions, I let them out slowly, so they don't explode all at once. "It is."

"I don't want to be your friend, and I'm not interested in dating."

I step back.

I blink.

My gut drops like a violent avalanche, and wrathful thoughts emerge.

"You're a real asshole, you know that? And confusing as hell." Circling around him to the bed, I stuff my blue dress into the bag. I gather my shoes from the floor, shove them next to my dress, and then close up my luggage. Storming in his direction, I heatedly continue, "You tell me you love me. You make me admit that I feel the same, and now, you tell me that you want nothing to do with me?"

"No," he insists, grabbing me by the arm as I'm entering the bathroom to retrieve the rest of my things. "You're not listening. It's simple. I don't want anything less than being with you. I don't want to be friends or date or pretend or go through any more of these stupid motions that keep getting in the way of what I really want. You. I just want you. Anything else is without you."

"You want me?"

"Yes." His face softens. "So. Much." His eyes close.

I melt from the inside out, and the burn of frustration fizzles.

"Is this real?" I ask, drinking in his sincerity. "No deals or stipulations? No pretenses or rules?"

"No rules," Foster quietly utters, relaxing his grip.

Nodding, my body replies before the words can be formulated. "I want you, too."

He slides his palm down the length of my arm, tenderly dancing his fingertips with my own. "I love you, Evelyn." Leaning in, he grazes my earlobe with his mouth. "For longer than you might have known."

"Likewise."

He chuckles against my cheek. "That's all you have to say? Likewise?"

"Just shut up and kiss me."

"I was getting there."

Foster cups my face with both hands, and there's no question in my mind about how he feels. It's been there all along. He's been asking me to love him with his expressions for months, and I was too blinded by denial to see it.

His lips float across my own, teasing and just out of reach. I silently gasp in anticipation as he marks every part of my mouth with his phantom touch. Patiently, I allow the moment to build for what's to be our first kiss. The others don't count because they were just surface kisses— the kinds that happen without any care, skimming along the shield we carry before us. This kiss will consummate a part of myself with him that is newly revealed—the living and breathing substance pulsating between both of us.

With noted restraint, Foster lands his lips upon mine, moving them languidly so that every crevice and cell receives the same amount of care and attention. His tongue asks entrance into my mouth, and I willingly welcome it. The familiar taste of him is like a dull echo in comparison to the new flavor he possesses now that his kisses are tainted with affection, the truest kind. It's currently seizing my body with a keen insistence and searing its way into my heart.

We're finding one another in a new way, laced with a sense of commitment.

Foster lowers his palms down the length of my arms to the bottom of my tank. He flirts with the hem, his fingers skimming along the space just below my navel.

"Yes," I answer to all of the questions he isn't asking.

"I didn't say anything."

"Doesn't matter. My answer is yes, Fozzie."

"I like the sound of that."

My shirt is quickly swept up and over my head, landing on the ground. I help him out of his, adding it to the pile on the floor, and then I press my breasts against his glorious bare skin, returning his kisses and holding him tight. Foster grips the back of my thighs, just under my ass, and lifts me from the carpet, shuffling us to the bed. He lays me down, our lips still sealed, and scoots our bodies up toward the headboard.

"Evelyn," he enunciates, trailing his fingers along the curve of my waist.

"What is it?"

"It's just you." He presses his lips to the sensitive space above my collarbone. "That's all."

Branding my skin, Foster kisses me further down my body, between my breasts, to my navel, and lands a final pucker at my hip. I comb my fingers through his hair, along his cheek, and on the shape of his neck. He dips his fingers into the waistband of my sleep shorts, tugging them down the length of my legs and tossing them aside. Biting my lip, holding myself in place, I fixate on him as he drops his boxers to the floor, revealing his miraculous nude form.

Stepping away, Foster digs through his bag, pulls out a condom, and then crawls over my body where I'm waiting on the bed. I take the contraceptive from his hand as he dots delicate kisses across my neck.

"Foster?"

"Hmm?" he mumbles.

"I don't want to use this."

He releases his mouth from the space just below my chin. "Are you sure?"

I hold the unopened square wrapper between us. "We're both clean. I'm on birth control, and I haven't been with anyone else since you and I started sleeping together."

"I haven't been with anyone since you either."

"Sounds like we've been exclusive for some time then."

Foster wraps his hand around mine, crinkling the object in question. "Are you saying that we're a couple?"

"I think we'd make a pretty good one."

"I'd have to agree with you on that."

He snatches the condom from my hand, tosses it to the ground, and then laces his fingers with my own as we gaze intensely into one another. Circling an arm around my waist, he presses his body flush with mine, every inch of my front touching his. I hitch my leg over his hip, glide an arm into the space between his ribs and bicep, and kiss him lustfully, inviting his tongue into my mouth.

Sliding an arm between us, Foster guides himself into my entrance, slow and steady, breathing jaggedly through every inch of the procession.

"Just so you know," he states with evident control in his voice, his mouth on mine, "I don't think I'll be able to last very long. This no-condom thing is like night and day."

"No worries." I nibble gently on his lip. "We can do round two in a little bit. Let's just call this appetizer sex."

Holding me tight, Foster rolls to his back so that I'm on top. "An all-nighter then?"

"If you're up for it. We do have some time between the sheets to make up for."

He thumbs my lower lip. "Not to mention all of the missed I-love-yous."

"Especially those." I kiss his sweet mouth. "I love you, Foster Blake."

Thirty-Four

Taking a step back, I fiddle with the ends of my hair and look over my installation in the classroom studio. It's all or nothing from here.

"Looks good," Wolfgang comments as he assesses my fully set-up project ready for inspection by Professor Turner.

"Do you mean the work is good, or it's ready?" I ask, my focus roaming up and down the colorful sculpture of Foster's bust depicting an artful array of human elements.

"Both."

"Be honest. What do you think?"

"It's different for you." He circles the freestanding art piece. "Definitely a new direction."

"You say that like it's a bad thing."

"It's not. It's good to see that you're growing. I never would have expected something like this from you. Most of your work in the past has been more fanciful."

I join him at his side. "Like a bit of whimsy?"

"No, like from another world. This is more grounded."

"I still don't know if it's a good thing or a bad thing."

"Trust me, it's good," he confirms. "This is one of the most serious pieces you've ever done. It's extremely well thought out."

"Figures, given my muse." *Foster.*

It's been a few weeks since Foster and I solidified ourselves as a couple, taking out the guesswork of what we are and filling in the grayness of our relationship. It's comforting to finally have the freedom to express our true feelings to one another.

"How is Mr. Molecular?" Wolfgang questions, straightening his canvas on the wall. "Still working out chemical theories?"

"Pretty much." I tie my hair into a ponytail, nervously waiting for our teacher's arrival. "His last final exam is today."

"Any big plans for you two over break?" he asks, referring to the week hiatus between quarters that begins tomorrow.

"I wish. He's going out of town for most of it."

"What did you do? Scare him off with your wild ways in the bedroom?"

I give him a bite-me look.

"Don't pretend you aren't a sex-tress," he teases. "You can always tell who's a minx in the sheets, and you, my friend, are a crazy kitty."

"Are you trying to get a rise out of me before this critique?"

"Maybe," he singsongs. "Is it working?"

"No, just the standard eye roll."

"I guess that will have to do."

With everything set in place, Wolfgang shoves his hand in his pockets, and we both focus on our final projects awaiting judgment.

"So, who's up for crit today?" he asks me.

Two students, one guy and one girl, pace and wait on the other side of the room.

"Just you, me, Grayson, and Tawnya," I tell him. "We're the last ones. Everyone else is done already. He did them earlier in the week."

"Do you know if he's been accepting many for the show?"

"I do, and it's less than I expected."

"Really?" he asks, astonished.

"Yeah. Grayson told me earlier that he's turned away over half of the class, claiming their work wasn't good enough for installation. That surprised me because some of the pieces were noteworthy."

"Does that mean they failed?"

"No." I shake my head. "Everyone who completed the work and has given a reasonable defense passed. So, that's everyone, except for Brad, who didn't even bother to turn anything in. He was a no-show."

"Da-amn," he mutters, emphasizing the second part of the one-syllable word.

"Mr. Turner is making me kind of nervous." I bite the inside of my cheek.

"Why? Based on his criteria, sounds like you'll easily pass. Plus, your work is respectable and will speak for itself."

"I'm not worried about passing. It's the show I need," I stress with the realization that this is an undeniable opportunity. This show will validate my work—not only to my peers and my family, but also to myself. "It's make or break for me, Wolfie."

Professor Turner enters the room with very little grandeur, plopping a tattered leather briefcase on the front desk.

"Save the best for last," says our opinionated professor, circling around the studio space. "I hope that saying holds some weight because not much has impressed me in your group." He rubs his hands together. "So, who wants to go first?"

"I will," Grayson, the small-framed guy with bleach-blond hair, states.

"Brave of you." Professor Turner pivots in Grayson's direction. "Let's see what you've got."

Wolfgang, Tawnya, and I corral toward our respective projects while our teacher interrogates Grayson about his work—a mixed media piece comprised of photographs and metal. Bold and sure, Grayson presents his ideas on industrial society over the next few minutes.

My palms sweat.

I fidget.

The whole process is nerve-racking, and I'm beginning to wish that I'd presented first instead of my classmate because anticipation sucks.

After some dialogue, Professor Turner shakes Grayson's hand, congratulating him on excellent work, and welcomes him to be a part of his gallery show in a week. He then steps toward Tawnya's project without any announcement.

It's immediately apparent that our professor is not impressed with her work—a display of paper airplanes to represent the transient nature of human life. I overhear words like *simplistic* and *underwhelming*, and my anxiety intensifies. After a few short minutes and little conversation, the professor tells Tawnya that her work is passable, but he doesn't have a spot for her in the gallery show at this time.

Leaving Tawnya with unshed tears, Professor Turner continues down the line and pauses in front of my work.

"Okay, EJ," he says, observing my sculpture full of lines and color. "Explain to me what you've got here."

I swallow and then begin to present my work as confidently as possible. "This is a representation of man as science."

He rubs the scruff on his chin. "Go on."

"Humans are all made up of the same substances, a balance of elements and molecules, crafted together in a similar pattern. In some ways, the human race is nothing more than a series of clones."

He steps closer to my work.

"Chemically," I continue, "we're all the same, but there's an aspect of each individual that can't be quantified. It can only be qualified. As humans, we're scientifically similar, but perspective is what makes us unique. That is what I'm exploring here. The perception of man's individuality and likeness to each other and how, essentially, they're rooted from the same source."

"And this is something that interests you?" He scrutinizes my work. "Something you have a passion for?"

"I think we all have a desire to know what makes us what and who we are, and I'm no different."

"Is that all?" His head tilts.

A cold sweat erupts at the base of my neck. "It is. That, and what you see before you."

"Okay then."

Professor Turner silently cocks his head from side to side. He steps even closer to my piece and then further away, looking at it with one eye open and then both. The prolonged lack of words streaming across the space of the ticking minutes builds a considerable doubt within me.

"I'm at an impasse, Ms. Cunning," Professor Turner finally announces, still focused on my piece.

"How so?" My voice shakes. *Fuck.*

"Technically, the work is very strong. Your brushstrokes and use of color are extremely compelling. Your message is undoubtedly clear, and it's definitely passable work."

"Thank you."

He nods.

"But," I breathe, "it's not good enough for the show, is it?"

"You see, this is the conundrum, EJ." He circles to face me. "Your work is definitely good, good enough to show, but..."

"But." I seal my lids shut. "But is never good."

"I'm sorry, but it doesn't move me in the way it should, and I tend to follow my instincts on these things." He observes my work once again. "It's a pity, too, because the composition is so close."

My world comes crashing down. "I'm sorry to disappoint you."

"You haven't disappointed me. You just haven't convinced me."

"Of what?" I question, always the pupil.

"That it means something...or rather, that it answers any questions."

"But isn't that the point?" I stress, calling forth one of the many lessons I've learned over the years. "Not necessarily to find the answers yet to ask the questions?"

"True."

"And have I failed at that?" I debate, unable to submit to defeat. It's not in my blood.

"No, you haven't."

"But it's still not good enough for your gallery show?"

"No." He exhales audibly. Staring at the colorful bust, he cocks his head in thought.

We're all silent.

Finally, he turns to me and says, "See me after class."

"Sure."

"You've passed, in case you were wondering."

"Thank you."

Professor Turner then moves down the line of students, focusing on the final piece presented by Wolfgang.

My friend has one of the oddest and most unique works I've ever seen. His depiction on violence in society is shown using real dyed locks of hair tightly braided, scattered, and strategically placed across a sticky-looking canvas that drips with hues of bliss and blood, all at once. It's weird and amazing.

The two men discuss the project at length. It's clear as day that our teacher is in awe of Wolfgang's strange and intriguing work. Quickly, I gather that my friend will earn a spot in the coveted show. The professor can't stop boasting and asking questions. He's come alive in front of the piece. He's obviously moved.

When their laughter and excitement dies down, the professor shakes Wolfgang's hand and welcomes him to the show. The invitation is of no surprise to me or anyone else in the room. Wolfgang has always excelled in the art arena.

Professor Turner meanders back to the front desk and opens his briefcase.

"Thank you everyone for your work," he states, pulling out a small stack of papers from the leather case. "Please take your pieces with you now if you can. If not, be sure to have them removed by the end of the day. The staff will be cleaning out this space over the break, and they have been instructed to dispose of anything left behind. If you will be showing at the gallery, please be sure to stop by my desk and pick up a sheet for instructions on setup times. Everyone else, I hope to see you there, supporting your fellow classmates."

The weight of defeat settles in, like a sinking battleship in the middle of the ocean. I turn on my heel and take one more look at my work—a bodice of Foster covered in everything he emanates. I love this piece, yet it wasn't good enough.

"Sorry, EJ," Wolfgang consoles at my side. "It's still really good."

"But not great," I say with resolve.

"You know art is subjective and not everyone sees the same piece the same way."

"I do." I ball my hands into fists. "But damn, if I didn't subjectively want this."

"I wanted it for you, too." He sympathetically rubs my back. "Are you breaking it down now or coming back later?"

"Later would be better." I gather my bag from the nearby table. "I need a break."

"C'mon then."

With an arm draped over my shoulder, Wolfgang leads me to the front of room and toward the exit.

"Aren't you two forgetting something?" Professor Turner calls to us as we reach the threshold.

Stopping in our tracks, we both glance behind us where our teacher is sitting at the desk, holding out a sheet of paper.

"Right," Wolfgang says, leaving my side and taking the instruction sheet in his hand.

"You wouldn't want to forget that." Professor Turner peers around my friend. "Ms. Cunning?"

Wolfgang backs away from the desk and says to me in passing, "I'll just wait outside."

"Thanks." I pause at the edge of the desk, remembering his request from earlier. "Sorry. You wanted to see me?"

"I did." Professor Turner holds out one of the instructional sheets for the gallery showing. "You should take one of these, too."

"But I thought…" I reply, staring at the tempting white paper.

"This is conditional."

"What do you mean?"

"Your work is good, very good, but you can do better. I've seen you do better."

I'm befuddled. "You've seen me do better? I'm sorry, Professor, but this is the first class I've ever had with you. I'm confused."

"Don't look so surprised, EJ. I do my research on each and every one of my students, including you." He takes a look at the work still remaining on the floor. "I want to know who I'm backing in my gallery, and I'm confident you have more in you than you're showing. I've looked at your slides from previous classes and spoken with the rest of the staff."

"I had no idea."

"Of course you didn't. I don't exactly announce it to everyone."

"And your sleuthing is the reason you're offering me this?" I ponder, hanging on his every word.

"That, and the fact that you're even in this class in the first place. You do realize that this is an upper-level course for fine art majors, not art history ones?" He lifts his brows, challenging me. "I'm actually surprised you're in this class in the first place and curious how you managed it."

"A lot of hard work and determination," I tell him plainly.

"Ah, a passion." He taps my hand with the instructional page, urging me to take it, and I do. "That's what I figured."

I peruse the instructions, and my blood begins to loudly echo each pump from my heart into my ears.

"The show is in one week," Professor Turner continues. "If you can improve on your work in that time and illustrate more passion, I'd be willing to grant you a spot. You have to prove it though."

"A new piece?"

"If you like. Or work from what you already have."

"That's not a lot of time."

"Are you not interested?" He turns over his palm, willing to take back his offer.

"No, I am," I state quickly, inching the paper closer to my body.

"I thought you might be." He rises from his chair. "Just email me when you are ready for me to have a look at what you've got. I'll be around over the break."

"Thanks," I utter in a tiny state of shock. "Will do."

"Good luck, EJ." The professor picks up his briefcase and exits the classroom.

A few moments later, Wolfgang joins me in the classroom. "What was that all about?"

"He's giving me a second chance," I state, showing him the paper identical to his own.

"So, you get to be a part of the show?"

"I don't know yet. I need to re-present to him first."

"A new project?"

"Yeah. I believe so."

"The show's in less than a week," he states the obvious with his voice rising an octave. "Girl, you are going to be busy."

"Tell me about it…and I'm clueless as to what I'm going to do."

"It'll come to you. Just give it time."

"I really don't have much of that," I grumble.

"True." He rubs the top of his shaved head. "Damn, let me know if you need help."

Adjusting my bag over my shoulder, I say, "Thanks. I appreciate it."

"C'mon. Let's get out of here, so we can talk about what you're going to do," he says, turning on his heel and leading me to the door. "Coffee will help. Coffee is always the answer."

"Is that right, Caffeine Buddha?"

"It never steers me wrong."

We leave the classroom, walk down the art building's empty hall, and exit into the warm spring air toward the campus cafe that's only two buildings away. The sun is shining bright, and the tulips are in bloom, creating a rainbow of hope across the verdant green grass.

As Wolfgang and I quietly walk together, I contemplate what could be done to prove my talent to Professor Turner, but I come up with nothing. I need to impress him, but my mind is drawing a blank.

"Don't think about it too much," Wolfgang says when enough silence has passed.

"That's it?" I sass. "That's all you've got? Don't think?"

"You got it."

"Do you have any other brilliant advice?"

"Be true to yourself," Wolfgang announces with mock theatrics. "Love thyself. And always practice safe sex."

I laugh. "Thanks, oh wise one."

"Anytime."

About halfway to the cafe, my phone rings out of the blue with my father's ringtone. He rarely calls.

"Let me get this," I tell Wolfgang. We pause, and I fish out my cell to answer it quickly. "Hey, Daddy," I greet him, adjusting the weight of my bag.

"Afternoon, E," he replies kind and conversationally. "How are you doing?"

"Well. Thank you."

"Good. I hope exams have gone as expected?"

"Yes, for the most part."

"I'm glad to hear that." He harrumphs. "I was calling because I have a favor to ask."

"What is it?"

"How would you feel about joining your mother and me for brunch tomorrow? We'll be in town."

Thirty-Five

It's the end of my shift, and everyone has left the library, except for Foster and me. He's currently downstairs, locking up for the evening, while I continue the task of organizing the stacks.

Today's final critique with Professor Turner was a hard hit and somewhat of a reality check. I'm likely taking the initial rejection a little too much to heart, but for the first time, I'm questioning whether art is really a worthwhile pursuit. Life is nothing but obstacles to overcome, and I'm no stranger to being spurned, but I'm gutted by today's events. Not to mention, after brainstorming with Wolfgang over coffee for an hour, I'm still no closer to creating a presentable piece for Professor Turner. I despise the growing doubt. It's a foreign feeling and not welcomed. I wish it to leave.

Then, there's my parents' sudden announcement of a visit tomorrow weighing heavily on my mind.

Nothing like short notice.

Of course, I agreed to meet with them. They'll be flying in town on business, and they asked that I join a social brunch with potential clients, which I don't do often, but it'll be easy enough to attend since the meeting is local. My father does this occasionally to show the human and family side of the company. Apparently, that family aspect is a selling point for some clients.

In this same request for brunch, he also stated that he would like an update on my plans for after I graduate. My parents are aware of my acceptance letters to now four MBA programs. I'm dreading the conversation, having no firm answer.

"How's it coming?" Foster asks, joining me in the stacks.

"Dandy," I comment pseudo cheerfully, shelving a book and then joining him at the cart. "All locked up?"

"Yep. Just you, me, and the bound words of a few hundred geniuses."

"Sounds intelligently creepy."

"It wasn't meant to be seductive." He lowers his voice. "But we are alone."

"Get to work," I tease, pulling another volume from the cart. Then, I make my way down the aisle to put it in its proper place. "I don't want to be here all night."

"I thought you enjoyed my private company."

"I do, but I'd rather enjoy it one last time in bed before you leave. And the sooner we're done here, the sooner we can get there."

He teases me, "You sound so determined."

"I am somewhat."

"Now, you're being modest."

"I didn't even know I possessed that trait." I lean a hip against a series of books perched on metal shelves.

"You always have. You're just now learning to embrace it." He eases a book into its proper place.

"Don't tell anyone. I wouldn't want my reputation to be tainted."

"Never." Foster picks up a book, ponders its cover for some time, and then adjusts the dark-framed lenses over his face. "Evelyn?"

"Yes, Fozzie?" I reply, unabashedly staring.

He's so fucking sexy. Who knew that geek was my type? Maybe it isn't, but Foster certainly is.

"When I get back from visiting my sister"—he rests the book back in the cart—"I was wondering if maybe you'd like to come with me to meet my family."

"I already met your parents," I say, closing the distance between us.

"A drive-by at a wedding doesn't really count. I was thinking, I'd like for you to meet them more formally, like for dinner possibly."

"You make it sound like we're a serious couple," I tease.

"Is that a problem?" he quickly quips back.

"No. I take you very seriously."

"The feeling is mutual." He slips his palm to my lower back and tugs me close. "My family is a little…different, but I don't want you to be scared. They're really down-to-earth."

"Now, you have me curious." I circle my arms around his waist. "Is there something I need to know?"

"Not anything of importance." He seals his chest to mine. "We can talk about it when I get back."

"You know, your vagueness will be your detriment."

"How so?"

"My imagination is very vivid." I kiss his temptingly kissable lips. "You're not part of a mafia family, are you?"

He laughs. "No, nothing like that. We're just normal everyday people."

"With giant brains, I assume?"

"Now, that is an insult. Giant doesn't even come close. They're gargantuan."

"Of course. My mistake."

He playfully smacks my ass, and we both get back to work, making a dent in the pile of returns that need to be shelved before we can leave for the night.

"So," Foster begins, "you're meeting with your parents tomorrow?"

"Yes. So nice of them to spring a surprise visit on me."

"Do they do that often?"

"No. My father has some business he needs to attend to in town, and I get to reap the rewards of that."

Crouching down to the bottom section of the cart, Foster says, "I never asked, but what kind of work does your father do?"

I thumb through the pages of a book, contemplating how much to divulge. Knowledge of wealth changes opinions so quickly, and I'm not sure if I'm ready for Foster to know that part of me just yet. I don't plan to keep it a secret forever, but maybe after I meet his parents would be a suitable time to reveal that portion of my life.

"He's in a kind of public relations," I tell him vaguely, leaving out that it's one of the largest international firms in the business. "Advertising mostly."

Foster examines me, confused.

He opens his mouth to speak and then quickly shuts it, shaking his head.

His perplexity fades away.

"That must be where you get your creativity from," he states.

"Possibly."

"Are you excited at all to see them?"

"Not really. I'm just hoping it goes by with little friction. They want to discuss grad school."

"And what do you plan to tell them?"

"Not sure." I smooth my hands across the front of my skirt. "I'm hoping to put it off a little longer, if possible."

"Why don't you just tell them you don't want to go?"

I chuckle. "That's funny."

"I'm serious."

"It's complicated and…"

"You do realize you're an adult and you can make your own decisions?"

"Decisions come with the risk of consequences," I echo back.

"Or with the risk of happiness," he counters. "Just look at you and me."

"True. You were a great decision." I smile. "Anyhow, it should be a short visit. They're planning to head south afterwards to go on vacation."

"Sounds exotic."

"Maybe." I slide a blue book onto the shelf. "So, what time is your flight tomorrow?" I ask, referring to his family trip to Georgia to visit his sister, Camille.

She recently had a baby, and they're all going down to meet the new arrival.

"Around two. I'm meeting up with my parents, and we're all going to the airport together."

"You must be excited to see your nephew."

"I am. And Camille. I told her about you."

"I hope it was all horrible and nasty stuff."

"Absolutely. Nothing but the truth." He scratches the side of his head. "Maybe you'll get to meet her one day."

"That would be nice."

Grabbing the second to last book, I exit the aisle and enter into another row, on the opposite side of where Foster still remains.

"How many days will you be gone again?" I ask through the empty space over the lined up volumes on the shelf.

"Just a few," he answers. "I was planning to be back for your show at the end of the week."

"Well, that's still up in the air."

"I'm sure you'll make it happen," he says encouragingly. Foster peeks through the shelves. "Do you have any idea what you're going to do yet?"

"No," I grumble. "I'm still waiting for that miraculous moment of inspiration that's supposed to come to all artists."

"You're waiting for a miracle?"

"Is that too much to ask?"

Foster walks down to the end of the row, rounds the tall stack, and joins me where I shove the final volume away.

"You know," Foster says like he's beginning a lesson plan, "scientists believe there's an explanation for everything, and miracles are simply a myth. People just need to know where to look."

"Is that right?" I mock. "Then, tell me where to look. I'm open to suggestions."

"You're grouchy," he teases, sliding his palm around my waist. "Maybe what you really need is a healthy dose of oxytocin."

"Of what?"

"It's a pleasure chemical."

"You know I love it when you talk nerdy to me," I jest at his playfulness. "Forget dirty wordsmithery. Science is where it's at."

"Is that so?"

I nod.

"You could also benefit from a little serotonin," he utters in a seductive tone at my ear.

"Keep talking."

"Dopamine." He trails his warm tongue along the length of my neck.

"That's so fucking sexy."

"You're not kidding, are you?" Foster nips at my chin. "You really like this?"

"Shut up." I grab his ass, tugging him against me. "What else do you have?"

"Endorphins." His mouth seals to mine. "Lots of endorphins." He kisses me soft and slow, like a drawn-out dream playing across my lips.

"What are they?"

"An endurance chemical that keeps me going all"—his lips press to my neck—"night"—his fingers slide under the fabric of my shirt—"long." His palm cups my breast.

"I love endorphins," I sigh, unfastening his belt buckle as he continues to slay the sensitive skin on my throat. "Bless endorphins and all their dorphi-ness."

"You might be more partial to oxytocin."

"Oh, yeah?" Unbuttoning his pants, I reach down into his shorts and grip his ready erection. "What does that do?"

He grunts. "I'll show you."

Foster dips his palms under the hem of my skirt and trails his hands along my thighs. He hooks his fingers around the elastic of my panties, pulling downward until gravity takes them. I step out of the small piece of fabric while he tries to make haste of my top.

"Aren't there security cameras we need to worry about?" I question, mid lift of my shirt.

He peers over both shoulders, scanning the walls and ceiling. Hauling me up by my ass, he carries me about ten feet to the left and into a shadowed portion of the stacks. Foster assesses the area one more time and then continues where he left off, relieving me of my blouse.

"We're out of view here," he states, unhooking my bra. "It'll be our little secret."

"I've never had sex in a library before," I admit, helping his pants and boxers find their way to the floor.

"You think we're going to have sex?"

"Why else would we be taking off our clothes?"

He tightens his mouth, withholding his enjoyment.

"Don't you tease me, Foster Blake."

He grabs my thighs, wraps them around his waist, and then presses me firmly to the bound volumes at my back. I hold tight to his shoulders as he tauntingly slides his length through my folds.

"Do you mean like this?" he asks.

"No." I bite my lip, struggling with patience. "Not like that."

"What do you mean then?"

"You…in me…now."

289

He chuckles against my cheek. "I love you and your crazy mouth."

"And I love you inside me."

As if it were a command, Foster finds my waiting entrance and thrusts himself deep into me.

"Like that?" he asks at my hair, slowly pushing in and out of me.

"Yes," I respond, breathless. "Just like that."

Foster presses his lips to mine and seduces my tongue with his own as we make love among the words of geniuses, their thoughts and ideas stamped in the pages surrounding us. I savor his taste and the comfort of his body commingling with my own, taking solace in the relationship that I don't think either of us ever fathomed. I'm not sure how or when it happened, but this man snuck his way into my heart. He's the answer to the questions I never thought to ask.

We gyrate our hips in unison, steadily letting the heat coarse between us. I cling to his shoulders when the euphoric sizzle grows from within and spreads throughout my entire system. Foster pounds into me hard and fast when I grip his hair and call out his name, shattering around him. He grunts loudly, reaching his own climax.

I love that sound.

"Do you feel that?" he asks, holding me close.

"It's challenging to miss."

"No, not this." He moans, pushing deep inside me for emphasis. "The way your skin feels like it's battling hot and cold? The way you can't catch your breath?" Foster caresses the space where my heart lies. "And the warmth pounding from here?"

I smile, savoring all the sensations he's describing. "Yeah, I feel it."

"That's oxytocin being released through your system."

"You make it all sound so mechanical," I utter, humored. "Like there's an equation or formula for everything."

"There is for the physical part." He touches his forehead to mine. "But I don't think there could ever be a formula to define what makes you and me."

Thirty-Six

"EJ!" Chandra calls as I slip on the second emerald earring. "Your ride's here."

"Coming!" I shout back, shrugging into a light jacket. Then, I grab the coordinating clutch from my dresser.

My mother was kind enough to have them both delivered for today's brunch, still making sure I dress the part even though I'm clearly an adult. At least she takes the guesswork out of what she expects. I will give her that. I found the package with the new items on my bed when I arrived home from Foster's place earlier this morning.

I exit my room and make my way to where Chandra is standing at the door with the formally dressed driver peeking across the threshold.

"That's really pretty," Chandra comments. "Your mom certainly does have good taste."

"Thanks," I say, stepping into the hallway. "I'm sure she just hired a personal shopper. I'll see you later."

"Later."

We wave good-bye and then the driver and I descend the steps to the car waiting at the curb. He opens the door, and I slide into the black interior. I greet my mother sitting on the far side of the vehicle, examining her nails.

"Good morning, Evelyn," she says conversationally, exuding properness and esteem. "You look very pretty today. I like your hair down like that."

"Thank you. You look nice as well," I compliment her.

The driver turns over the ignition and proceeds to pull away from my apartment building, taking us to our brunch destination with my father's potential clients. Seeing how the company is family-based, it was stressed to me that a family front would go a long way in sealing the deal. This isn't the first time I've helped my parents' business like this and likely won't be the last. Even though we might be divided on some of our views, we are still a unit, and I would never turn my back on that.

"I assume you got the email with the information about the client?" my mother asks, tucking a loose strand of hair back into place. "Your father's assistant was supposed to forward it to you."

"Yes," I confirm, recalling it landing into my inbox earlier. "She sent it to me this morning, but I haven't had a chance to look it over." I cringe, knowing she won't be pleased with my lack of knowledge. I try to brush over it by saying, "I was hoping you could brief me before we got there."

"I wish you had at least perused it," she scolds.

Just keep the conversation flowing. "Daddy already told me it's a family company, and they like to work with family businesses. I wasn't really sure the rest mattered too much."

"You should know better, Evelyn." She glares at me. "Of course it matters. This is a huge client, and your father has personally been working to get this account for months. You know he doesn't usually scout and cater like this for prospective clients, but this one needed some special hand-holding."

"Yes. You're right." I set my eyes on the seat in front of me. "Could you please inform me, so I don't embarrass myself or anyone else?"

"Fine," she huffs, straightening in her seat as the driver turns onto the highway to take us downtown. "Blake Laboratories is a multibillion dollar family-run company that specializes in drug manufacturing. Deidre and Foster Blake started the business a little over fifty years ago, and it's now run by their son, Clayton, and his wife, Susan. Their main office is here, but they also run two other labs—one in Georgia and the other in Texas, headed by two other family members."

Blake Laboratories?

Blake Laboratories…

Blake.

"Evelyn?" my mother prods. "Are you listening?"

I gulp. "Yes, sorry. Go on. I'm just taking it all in."

"Maybe you should have gotten a good night's sleep, and then your attention span would have been better."

"You're right," I agree, not wanting to argue. "Tell me, what else do I need to know?"

"This is the first time the company is in need of assistance with grand-scale advertising and marketing. It's not like drug manufacturers really need advertising, but they're launching themselves into the health and wellness market. The company is planning to release a revolutionary skincare line over the next year—combining scientific research with natural products. Your father is working on a proposal that will effectively promote the line as the perfect combination of Mother Nature and man-made beauty. It's going to do very, very well and even better with our company's help. This morning, your father met with Clayton and Susan along with their son, Foster."

"Foster?" I question, quickly making the connection.

"Yes…" she drawls like I possess a low-mental capacity. "Do I need to repeat myself?"

"No. I thought you said that was the grandfather's name," I state, trying to cover my growing anxiety attack.

"It was. He's passed away, but it's the grandson's name as well." She pops open her purse, pulling out a compact to freshen her makeup. "Clayton and Susan are the owners now. Anyhow, they all met this morning to go over the proposal, and now, it's our turn to cozy them up a little more and hopefully seal the deal. Their other son, Harold, will be joining us, too. He's still in high school. Just be nice to him."

The driver takes the downtown exit off the highway, and my brain is working on overdrive, trying to connect all the dots.

Are there dots to connect?

Blake Laboratories.

Multibillion-dollar company.

Foster Blake.

I know a Foster Blake—and his penis—but he couldn't possibly be associated with the business the woman to my left is describing.

"This is for a huge campaign, Evelyn," my mother stresses again as the vehicle brakes at an intersection. "And I'm confident you will help your father in any way you can."

"Of course," I say on autopilot. "Absolutely."

Two more blocks down the street, our car stops in front of a historic hotel. The driver opens the door and assists us to the sidewalk. My mother then struts confidently through the revolving doors of the old building like she owns the town with me fast on her heels. We check our coats at the host station of the restaurant, and then a tall woman leads us to the back of the dining room, opening a set of mirrored doors to a private space.

Talking within the room ceases.

Everyone turns to greet us.

Time stands still—or maybe it never truly started.

Five people sit at the formal table, dressed and suited for business.

I recognize all of them, save for one—a young man. I assume he is Harold Blake.

I see Foster.

My Foster.
My Fozzie.

I'm at a loss for words. He doesn't move, and neither do I—caught in this surreal moment of secrets, half-truths, and the mother of all coincidences.

Thirty-Seven

Everyone rises from their chairs as my mother and I take the final steps to join my father and the Blake family. My gaze never wanders from Foster's, like a child glaring at the sun during an eclipse, mesmerized.

My father takes my mother's hand, kisses her on the cheek, and then introduces her to Susan, Clayton, Foster, and finally, Harold.

The Blake family.

The owners of Blake Laboratories.

A motherfucking drug-manufacturing empire.

"And this is our Evelyn," my father announces. "She actually attends college nearby."

"We've met before," Foster's mother says warmly, genuinely happy to see me.

"Is that so?" My mother speculatively peers at me.

"Yes. Foster introduced us about a month ago at a family friend's wedding."

"Oh." My mother smiles, taking noted interest in Foster on the other side of the table. "I had no idea."

"It's a pleasure to see you again," I say to Mr. and Mrs. Blake. Then, I peek at Foster. "And quite a coincidence."

"A good one though," my mother offers.

"Yes," Susan agrees. "Definitely."

"Shall we all have a seat?" Clayton suggests.

My father pulls out a chair for my mother and then takes a seat across from Foster's father. This is a tactic I've seen my dad use for years, never taking the head of the table to keep everyone feeling equal in these settings. Before I sink down into the chair next to my mother, Foster circles around the table and sidles up next to me.

"Allow me," he insists, scooting the seat back.

I lower myself onto the cushion. "Thank you."

"You're welcome." He leans down, whispering into my ear, "You look very beautiful...and not yourself."

"You look different, too," I comment, equally as quiet.

"Did you know about this?"

"The meeting?"

"You know what I'm asking." His breath brushes softly at the shell of my ear. "My family."

"No." My disillusioned eyes meet his own, free of their glasses. "Why didn't you tell me?"

The corners of his mouth turn downward. "Maybe I should ask the same of you."

"Foster," his father says, "why don't you have a seat, so we can order? We don't have much time before our flight."

"Right. Of course." Foster pushes my seat inward and then rounds the rectangular table, taking a place across from me, next to his mother and brother.

"Evelyn," my mother says secretly into my ear, "you never mentioned that you went to a wedding."

"I didn't think it was important."

"Well, it is when it's with someone like Foster Blake. How do you two know one another?"

"We work together at the library."

"Is that all?"

"What are you asking me?"

She measures Foster, who is sitting across from us. "He's a very handsome man." She pauses. "And comes from a good upbringing."

I groan. "He's nice, Mother," I state, giving her zero satisfaction.

As the server fills the water glasses, my mother leans forward, addressing Foster, "So, you and my daughter know one another?"

"We do." Foster narrows his brows. "We know each other pretty well actually."

"She tells me that you work together?"

"Yes. I've had the enjoyment of working with EJ since early fall quarter."

"EJ?"

"I thought that was how she liked to be addressed?" he challenges, unfolding the napkin and placing it on his lap.

"Oh, that's right," my mother politely plays off, lightly dabbing her brow. "I forgot. I've always called her Evelyn."

I give Foster an angered look, begging him not to prod the cow next to me any further.

"Maybe it's time for a change?" he suggests, ignoring my silent cue.

My mother stiffens. "I'm always open to new ideas."

"That's very…proactive of you."

Resisting the urge to kick him under the table, I turn my focus toward the polite conversation happening between my father and Susan. Always the charismatic man, my dad is attentive during the discussion. My mother finds the appropriate places to comment as well, keeping everyone engaged. She executes social grace with effortless perfection.

Foster partakes in idle conversation with his brother, sporadically peeking in my direction.

For possibly the first time in my life, I'm at a loss for how to behave in a situation. I've been groomed and trained for these occasions, but the man across the table has pulled the wool over my eyes, leaving me in a stupor. Foster continues to surprise me—first, with what he is, and now, with who he is.

When the first course is delivered, the table falls silent to enjoy the meal. Foster and I share many wordless looks, both of us playing the polite counterparts in order to get through this awkward and somewhat revealing ordeal. We definitely need to talk once we have a private moment—to clear the air, if nothing else.

He's kept his wealth hidden, as have I. There are many reasons to do so—privacy, judgment, and protection, to name a few. Mine is to protect the fantasy that I can lead a typical life.

I wonder about his reasons.

"Evelyn," Susan addresses me when she finishes a bite of her salad, "your mother mentioned that you'll be heading to graduate school come this fall. That must be very exciting for you."

Foster audibly drops the fork to his plate.

"I'm weighing my options," I politely tell her. "There's still time."

"Oh, yes, of course. You wouldn't want to make a hasty decision."

"I couldn't agree more," Foster adds loud enough for everyone to hear.

"How about yourself?" my father questions the man across the table from me. "What are your plans for the fall?"

"I'll be heading to the Knight Management Center."

"Stanford Business School," my mother states, her tone laced with respect. "That is quite impressive."

"Foster is very adamant about his studies," his mother comments. "He's quite determined."

"Diligence and a strong work ethic will always get you far."

"We tend to agree."

Foster glares at me across the table, like he's urging me to say something.

"Have you ever seen Evelyn's work?" Foster asks my father.

My mother perks up, giving Foster her full attention.

"Yes," my father states, wiping his mouth. "Evelyn has been creating beautiful things since she was a child."

"She's very talented. Wouldn't you agree?" he says, insistent.

"Yes. I've always enjoyed seeing her pieces."

"Her pieces?" Susan questions.

"Evelyn is an artist, and she has quite a unique way of seeing things. I've never seen anything like it. She takes some of the simplest subjects and puts a new twist and perspective on them, telling an unseen story. I've been helping her with a project over the past few months." He turns his focus to me. "She's even inspired me."

Susan shifts her eyes between Foster and me, expressing affection.

The server returns, clears our plates, and refills our drinks. My father begins a new conversation at the table, engaging everyone on the casual topic of their favorite vacation places.

"Foster is enamored with you," my mother echoes softly, only for my ears. "You really should consider getting to know him better."

I close my eyes, stifling out her constant meddling. There's no doubt in my mind that she wouldn't even give Foster a second thought in regard to us *courting*, if it weren't for the fact that his billionaire family has…well, billions.

"And he even likes your artwork," she adds. "Not that it has as much value as an MBA, but I'm happy it was able to grab his attention. I might have underestimated its draw."

Mortified by her words, my jaw goes slack, dropping open. *She's happy about my art hobby, as she would put it, in the process of landing a man, but she still finds it beneath anything she deems of importance.*

Foster releases a tentative grin in my direction and then returns his attention back to our fathers, who are in deep conversation about their golf handicaps and the possibility of a future game together.

My mother gawks at Foster likes he's some sort of gift that's been handed into her lap, and my stomach goes ill.

He circles his long fingers around the water glass, and I'm drawn to the clear substance contained within the crystal. I become lost in the small ripples creating a tiny tide within the brittle shell.

Daydreaming.

"Stanford is impressive," my mother repeats again, as a reminder to me, while everyone is engrossed in their own discussions.

I need to escape this moment.

I dive deep into the fluid, allowing the bubbles and thickness to surround me in my mind, clouding out the noise of my mother's encouragement toward a man she knows absolutely nothing about, other than his favorable prospects and bank account.

"I was upset about Gerard," her shrilling voice echoes in my ear, "but there might be hope for you yet."

My body morphs into a clear stream and becomes one with the cool substance, drowning to the depths.

"Foster and his family are fine people," she adds. "And they already seem to like you so much."

Gasping, I try not to let it consume me.

"Did I mention you look very pretty today?"

Enough!

I carry myself upward, breaching the surface of what everyone sees, ignorant to the fight below. Everything is calm and clear through their one-dimensional perspective. They see nothing—only what they want. They know nothing.

Out of my mind and into reality.

I am not the water.

I'm something else.

More than water.

The woman at my side sees me as a pawn in her game, a plastic piece to be maneuvered in the right direction, and now, she's plotting to send me straight toward a new prize.

Foster.

My—

Suddenly, he doesn't feel like mine anymore.

He's her choice.

We are just water to her—pretty and pristine and contained within the glass of her making.

"You're almost perfection," my mother says proudly.

"I'm more than water," I say just above a whisper.

"What's that, Evelyn?"

"I'm more than water!" I shout, surprising even myself, garnering everyone's attention at the table. "I'm more than water."

She nervously laughs, making light of my obvious temper. "I don't understand."

"No. You wouldn't. You understand nothing about me." As gracefully as I can muster, given the angst pumping quickly through my veins, I empty myself from the seat and take my clutch into my hand. "Excuse me. It's best if I leave." I glance in Foster's direction. "This was a mistake." I address Foster's parents, "It was good to see you again." I turn to my mother. "I'm not a prized mare for breeding. And you likely don't want to hear this, but I won't be getting my MBA from Yale or any other college. So, you can stop pestering me about it. It's done. I'm not going."

"Evelyn—"

"If you cared about my happiness at all, you would know why." I step around where she's seated and pause in front of my father. "I'm sorry. I hope I haven't ruined anything."

With those last words, I turn on my heel and hastily exit the room. My body quivers with elevating adrenaline levels. I quicken my steps in hopes of alleviating some of the jitters. When I'm almost at the host stand to retrieve my coat, I'm alerted to hurried footfalls trailing behind me.

"Evelyn," Foster calls. "Wait."

I pause in my tracks and wait for him to catch up.

"Hey..." I utter with measured control.

"You didn't say good-bye."

"I'm sorry. Good-bye, Foster."

I step away, and he grabs my arm, not allowing me to leave.

"We need to talk about this," he insists.

"I'll apologize to your parents and mine about my behavior. I'm sure a note will suffice."

"No," he stresses, "it was good to see that. It was killing me to watch you so...muted."

"I should go."

"I'll go with you."

"No." I run my hand down his suit-covered arm. "Good-bye, Foster."

"Good-bye? Wait, what's going on?"

"I can't..." My lip quakes.

"You can't what?" His mouth tightens. "Evelyn?"

"I thought you were smart."

He's taken aback. "Apparently, not smart enough. Maybe you need to educate me."

"I'm not living like this anymore."

"Like what? You're confusing the hell out of me."

"This." I motion to my outfit, then to his, and then to the room from where we came. "That! All of the society bullshit."

"I never asked you to be a part of that. Hell, I never even expected it."

"Why didn't you tell me?"

"Tell you what?" He runs his fingers through his hair. "About my family? The money? God, I don't know.

Maybe because it's impolite to talk about? Because I don't want people to know? Because when they do know, all they see is a future for themselves and a giant bank account? Or maybe it's because I wanted to make sure you loved me for me, first and foremost? Take your pick. All of them are the truth."

"Never mind." I shake my head. "It doesn't matter."

"It doesn't matter?" he echoes back, trying to follow.

"Don't you get it? You're exactly what they want for me. You fit the mold. My mother was practically marrying us off to each other while we were sitting at the table. I swear, from the way she looked at you, she could see diamond-studded babies being spawned between us."

"Is that a bad thing?"

"Yes!"

"Why?"

"Because you're their choice!"

"Their choice?" he groans. "Why in the hell should that matter? What's your choice?"

My blood hammers heavily in my chest.

Tears threaten to expose my plight.

"I've never had one."

Thirty-Eight

I left. I walked away without one more word, and Foster let me.

There was nothing more to be said.

He understood.

After exiting the hotel, I grabbed a cab and had it drop me off at a park about a mile from my apartment. It wasn't a place I frequented often, but I wasn't ready to go home. My phone rang numerous times. I ignored it and finally turned it off.

Decisions come with the risk of consequences, and there's no doubt that there are many waiting for me after today.

Brunch was a disaster on many levels.

My parents will hate me.

Foster will, too.

It's been a few hours since I left the hotel. On foot, I meander along the sidewalks, back toward campus, and I lazily tread down the hill to my apartment. Parked at the curb, near my building's entrance, is a luxury town car with no occupants, other than the driver. I gather myself and enter the brick structure, knowing that my mother and father are waiting for me upstairs.

I'm emotionally spent and give zero fucks.

Opening the door, I find my parents sitting casually on the couch, and Chandra is in the kitchen, flipping through a magazine.

"Hello," I say, shutting the door.

My parents rise from their seats.

"E," my father says in absence of my mother's greeting.

"I'm going to head out for a bit," Chandra announces, emptying herself from the kitchen. "I'll be back in an hour or so." She slips on her jacket and then embraces me for a brief wordless moment before exiting.

I shrug out of my coat and fold it over my arms, waiting for the expectant onslaught of disciplinary words from my mother and father. There's no doubt in my mind that they're here to scold me for my behavior and for blowing any potential business dealings with Blake Laboratories.

"Apparently, you're still in town," I state the obvious.

"Yes," my father replies. "Your mother and I would like to have a word with you."

"Is this the part where I'm supposed to apologize for my behavior today?" I snip. "Because if it is, let's just get it over with. I'm sorry, and I'll apologize to the Blakes as well."

My parents share a look.

"Why don't you sit down?" my father suggests, gesturing to the red chair.

"Fine," I submit, taking a seat where indicated as they lower back into the sofa. "I'm listening."

Taking my mother's hand in his, my father begins, "We've spoken to the Blakes about your outburst, and they are willing to overlook it. We've already apologized for you, but I'm sure they would appreciate hearing it from you as well."

"Of course. Anything else?"

"Yes, actually, there is." He sits up straighter. "Their son had a few choice words for your mother and me about you. I won't go into details because he wasn't exactly tactful in his delivery, but we were very surprised, to say the least."

"By what? That someone could speak so rudely to you?"

"Hardly." My father guffaws. "I've been called worse over the years. However, the vitality that man possessed in regard to anything related to you was noted."

"So, it got heated? Awesome. I'm sure that's my fault, too."

"No, he was very adamant that his opinions were his own and that he cares for you very much."

"Very much," my mother echoes in a familiar tone of insistence.

"Oh, give it a rest," I implore. "If you're here to ask me to fix this by dating their son, you can forget about it. I'm through with playing the part."

"E, we're not asking anything of you," my father insists. "We're just telling you as your parents that—"

"He loves you, Evelyn," my mother states. "EJ, I mean."

I focus on a vacant space near the window and whisper, "What do you know about love? I thought you only specialized in etiquette and breeding, which is a fairly sterile practice."

"E, that's unfair," my father scolds. "First of all, those were his exact words. Second, your mother loves you more than you know."

"She has a funny way of showing it."

My mother lowers her lids. "I realize I might come off a little...pushy—"

"That's an understatement."

"But it's only because I want the best for you."

"How could you possibly know what's best for me when you know nothing about me? All you care about are the right shoes and purse and table manners and galas and the right school and marrying me off to someone with a large quantity of stock shares. I'm not some doll you can dress up and play life with. I'm your daughter. A person."

"Ev—EJ," she utters, stumbling over my name, "I was just…I was trying the only way I know how, raising you and your sister just as I was."

"But I'm not you or her. I'm nothing like either of you. We're so different. You care nothing for my interests or my dreams. You've only seen your own wishes for me."

"That's enough of that," my father sternly interjects. "Whether you like it or not, you, your mother, and your sister have a lot in common. You're all beautiful, passionate, driven, and wonderful women. That being said, your mother and I might have been wrong when it came to the direction we've been leading you." He wraps his arm around his wife's shoulder. "We were only trying to guide you the best way we knew how, but in retrospect, it might have been detrimental. We had nothing but your long-term happiness in mind. You can't fault us for wanting you to have a secure future. That's all we've wanted for you."

"Your father and I care for you more than you realize," my mother states, emotionally fragile. "You've made it clear how you feel about me. I accept that, but know that I love you, regardless of any of your decisions."

"And that includes graduate school," my father adds. "As much as we think you going would be for the best, it's your decision. We will still love you."

"That's it?" I ask, stupefied. "Just like that, you're letting it go?"

"No," my father responds. "But I accept when a negotiation is over, and there's no more room for debate. You've made your opinion loud and clear on the matter, and I'm man enough to submit to defeat."

He rises from his seat and assists my mother to her feet as well. Assessing that this conversation is coming to a close, I stand, too. They quietly make their way to the door, and I follow to let them out.

"We're still family," my father says with his hand on the knob. "That hasn't changed, and we will always back you even if we might not agree. We're here for you. Don't forget that."

"I won't," I say, agreeing to the simple request.

"Here," my mother says, pulling a small brown envelope from her handbag. "Foster asked us to give this to you."

"What is it?" My hand tentatively takes the rectangular package.

"I'm not sure. He said he'd planned to show these to his sister, but you needed them instead. He gave it to us right before they left for the airport."

"Thanks."

"You're welcome." She offers an apologetic and hopeful smile. "Take care, EJ."

"You, too."

With that, my father opens the door and escorts my mother into the hallway and down the steps, leaving me alone in my apartment. I take a seat on the sofa and anxiously stare at the envelope in my hand. With trepidation, I unhinge the metal prongs, reach inside, and pull out the flat contents.

His eyes.

His mouth.

Foster's face.

I took these. They're mine. They're him.

My vision blurs from wetness as I shuffle through the images. The four enclosed photographic copies I sent to Foster a few months ago bring back memories of one of our most intimate moments together. We've had many, but the day I painted scientific shapes and elements on his body is one to be remembered forever. It feels like the first day we ever truly met.

The pictures he's sent for me to see are not the ones I took of his torso, which display my colorful work.

These are him.

His unique characteristics.

His face.

His soft gaze.

His vulnerable self.

Seeing him through the lens was like finding him.

I saw him that day. He was stripped bare.

He showed himself.

It scared me.

I unfold the attached note.

THIS IS THE FACE OF A MAN LOOKING AT A WOMAN HE LOVES. HE HAS NO MONEY OR PRESTIGE, ONLY A HEART.

Thirty-Nine

The gallery doors have been open for nearly two hours. As promised, in attendance are many influential people from the art world, both locally and nationally—buyers, sellers, dealers, and individuals—looking to commission pieces by up-and-coming artists.

"Congratulations," I tell Wolfgang, wrapping my arms around him. "A buyer and a new commission! That's impressive."

"Thanks," he responds, clinking his champagne glass with mine. "I'm kind of in shock."

"Why? Your piece is spectacular. I'm not surprised one bit, and I couldn't be happier for you." I sip the crisp liquid from my flute. "However, if you don't want to do it, I'd gladly take the work off your hands."

"You're such an opportunist."

"It's a dog-eat-dog world, Wolfie. You'd better get ready for the wolves because it's gonna be a fight."

"Is this part of your business teachings?"

"Possibly. I'll send you a handbook on the rats in the industry."

It's been nearly a week since reality took on a new meaning at brunch with my parents, Foster, and his family. It took me a few days to come to terms with what had happened, who Foster was, and what I truly wanted. Having a free choice for the first time in my life was new territory, and I wasn't sure how to focus, but soon, my decision and direction became clear—once I let myself see beyond all the barriers.

Like second nature, I emerged myself into my art as a means to reveal my desires, and it helped in more ways than I'd expected. I enlisted Wolfgang's help in making my project come to life because it was nearly impossible to cast my own body, and Chandra was on vacation with Jeremy for the break.

Wolfgang was also a supportive ear, allowing me to vent all of the untold truths about my family, Foster, and myself. I revealed a part of myself, often held in secret, and the physical act of creating something new helped me to truly know what was in my heart without any obstacles. The product of this process was also able to impress Professor Turner enough to land me a coveted space in his show.

He called my piece "a vehement beauty."

Being at this event is truly an opportunity of a lifetime for many, including myself. Earlier in the evening, I was approached to create a piece to be displayed in a well-known aquarium. I'm truly honored.

Mid sip of my drink, I'm tapped on the shoulder.

I turn around.

My mother and father have genuine smiles plastered across their faces while they stand side by side as a pillar of properness with their coats in hand.

"We need to get going," my father states, looking at his timepiece. "We have a plane to catch, but we wanted to say good-bye first."

"I really appreciate you coming," I say wholeheartedly. "I know it wasn't on your schedule."

"Thank you for inviting us," my mother adds. "We wouldn't have missed it. There are a lot of really wonderful pieces here tonight."

I'm unsure if she's being polite or honest, but either way, she's making an effort.

When they were last in town, we parted with a bit of unease, but there was a sense of hope.

It was Wolfgang's suggestion that I extend an invitation for them to come even though they were on vacation, but I didn't expect them to attend. Their presence is an encouraging surprise, and deep in my heart, it's a welcomed one. It's a first step. For possibly the first time in my life, they're showing an interest in something that truly matters to me, and it has no benefit to them, other than knowing that it makes me happy.

"Have a safe trip," I say, hugging my father and then my mother.

She kisses me on the cheek.

"Congratulations," my father says for possibly the fourth time this evening. "You've done very well. We'll talk to you soon."

"Enjoy the rest of your evening, EJ," my mother adds. "And it was a pleasure meeting you, Wolfgang."

"You, too, Mr. and Mrs. C.," Wolfgang replies, somewhat aloof, causing me to snort.

The look on my mother's face in response to his informal address is priceless.

"Come on, dear," my father encourages my mother, taking her by the arm. "It's time for us to head out."

We all say one last final farewell, and my parents leave through the crowd of guests. Wolfgang and I wander around the room, studying everyone's work one more time, discussing what we think the artist is trying to convey and the execution. We're both on our second glass of champagne, so our observations aren't very technical at this point.

"Well, isn't that just phallic?" Wolfgang states in examination of one artist's depiction of a weeping woman on a log.

"I guess we all see what we want to see." I laugh.

"It's wood," he deadpans. "And the leaves are ejaculating."

"It's a very excited little log."

"Now, girl, you know better than to ever call a piece of wood little. That's just plain old insulting."

"Well, somebody likes it." I point to the red dot next to the title of the piece, indicating that it has been sold. "Enough to buy it."

"Porn always sells."

"C'mon." I loop my arm through his. "Let's keep moving."

We proceed to the next installation—a high-speed video display of a man on a roof as the sun rises and sets. Of course, he's naked.

Why is there always so much nudity in art? Maybe we are a bunch of horny people.

"So, I haven't seen Foster," Wolfgang states, probing. "I guess he didn't make it?"

"No." I smile, hiding the splinters in my heart. "I guess he didn't."

"Have you talked to him?"

"Briefly. He called yesterday when he arrived back in town."

"And how did that go?"

"It was okay." I bite my lower lip. "I really hurt him."

"I'm sure he'll forgive you. He has to understand what you were going through."

"I think he does, but it's no excuse." I shake my head. "I pushed him away, simply for what he is. It was completely hypocritical of me, judging him on his family's stature."

"Man, you rich people have it tough," he kids. "Money trees and vapid dreams."

"We all just want to be seen as people, Wolfie. What do you think we do all day? Roll around on the bed, covered in hundred-dollar bills?"

Wolfgang takes my hand, winks at me, and then leads us toward the next collection of students' work in a smaller space brightly lit to showcase the five brilliantly colored canvases on the wall. Within the room, Professor Turner nonchalantly speaks with a couple about the compositions, signaling and waving his arms in an animated fashion. When he spies my friend and me, he excuses himself from the attentive pair.

"I was just looking for you," Professor Turner says, addressing me. "You have a buyer interested in your piece, and he'd like to meet you."

"Oh," I utter, surprised. "Well, it's not exactly for sale. Is it mislabeled?"

"No, the label is correct, but he insisted on meeting you, in hopes of changing your mind."

Wolfgang and I share a look.

"I doubt I'll budge," I confess, "but I'm happy to speak with him."

"Come"—he gestures to the left—"I'll introduce you."

With Wolfgang by my side, we follow the professor toward the space where my work is displayed. A small number of people are gathered around my sculpture installation, but I'm only drawn to one. A man dressed casually in a pair of jeans and a T-shirt, his warm-brown hair falling just over his brow while sporting a pair of familiar dark-framed glasses, stares intently at my creation.

Foster.

He came.

Cutting through the crowd, Professor Turner approaches Foster and signals toward me. "Mr. Blake, I believe you wanted to meet the artist. This is EJ Cunning."

"Hello," Foster says, the hint of a smile flirting at the corner of his mouth.

"Hi," I respond, a surge of relief spreading across my chest.

"I'll let you two get acquainted," the professor says to us. "Please let me know if you have any questions, Mr. Blake."

"I will. Thank you."

Professor Turner nods and then makes his way back into the crowd.

"Looks like it's time to refresh my drink," Wolfgang says, raising his half-empty glass and taking mine from my hand. "I'll take care of these." He then leaves Foster and me alone in front of my work.

"You made it," I state, unable to contain my exuberance.

"I did." He smirks. "I was trying to find the right outfit. I didn't want to seem too...professional. It's not really my style."

"Mission accomplished." My eyes sink into him as he stands before me. "You look perfect."

The crowd around us begins to dissipate.

All that's left is Foster.

Me.

Us.

"So, tell me about your work," Foster says, stepping closer to the castings of a man and a woman's torsos. "It's different than the last time I saw it. You've gone in a new direction."

"Foster...I..."

"It's an interesting title." He spares me a glance, ignoring my incomplete thought. "You call this one *More Than Water*? I'd like to know a little more about that."

"Fozzie..." I implore, trying to find the words to express the elephant sitting its ass firmly between us.

"I don't recall a woman in the original piece. Why the change?"

I sigh, resigned, and join him as he ponders over my piece. "I wasn't looking deep enough before."

"And now?"

"Now, I see what was there all along."

"Tell me more." He pauses. "Evelyn." A moment of silence. "I want to hear it all."

Together, Foster and I speculate over my work, a colorful casting of two figures, a man and a woman, covered in a dripping blue-and-green substance to simulate water. The male counterpart is the original cast of Foster that I submitted for review—a vivid display of the science of man with his palm resting over his heart. Now, in addition to that is the cast of a woman, modeled after my own torso, her hand resting over his heart with her chest angled toward his. Her body is covered with various shapes and vibrant colors, a unique design of her own making. In the space where their hands are joined, an energetic and fiery vermilion flame pattern seeps through both of the figures, gradually fading into their individuality. Just beyond the last licks of the scarlet heat, the water that covers them both melts away over their shoulders and along their lines, sluicing down toward the ground.

"These two individuals," I begin to tell him, "live under a mask, but it's not of their doing. They're both caught in the wave of limited vision. It's heavy and clouded. It often weighs them down. Sometimes, they feel like they're drowning. However, there's more to them than what meets the eye. It's all about perception."

"And the place where their hands meet?" he asks, not looking at me. "What is that?"

"It's something else altogether. It's the catalyst for them to truly find themselves and each other. It's the strength they need to fight away the pretenses, the wave."

"Does it have a name?"

"Not officially, but it stems from their love for one another. It trumps everything else. It cuts through barriers, allowing them to break free as individuals and as a unit."

Foster's hand finds mine, weaving our fingers together. He leans down and presses his soft lips to my cheek, and the air passing through my lungs hitches.

I imagine the heat building in the places where our bodies unite, growing and expanding through both of us, as we shed away the exterior that each of us carries.

"And this is how you see us?" he asks, skating his mouth to my ear.

"Yes." I nod. "Neither one of us is the water. You're not, and neither am I. We're more than water."

"It all sounds very wet," he jests. "And watery."

"The combination of hydrogen and oxygen is off the charts. We might be swimming in it for days."

"Are clothes required?"

"Completely optional."

"Evelyn," Foster carefully pronounces, like it's the most precious word to ever cross his lips. His fingertips delicately graze along the shape of my cheekbone. "Just my Evelyn."

"Yes, Fozzie," I reply in confirmation.

Slipping his palms to the base of my neck, Foster connects his lips with mine, fervently kissing me and sealing together who we are outside of our stature and status, beyond his science-oriented mind and my free-spirited one. I swim into his depths as we drown ourselves in one another, underneath what the world perceives.

There are many factors that make us an unlikely pair—my own predisposition toward any kind of society, his geeky way of thinking, and the vibrant way I express myself—but we have a chemistry that cannot be denied.

Like a flame breaking the boundaries to survive underwater, we, too, are something beautiful.

We are a substance of our own design.

We're more than water.

We're more than fire.

We're a miracle, a living and breathing combination, with no formula to define us.

AUTHOR'S NOTE

Almost fifteen years prior to writing this story, and before digital photography was common practice, I took a photography class in college that sparked a love to last a lifetime. Having been an artist all of my life, finding stories through the lens was like opening up my imagination to the layers of the everyday world with a new and exciting medium.

I took the following images for a project similar to EJ's, with a friend watching my back during not-so-safe hours. Never in my wildest dreams did I imagine that my own art would inspire a story to be written later in life.

Look into the depths for what's hidden within.

It's more than water.

It's a story.

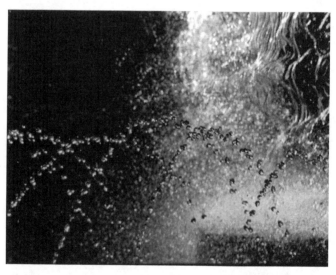

ACKNOWLEDGEMENTS

The only way for a new venture to happen is with an amazing support system. I'm so lucky to have one of the best.

Alyssa—Thank you so much for your constant enthusiasm toward my stories, for reading my works critically and open-mindedly, for talking through plot points at any hour of the day, and for your willingness to help me fine-tune the details over and over again. You're an amazing person, and I'm lucky to call you a friend. Also, I will never use the word *piston* in a draft ever again. I promise. Hips should never do such a thing to one another.

Thank you, MJ, Mendy, Evette, Kristin, Mandy, Renee, and Amanda—my super amazing cheerleaders and beta readers! You were there for me to answer my *many* questions, patiently waiting as I wrote and tweaked this story, and you loved EJ and Foster even more than I anticipated. I love you all so much and appreciate you more than you know. I value your opinions and friendship unconditionally.

My amazing Street Team—Thank you for your continued support.

My husband—I love you.

My children—Thank you for cheering me on daily. I never thought my love for writing stories would inspire you to write as well.

Jovana with Unforeseen Editing—You always make my words shine.

The University of Cincinnati, College of Design, Architecture, Art, and Planning—My time with you as an undergrad opened my eyes to many forms of art, allowed me to see things differently, and helped me to understand the value of a critique. Thank you.

And finally, Humor—Without you, the world would be boring and exhausting. Thank you for getting me through each and every day.

ABOUT THE AUTHOR

Renee Ericson is the author of the These Days series.

Originally from the Midwest, she now resides in a small town just outside of Boston with her husband and three children.

Most winters, Renee can be found on the slopes of the White Mountains skiing with her family. During the summer months, she likes to spend every spare minute at the beach soaking up the sea air. All those moments in between, she is talking to imaginary characters and caring for her children.

Made in the USA
Middletown, DE
24 June 2015